The World Turned Upside Down

The World Turned Upside Down

by
Léonie Rouzade

translated, annotated and introduced by
Brian Stableford

A Black Coat Press Book

Edited by Peter Gabbani

English adaptation and introduction Copyright © 2014 by Brian Stableford.
Cover illustration Copyright © 2014 Jean-Félix Lyon.

Visit our website at www.blackcoatpress.com

TABLE OF CONTENTS

Introduction 7
A VOYAGE TO THE ISLE OF UTOPIA 13
THE WORLD TURNED UPSIDE DOWN 119

Introduction

Voyage de Théodose à l'île d'Utopie and *Le Monde renversé* by Léonie Rouzade, here translated as "A Voyage to the Isle of Utopia" and "The World Turned Upside Down" respectively, were first published in Paris by Lachaud in 1872. They were the third and fourth, and the two most substantial, of five items issued by that publisher in rapid succession, following *Connais-toi toi-même?* [Do you Know Yourself?] (1871) and *Le Roi Johanne* [King Johanne] (1872), and being followed in their turn by *Ci et çà, çà et là* [This and That; Here and There] (1872). The first and last were non-fictional pamphlets, more akin to meditations than essays, whereas the second, which had a considerably lower page-count than the two novellas that succeeded it, was a visionary fantasy reflecting the same socialist and feminist concerns as its successors in a similarly oblique fashion.

Given that the total wordage of the five Lachaud volumes is not much over 100,000, it is possible that they were written in much the same interval of time as was taken up by their publication, but it seems more probable that at least some of them had been written some time before publication, and the order of their composition might not be the same as the order in which they appeared. *Voyage de Théodose à l'île d'Utopie* is dated September 1872 at the end, but the last chapter of the novel is radically different from the remainder, and it might be the case that the chapter in question was added at that date to a story that had been written some time before, and had originally been thought to be complete once the protagonist had landed in France; indeed the final section might have been a separate story that was somewhat awkwardly grafted onto the remainder. The epilogue of *Le Monde renversé* suggests strongly that the author had experimented with more earnest utopian fictions before developing the more adventurous rhetorical strategies applied tentatively in *Voyage de Théodose à l'île d'Utopie* and far more wholeheartedly in the second novel—in which the author's scathing sarcasm and righteous wrath are given much freer rein—but that her earlier efforts had been unappreciated.

It is not obvious that her more strenuous efforts were much better appreciated; Léonie Rouzade has never been well-known as a writer of fiction, although she did become famous—or at least notorious—during her lifetime because of her activities as a crusading feminist. Her political career did not take off until some years after the publication of the five Lachaud volumes, and her later writings are by no means as quirky and enterprising as those works, although she never abandoned her penchant for brutal sarcasm. *Le Monde Renversé* remains outstanding not only among her own works but in the canon of feminist fiction in general; it is not only the earliest fantasy of sex-role reversal ever penned, but is far more striking than almost all of those that came after it, in terms of its flamboyant imagination of the operation of that reversal and its description of its possible consequences. It is a grandiose Voltairean *conte philosophique*, but it takes its satire to a comic extreme that is on the edge of absurdism, and can now be seen as a work that was far ahead of its time in its method as well as its angry intent.

The author was born Louise-Léonie Camusat in Paris in 1839, the daughter of a watchmaker; she liked to boast that she was the grand-daughter of a delegate to the 1789 Estates-General. She apparently worked as an embroideress before marrying Auguste Rouzade, the municipal accountant of the wealthy suburb of Meudon, at the age of twenty-one. He was presumably older than she was, but the final section of *Voyage de Théodose à l'île d'Utopie* is highly unlikely to be a transformation of her own marital situation, as her husband bore no resemblance to the ridiculous Théodose, being a Utopian socialist in the tradition of Charles Fourier and Étienne Cabet, who undoubtedly encouraged her interest in such matters and supported her writing and political activism. According to

Rouzade's lifelong friend, Hubertine Auclert, who introduced her to socialism, the marriage was happy from its beginning until Auguste's death in 1901.

Léonie Rouzade's activism apparently took considerable inspiration from her attendance at the International Congress on Women's Rights held in Paris in 1878. In 1880, she was a co-founder, with Eugénie Pierre (later Potonié-Pierre) and the ex-Communard Marcelle Tinayre, of the *Union des femmes* [Women's Union], a group designed to obtain representation for women in the *Parti ouvrier* [Workers' Party], and she was one of the authors of its manifesto. In 1881, she stood as a socialist candidate for the Municipal Council in Paris—the first woman to do so (women had been allowed to vote and stand for election in French municipal elections since 1872, but were not allowed to vote and offer themselves as candidates in legislative elections until 1944). She had no chance of being elected, especially as one of the two main socialist parties in Paris refused to support her, but the mere fact that she stood and campaigned was a landmark in the political progress of women in France. Contemporary reportage of her political activism suggests that she was an outspoken and controversial figure—the *Evening Post* described her in 1896 as "notorious for her combative nature"—who annoyed many of her fellow feminists almost as much as the male socialists she continually castigated for their lack of concern regarding the oppression of women. She was one of the most radical of the Parisian feminists of the day, notably in her advocacy of the collectivization of motherhood.

Rouzade published a number of articles in left-wing periodicals, and some of her speeches were printed, but her most successful work by far was the anticlerical *Petit catéchisme de morale laïque et socialiste* [A Short Catechism of Secular and Socialist Morality] (1895), which went through several further editions in isolation, and several more in tandem with *La Femme et le Peuple organisation sociale de demain* [Women and the People: The Social Organization of Tomorrow] (1896), which was her only full-length work of non-fiction, and was reprinted twice. The former item was translated into English—advertised in its subtitle as the "last chapter" of the latter—as *The Feminist Catechism* (1911). She died in 1916.

Her literary reputation might well be more considerable nowadays had the five Lachaud volumes not become so hard to find. A review of *Le Roi Johanne* in *La Renaissance Littéraire et Artistique* in 1872 was extremely complimentary, comparing it to the early work of George Sand, but all of the Lachaud volumes had probably languished virtually unread for a hundred years before the Bibliothèque Nationale reproduced the two volumes translated here on *gallica*, even though Charles Sowerwine had summarized the plots of both novellas in *Les Femmes et le Socialisme* (1978; tr. as *Sisters of Citizens? Women and Socialism in France since 1876*) and had warmly recommended *La Monde renversé* to the attention of contemporary publishers—to no avail.

The French tradition of utopian fiction is a strong one, and after its 18th century heyday, it had continued with a certain residual vigor throughout the 19th, fuelled by the followers of Fourier and Cabet. In spite of the suppression of radical thought between 1851 and 1870 by the Second Empire's censors, the list of notable French utopian fantasies had been supplemented in 1869 by Tony Moilin's socialist vision of *Paris en l'an 2000*,[1] which Rouzade probably read, although there are no echoes of it at all in her own works. The fall of the Second Empire undoubtedly encouraged radicals to believe that it might be easier to publish such works in the future—all the other works advertised by Lachaud in the Rouzade volumes are accounts of the siege of Paris, the Commune and its aftermath—but any aspirant writers of didactic fantasies would have been well aware, as Rouzade clearly was, of the criticism that utopian writing was generally considered to be dull by virtue of being essentially deprived of drama and action. Various writers adopted different strategies to contend with that

---

[1] translated as *Paris in the Year 2000*, Black Coat Press, ISBN 9781612271606.

difficulty and attempt to overcome it, and Rouzade might have been aware of Hippolyte Mettais' *L'An 5865* (1865)[2]; although she would not have been sympathetic to its politics, she might well have found its narrative strategy interesting.

The narrative method adopted in *Voyage de Théodose à l'île d'Utopie* is a simple and relatively straightforward one, employing an unsympathetic narrator to whom everything about the isle of Utopie—which is not Thomas More's hypothetical island but one that has adopted the name for a different reason—seems tedious. When its inhabitants explain to him how things work there, he simply switches off mentally, much as many readers of utopian fictions are assumed to do, and concentrates on his own narrow concerns and prejudices—which thus form a standard of wry comparison with those of the islanders, tacitly assembling a scathing critique of his attitudes, aspirations and intellect. The tactic carries the danger, of course, that the reader might react in the same way as Théodose to the didactic lectures, even while deploring his ignorance and arrogance. But it has the advantage that the novella possesses a certain amount of energy as a satirical character study, and the scenes in which the protagonist is pursuing his own ends, without anyone attempting to explain things to him, have a zest and intrinsic interest that is often lacking even in relatively boisterous utopian satires.

Le Monde renversé is, by comparison, a far more ambitious and enterprising work, which modifies its rhetorical strategy to a far greater extent than any previous utopian satire, or anything published for a hundred years thereafter. In essence, it employs the simple device of conferring dictatorial power upon its protagonist in order that she can become potentially capable of putting the world to rights by edict, but it does so with deliberate perversity, employing as a protagonist not some well-intentioned philanthropist but an ultimate *femme fatale* suffering from terminal ennui, whose one and

---

[2] translated as *The Year 5865*, Black Coat Press, ISBN 9781612271002.

only concern is to continue, for as long as she can, the ultimately hopeless quest to stave off boredom. The heroine in question turns the world upside down not in order to set it to rights, but merely to provide herself with a little amusement that cannot possibly last, so that any moral lesson that emerges has to do so on the principle that many a true word is spoken in jest.

The wonderful Celestine is an unashamed absurdity, who plays her part to the very end, in a fervent spirit that goes beyond the Voltairean to the Rabelaisian, for which significant precedents in the utopian tradition can only be found in the more outré works of Restif de Bretonne and Théophile Gautier's *Mademoiselle de Maupin*. The novella is as much a phantasmagorical comedy as an item of didactic fiction, and one can hardly be surprised that it failed completely to find a sympathetic audience in 1872, when it must have seemed to many readers to be bizarre, incomprehensible and not at all the sort of book that a decent young woman ought to write. Nowadays, of course, we live in a different age with a very different spirit—the era, among other manifestations, of Jody Scott, Josephine Saxton, Riot grrrl and Pussy Riot—and there would probably be no problem in finding a sympathetic audience for the antics of a modern equivalent of Celestine. Perhaps it has taken far too long to arrive, but *Le Monde Renversé* has certainly found its time now, and it can and ought to be recognized and hailed as the ancestor—the mitochondrial Eve as it were—of a great deal of modern feminist satire.

These translations of *Voyage de Théodose à l'île d'Utopie* and *Le Monde renversé* were made from the copies of the Lachaud edition reproduced on the Bibliothèque Nationale's *gallica* website.

Brian Stableford

A VOYAGE TO THE ISLE OF UTOPIA

Chapter I
The Shipwreck

Théodose, majestically framed by that forename and his side-whiskers, and preceded by the ample sphere of his potbelly, was gliding over the waves aboard the *Poussah*,[3] *en route* for the Indies.

The sea was calm, the crew tranquil; the passengers were chatting.

Théodose, standing up, gazed around him in a dignified manner; there were people there of the very best appearance, all disposed to sociability, but Théodose thought that power surpassed all personal value; so, disdaining his peers, he went to bow to the captain of the vessel, and, as if he were saying "My king" he said: "Captain, the wind seems fair to me." Then, slowly, he turned his head toward the passengers, hoping to find them attentive in contemplation of "the gentleman who was conversing with the chief."

The society, however, divided into little groups, was pontificating, laughing, arguing and singing, and did not seem to be paying any heed to anything but its laughter, its pontifications, its disputes and its songs: a check for Théodose, but not a defeat.

Meanwhile, the captain had replied, dryly: "Yes."

---

[3] A *poussah* is a kind of toy, usually consisting of a human figure on a rounded base, which always returns to an upright position if knocked over.

Piqued, Théodose riposted: "Do you know, Monsieur le Capitaine, that it's necessary to be born to your métier to remain in it. Certainly, I'm not an effeminate individual, but when I think about my apartment in the Chaussée-d'Antin, and my entirely Parisian habits, I tell myself that it's necessary never to have lived with civilization to accommodate oneself to your cage of wood." He added, bowing: "I only honor you more for it, and it's very fortunate for us, the people of the drawing room"—he dared not say *court*—"that a few men have conserved these simple tastes."

During these last words, the captain had looked Théodose up and down. Théodose, clad in the modern fashion, in fine cloth and beautiful linen, with a cascade of chain and trinkets at his belt, a diamond solitaire gleaming on his hand, tall of stature, about fifty years old, devoid of hair, his fresh skin tightly confined by a high white collar, with a face like the full moon and the stance of a crowned laureate, was, in sum, on the deck just as he was on the Boulevard des Italiens or in the intimate foyer of the Opéra; he blossomed under the captain's gaze.

Suddenly, however, a breeze rises, a cloud appears, and the captain's eye immediately quits Théodose in order to interrogate the horizon. In less than a second he has seen, he knows, and, drawing away promptly, he issues commands and is obeyed, before Théodose, who has not understood that abrupt exit at all, has resumed his natural pose.

As the passengers have immediately turned toward the captain, and the captain has disappeared in the blink of an eye, everyone, without premeditation, finds themselves contemplating Théodose, still bowing and smiling blissfully. Théodose straightens up and the crowd laughs. Profoundly shocked, Théodose hesitates between the scornful and the superb; during that hesitation, the society has recovered the politeness that a moment's surprise caused it to lose, and no one any longer seems to see Théodose. With his back more sternly braced than usual, he smiles to himself, feeling pity for those poor people, and, whistling an arietta, he blinks at the cloud with a sufficient expression, while directing his lorgnon at it with an utterly impertinent negligence.

But a bolt of lightning immediately erupts; that flash, in the midst of a clear sky, seems to everyone to be the effect of a glimmer in the eye; they all believe it to be an illusion and no one mentions it. However, everyone gazes attentively at the corner of the horizon suspected of disturbance.

A second flash of lightning... a third... cloud... turbulence... a thunderclap, and a gust of wind... and everything trembles, including the passengers, who look at one another in bewilderment.

Théodose has dropped his lorgnon; Théodose has drawn closer; Théodose is now pure nature. He queries with interest, listens attentively, and learns, to the detriment of his peace of mind, that in these regions the tempests are of the worst kind.

During those few minutes of uncertain anguish, the torment has become more complicated; it arrives with the exuberant force of its tropical constitution. Air, sun, birds, sea— everything is engulfed in the horrible flying crater. It seems that, having emerged from nature, it is intent on destroying it entirely.

The vessel spins, sways, rises up, falls back, disappears and re-emerges like a wisp of straw in a basin when one troubles the water.

Where did the tempest come from? No one knows. Where has it gone? Everyone is ignorant. The sky is as beautiful as before; the horizon is nothing but blue, the light nothing but golden; nothing has changed in the immensity, except perhaps, from the viewpoint of the travelers, the means of traversing it, for the ship resembles a nutshell emerging from the pressure of the thumb and forefinger of a Hercules.

The captain has the lifeboats put to sea and the passengers embarked. Ready to descend, Théodose suddenly remembers that there is a strongbox in his cabin that contains some 200,000 francs in bonds of various sorts; that sum is not his entire fortune, even nearly, but it is too considerable for him to reconcile himself to its loss. How long will it take to go to the cabin, get the box and come back? Two minutes. Théodose will be the last to embark instead of being the first, that's all.

He runs, arrives and grabs the box—but in his hurry, his feet trip over an obstacle. He falls, strikes his head, and, with the aid of fear added to the commotion, he faints.

Meanwhile, everyone has embarked. Night will not be long in falling; prudence demands that they make haste in order to navigate in daylight in search of land. Besides which, the vessel might sink entirely at any moment. As the lifeboats move away, the captain hails any remaining passengers; he listens, but no one replies; everyone is pressing him, making demands on him; he decides to abandon the mutilated remains of the *Poussah*.

Chapter II
The Isle of Utopia

What has happened?

Théodose extends one arm, and then the other, and then both at the same time. He stretches his limbs, yawns, opens his eyes slightly, closes them again, and peeps again, somnolence disputing with a vague idea of reflection. In brief, Théodose thinks that he is at rest, and, instinctively, meekly leaves body and mind to their own devices. Confusedly, he feels an inexpressible sense of wellbeing; he has glimpsed a harmony of colors and decorations—an ensemble, in sum, in which everything concurs in establishing a perfect quietude.

He delights in that impression and seeks to maintain it, but, by degrees, it escapes him, although nothing changes—except that, instead of an indefinite sensation, it is a reality that takes shape: the images acquire consistence; objects stand out clearly, and the more Théodose attempts to remain torpid, the harder reality grips him.

His gaze, initially unconscious, becomes curious, and then astonished, and then stupefied. Soon, his open eyes have widened; his mouth has followed the example of his eyes, and Théodose is gaping—and he stays still, only his thoughts pursuing their train.

It's extraordinary, he thinks. *Why, I'm in a bed! My hand is touching the sheet! However, I ought to be in the water. It's doubtless a vision; I'm delirious. Just now, I was about to sink to the bottom. What a misfortune! And to think that I've never felt so restful in my life!*

But could I have dreamed that I boarded the ship? Doubtless I'm at home; my voyage was a dream. Oh, what a nightmare!

However, it's very odd, but I don t see anything here that's familiar. Those curtains are lace; mine are damask; and then, the furniture is very peculiar—I've never seen its like. Let's see—where's my bell?

No, no, it's not there. Nothing can be found. I'm neither at home, nor aboard ship, nor in the sea. What can it mean? Oh, I'm lost!

Anyway, I'm quite certain that I embarked, and then that shipwreck...

Soon, I'll feel the damp. I'm on a plank, floating, and dreaming...

Oh. I'm going to get up, wake up; I don't want to stay like this; my head is all over the place. If I sink, well, I'll sink.

Théodose throws back the bedclothes abruptly. At the same time, a wooden wall panel rotates silently, and in the frame a man appears, dressed in a simple and elegant manner: nothing at all; or, rather, a kind of exceedingly rich loincloth comprises both the detail and the ensemble of his costume. The man's physiognomy is so cordial and so frank that, without analyzing his features, he seems immediately handsome and sympathetic.

Théodose and he look at one another. The stranger smiles, but Théodose is so astonished that he is incapable of the slightest articulation. The stranger, still smiling, advances toward the bed and stops at a small table placed at the head of the bed, on which there is a laden tray. He pours out a golden liquid reminiscent of wine into a cup, and fills a bowl with a succulent cream, which a Norman cow would not have denied. Having done that, he picks up the cup in one hand and the bowl in the other, and presents them both to Théodose.

In the grip of an involuntary confidence, Théodose mechanically closes his hand on the ruddy liquid. Immediately, the stranger sets down the bowl and picks up another cup. He pours a similar measure into that one, and then, raising the glass by way of a salute, he empties it in one long draught.

Théodose, utterly subjugated, imitates him perfectly, and when he abandons the empty cup, which the stranger takes back, the other seems satisfied by the fact that he has drunk. Then the man in the loincloth mimes the action of pouring again. Immediately, Théodose's face relaxes; he smiles and puts his finger to his forehead, in a jesting manner, expressing fear.

With that, Théodose's companion shakes his head, imitates an expression of astonishment and concludes by reclining his head on his shoulder, while emitting an emphatic snore.

"No, that's enough," says Théodose, laughing frankly. Then he stops short before the reflection that the other might not understand, and begins to sketch out an amiable pantomime.

Scarcely has he commenced, however, when he hears a sonorous voice pronouncing: "Oh! He speaks as I do!"

"What!" says Théodose, amazed. "You can understand me?"

"Word for word," the stranger replies.

"But where am I, then?"

"On the isle of Utopia, friend voyager."

"On the isle of Utopia! What's that? Where is it? In what country are you?"

"We are a country; a country is a country, and all countries are countries."

"Yes," says Théodose, ironically, "but to what people do you belong?"

"We are part of all the peoples we encounter," the native replies.

"Undoubtedly," retorts Théodose, impatiently, "but in sum, there are names to distinguish the different parts of the earth, and you must have a name?"

"Who has given these names, friend?"

"Us," Théodose replies. "Others...anyone...people!"

"Then it's up to you to tell me the name I ought to wear."

"That's a joke. How do you expect me to know, having fallen here from the clouds?"

"And how should I, friend voyager, know the name that it has pleased you to give me out there? Then again, why should a particular and insignificant name be so important to you? Call the quarters of the globe what you wish—will it change them? Do you want to know where you are? Interrogate nature; she will give you the same response that she gives to us." He drew back a thick curtain abruptly, and added: "Look."

A shaft of light with no possible name flooded the room. One might have thought it volatilized flame, or that the atmosphere was composed of impalpable diamonds. Its reflections seemed to contain the source of life within them, and simply to conceal the birth of the world, and then, enveloped within it as if in an adornment, an infinitely capricious and gigantically splendid creation: more than a dream, an ecstasy; not the admiration of the marvelous but the grip of the unknown, the unimaginable, the uncreated…and embracing all of that, an endless marine horizon; that was the limit, for the irresistible enticement was to go on to the end, to see whence that life originated.

"Well, friend," said the native, "my country is the neighbor of the sun, as you see; call it what you will, it will always be a translation."

"Oh, how beautiful it is, how beautiful!" said Théodose.

"Well, get up, since you've recovered, and soon we'll take you into the great shadows that you can see over there."

"But tell me," Théodose asked, "how did I come to be here? If I'm not mistaken, a few hours ago, I was on a ship; the tempest had damaged it, and as I went to get something from my cabin, I fell over. Since that moment, I can't remember anything more. Did someone carry me to the lifeboat, and we've disembarked here?"

"No, my friend. We're the ones who perceived a black dot on the sea after the tempest. We suspected that it was a vessel, and several inhabitants of the isle wanted to go to meet it, to see whether it was lost or simply passing by. That's how you were found, unconscious, and were brought here. Now you've woken up."

"Have I been here a long time?" Théodose asked.

"A whole night. You were picked up yesterday evening, and now it's morning."

"And my poor companions—what became of them?"

"You can be tranquil on their account. We perceived a boat in the distance, and as this region is dotted with a large quantity of islands, your companions will have reached land, all the more so as the weather was calm all night long."

"But they won't come to any harm?"

"What harm?"

"Well," said Théodose, embarrassed, "one never knows. If no one takes an interest in them...when one is a stranger..."

"I don't understand," said the native, severely. "When one is new, one makes acquaintances, that's all."

"That's true, that's true," Théodose hastened to reply. "Well then, I'll get up, since everything has worked out so well. Now that my mind is at rest, I've had enough sleep."

"That's right, get up. We've been waiting for you before eating, because we thought you'd wake up soon. Look, here's a garment that my wife has sent you; it's my daughters who embroidered it." So saying, the native unrolled a magnificent piece of white cashmere decorated with red and gold.

"What?" said Théodose, blushing.

"Well, what?" asked the other.

"But I'd be quite naked," Théodose added, timidly.

"Oh, I understand—you're used to being covered up to the chin. But it's too hot here, friend; you wouldn't be able to endure it. Everyone is like me, and as you see, I have a garment just like yours. Put it on without fear, and don't worry about it."

During that speech, Théodose thought to himself: *If I were twenty years old, I'd ask for nothing better than to content myself with that wretched girdle, but now, with my potbelly, and bald—no, I don't want to.* Involuntarily, he saw in anticipation his host's wife and daughters, and he refused to present himself before them in that way.

"No," he said aloud, "I'm sensitive to the cold, you see, and my clothes are light; I assure you that they won't inconvenience me."

"Try, since that's your desire," his host replied.

Then, indicating to Théodose the purpose of each item of furniture, he showed him a mobile panel that opened on to a small room with a marble washbasin and bath. A tap could be turned up above, and water flowed; a tap could be turned down below, and water flowed.

There was a dressing table with all its utensils, a full-length mirror all the way up to the ceiling. fine towels—a comfort, in sum, that would have been the envy of a respectable person. And having initiated Théodose into the secrets of operating each device, he left him alone, recommending him to come as soon as possible, because they were waiting for him.

Chapter III
The Meal

Théodose got up and went to look at himself in the mirror; he thought that he looked well. Satisfied on that score, he examined the furniture swiftly. It was, in truth, luxurious and well-designed; so, without further deliberation, he embarked bravely on the details of his toilette. Although he put the most minute care into it, however, he could not get rid of the creases in the collar of his shirt—and what a misfortune that was for a man like him, accustomed to linen immutable in its stiffness and dazzling in its cleanliness. There was no means of obtaining a substitute, though, the shirt not flourishing in the locality, and even seeming to be unknown there.

Théodose gave extended thought to his lost wardrobe, but that did not remedy anything; so, being obliged to make the best of things, he cast one last glance over his person, passed the crumpled linen through his fingers one last time, and, half sure of himself, opened the door through which his host had gone.

Four people were immediately presented to his sight: the man whose acquaintance he had made, a mature woman and two young women. The three women were endowed with physiognomies that could not have been more amiable; their figures were beautiful and naturally majestic. Their rich and brightly-colored costumes left bare the neck, the arms and the legs beneath the knee; their hair, beautiful and well cared for, was gathered on top of the head because of the excessive heat; pearls, feathers and flowers decorated their garments and their hair, but all those ornaments were tastefully disposed and not excessive.

As soon as Théodose appeared on the threshold, the man and the oldest of the three women came to meet him and, each offering him a hand, led him solicitously to the table in the middle of the room. One of the young women brought forward a chair, the other graciously offered him her hand, and Théodose sat down, thanking all the people who were eager to serve him.

"There," said the host, sitting down opposite, with the two young women on either side, while the lady of the house sat down next to Théodose. "Now let's share the meal. Whoever takes a place at this table takes a place in the family; the same bread will nourish us, as the same amity unites us."

He presented a full glass to Théodose, adding: "Greetings to our friend!"

Everyone present having picked up a glass at the same time, they all repeated cordially: "Greetings to our friend."

"I greet you in my turn," said Théodose, nonplussed. "I salute and bless you…I…"

His poor tongue could not finish; he was confused.

"Come on," said his host joyfully, "Let's eat; you must be hungry, and I confess that we've been generous in waiting for you, for there are ever-eager stomachs here." So saying, he gave a little tap to the chins to either side of him.

"Papa is pretending that he isn't thinking about eating, as we are," said the neighbor to the left to the neighbor to the right—and, laughing mischievously, the two gazes approached one another beneath their father's nose. The latter started to laugh.

"Well, my daughters," said the lady beside Théodose, cheerfully, "if you sit down at the table with such charitable dispositions, what will become of you, pray, by the end of the meal?"

"My dear mother," replied one of the two mischief-makers, "it's just to have an opportunity to kiss Papa: we annoy him, we argue with him, he forgives us." During that riposte, the neighbor took advantage of her sister's idea and kissed the paternal cheek on her side effusively. Seeing that, the speaker swiftly leaned toward the other cheek and deposited a sonorous kiss.

Théodose stared, but all those people were so lively, so simple and so natural that they left no scope for any observation. Meanwhile, the host, while laughing and chatting, had sliced up a magnificent piece of meat. He offered the dish to Théodose, and while the latter was serving himself, at the general invitation, the young women occupied themselves with serving like true housewives; they offered the father and the mother various kinds of *hors-d'oeuvre*, sliced the bread and maintained order on the table.

Soon, everyone had made their choices, and jaws were moving with appropriate activity.

During the first few moments there was nothing but "Take this...taste that...no thanks...pass me the bread, please...but you're not drinking..."—in sum, just enough words to make oneself understood, and not enough to interrupt the solemn operation. When the initial appetite had passed, Théodose sat back in his chair and, while examining the large and beautiful room in which he found himself, he uttered an exclamation of contentment.

As if at a signal, everyone replied in his or her own fashion.

"Oh, I was hungry," said the mother.

"Me, too," added three more voices, "me, too...and me..."

"Your cuisine is truly excellent, Madame," said Théodose, addressing his neighbor.

"I'm delighted that it pleases you, Monsieur," she replied. "You must have had a good appetite, moreover—that's strong seasoning."

"It's a fact, Madame, that I haven't eaten since noon yesterday...the middle of the day," he added, by way of explanation.

"Of course, Monsieur—we understand everything you say."

"But how is it," asked Théodose, looking at all of them, "that you speak exactly as I do?"

"Some years ago," the host replied, "one of our young people took advantage of a ship that had anchored off our coast to satisfy an impulse to travel that tended to excess, to the point of obsession. He succeeded in being taken away, and later, having become bored with the country to which he went, he came back with a cargo of books and instruments of every sort. Naturally, we pestered the voyager to get him to tell us something. To simple folk he said silly things, but he explained new points to the scholars, and as we gained confidence in him, he was soon given the means of executing what he explained.

"All his enterprises succeeded so well that the population, on the initiative of a few, declared that to honor the genius of the nation where our compatriot had been educated, we would henceforth use its language, and no other. Immediately, the voyager was asked to educate pupils in the language he had learned, in order that they could become teachers in their turn, and the plan was executed with so much enthusiasm that a few years later, the original language was no more than a memory." The host added: "You speak that language, so it's your people that we're honoring."

"I'm profoundly touched by it," said Théodose, with feeling. Then he added: "It's as if I were in my own country here."

"Absolutely," replied the host. "You only lack your nearest and dearest; we'll drink to their health—your glass, friend. By the way, what's your name? Mine is Verdin."

"Verdin," repeated Théodose. "What a name!"

"Why?" said his host. "Isn't the name Verdin as good as Polycarpe, Barnabé or Chrysostom?"

"Yes, but Verdin is a fantasy; why not also Jaunet, Bleuâtre or Noirot?"

"We do, in fact, have yellows, blues and whites."

"You have yellows, blues and whites? But in that case you have reds and crimsons? Perhaps even commu..."[4]

---

[4] In 1872, everyone in France would have jumped to the conclusion that the incomplete word is "communards"—who were, of course, familiarly known as *rouges* [reds] in the same way as modern communists. The memory of the 1871 Com-

Théodose did not finish; his mouth remained open, his eyes fixed, and all his tensed muscles expressing the most terrible fear.

"What does this terror for one name rather than another signify?" Verdin asked.

"Wretch!" exclaimed Théodose "Is a name not, in itself, the person, and can I be tranquil in the midst of individuals who bear bloody names?" And Théodose shivered.

"He's mad," thought Verdin, aloud. Compassionately, he said: "Come on, friend, you're not thinking clearly; it's the aftermath of the shock. How can you expect a name to signify anything, since it's given to a child as soon as he's born, and no one knows what he will become later? Instead of insignificant syllables, we sometimes receive denominations of things, of birds or plants. My mother liked spring best of all, so she called me Verdin, like many others."

"Ah!" said Théodose, who had listened anxiously. "Oh, my dear Verdin, I shall embrace you." Effusively, he went on: "Oh, my dear friends, how happy I am to be among you. But I don't believe that I've told you my name: it's Théodose, and I'd like to write it myself in some corner, in order that you'll remember me." He turned to his neighbor and continued: "My dear Madame, permit me to kiss that beautiful hand, which has served me the best and most agreeable of meals."

"That hand would have been to seek your family, if that had been possible," the lady said, with an expression of ineffable bounty.

"My family is here, where I have been treated as a brother, Madame; I did not know mine until today. Today, I have made its acquaintance, and I love it."

"So much the better, if your heart is in accord with what you say; at least we can soften your regret for absent dear ones."

---

mune would still be sharp and raw in Théodose's memory; its brief authority would have horrified him as much as it presumably gave hope to Léonie Rouzade.

"What absent dear ones, Madame?"

"Your wife…your children…I don't know. Are you alone?"

"Entirely alone, Madame."

"Oh, our friend!" said the lady, emotionally. "What, you have lost…! Forgive me for having recalled those memories."

"You haven't recalled any painful memory, Madame; I have, it's true, lost my father and my mother, but they were very old, and I couldn't hope to keep them any longer. Such a memory makes one think, but doesn't make one sad."

"But your wife, your children?"

"I have none, Madame," said Théodose, smiling.

"No children?"

"Nor a wife."

"No wife! She's dead, then!"

"No—I've never had one."

The lady and Verdin stared at him.

"Maman," said the two young women, taking advantage of the momentary silence. "Should we serve the coffee here or tell our friends that we'll take it with them?"

"That depends on our friend," said the mother. Turning to Théodose, she added: "Monsieur, the people who accompanied my husband when you were brought here have, like us, the desire to be agreeable to you; except that, as liberty is the best hospitality, it goes without saying that what will make you happy will make us equally happy. Would you prefer to remain alone or accept the invitation?"

"Madame," said Théodose, gallantly, "the company here is too good to have any taste for solitude; in any case, by surrounding a stranger with concern, you have taught him to love his fellows. I accept."

"My children," said the mother, "Go and inform the family; there's no need to come back. We'll join you at the spring soon, as usual."

At these words from their mother, the two young women got up, kissed their parents and drew away swiftly.

Chapter IV
A Stormy Debate

"They're your children?" said Théodose. "How charming they are!"

"They're our entire life," said the father, looking at his wife. The latter held out her hand to her husband and both of them, turning to look at Théodose, seemed to be pitying him.

"So, you're alone," said Verdin. "No children, no wife, nothing. What an existence! Have you not been able to find a companion of your choice, then?"

"I've never tried," Théodose replied, placidly.

Verdin reflected, and then suddenly, as if enlightened, said: "I see. You belong to those who have taken a vow of nullity. Our voyager mentioned them. If my memory serves me right, such people are called 'priests' or 'monks'—but my friend"—Verdin's voice took on a grave intonation—"how can you believe that you are honoring nature by holding in shame the work that has given you life? If creation is culpable, nature is therefore eternally culpable, since she has created you and everything that exists. Then again, if it were admitted that to develop existence is a crime, how would you dare to develop your life by nourishment and care, for if it is unworthy to give life to others, it must be unworthy to receive that existence for oneself. Only a boor pockets and keeps everything for himself."

"You're very prompt to criticize," said Théodose, angrily.

"A mine explodes in proportion to the powder put into it, friend. I see you in the latter part of your career, plump and fresh, as alive as an oak in the middle of a forest, and all that life is monopolized; you have only employed it in creating a void, a branch extended over the human race; you want being to conclude with yourself, and you're astonished that I'm indignant?"

"If you'd let me speak, you wouldn't have become indignant. I'm not a monk; I'm a bachelor."

"That you're a bachelor goes without saying. What did you think I believed?"

"I'm telling you that I've remained a bachelor because that status suits me."[5]

"You've remained a boy!" repeated Verdin, amazed. "Can one become a girl, then?"

"In truth," said Théodose, "you're too naïve, or you're being deliberately so. When I say that I've remained a bachelor, I mean that I'm not married. In brief, I don't have a household. Do you understand now?"

"Well then, what difference is there between you and a monk?"

"There's a great difference," said Théodose, laughing. "A monk lives in his cell, or, at least, is obliged to live there, while I revel in society."

"Yes, but you live alone there."

"Alone!" repeated Théodose, in a passably complacent tone. "It depends what one means by alone. I left a few regrets behind on my departure. People will be thinking of me in more than one place."

"What people? Who?" said Verdin, impatiently.

"Well," said Théodose, tiredly, "if it's necessary to dot the *"i"*s, do you want me to recount my escapades in front of Madame?"

Ah!" Verdin pronounced, slowly, almost talking to himself. "Is it the case then, that you live there like the traveler who takes shelter in the shade of a tree, refreshes himself and moves on? You imitate a creature, or a thing—and it's tolerated among you that a being lives alone in the midst of united beings?"

"Who, then, would oblige me to marry?"

---

[5] Théodose has referred to himself as a *garcon,* meaning bachelor, but the word has other meanings, including "boy"—hence Verdin's next remark.

"Moral law, nature and her executor when a man does not subscribe to it himself—society."

"Oh, I satisfy that law," said Théodose, sniggering. "I espouse all the beauties who want me to do so."

"Don't laugh!" exclaimed Verdin, imperiously. Then, sadly, he added: "In fact, what reproaches can I address to you, and what would be the point? To live thus, is it not necessary to be incapable of feeling? In which case, how could my reproaches touch you? All I can do is to pity you."

"This scene is perfectly ridiculous," riposted Théodose, losing his temper. "Everyone is free, I suppose, and if it suits some to remain unmarried, what business is it of anyone else's?"

"None, so long as the unmarried individual lives in pure unity with himself, that he isolates himself absolutely as a 'me'; but as soon as his being has become part of an 'us,' other individuals, the family, then society—the entire group, in sum—has rights over the individual who has allied himself with the group as one of them. If, through indignity or weakness, it pleases the individual to accept an outrage, it is not appropriate for the family to support him; and if the family, like the individual, is unworthy or weak, then society—which is to say, other families—should oblige everyone to return to the path of duty."

"You're forgetting, friend Verdin, that everyone has personal rights, and that no man can claim the obedience of another. If you say to me, your peer: I don't want that; I may reply: I do. Can a man be both free and not free at the same time? Beware of the mire into which you're sinking."

"Have you set out all your arguments? Have you none in reserve?"

"Do you need any more, by chance?"

"No, I believe them to be sufficient. So, when I have demonstrated their inefficacy to you, I hope that you will be convinced. But drink, then! Personally, I have a dry tongue by dint of chattering away! To your health! I'll continue. One is free; which is to say that one has all rights, and nothing but rights, so long as one lives alone; but as soon as one makes contact in any fashion with society, one belongs to that society, one is part of it, one has duties, and only a dishonest society can tolerate dishonest individuals in its midst. No one can prevent you from being whatever you please, but if you want to live with others, it is necessary to be what pleases them; otherwise, take your baggage and go, for people have to be subject to their will. Can you understand that, my dear Théodose?"

"Not very well. So it's necessary for me to be everyone's slave, then? And everyone, whose slaves are they, pray?"

"Everyone who lives according to their desires—and you, who oppose it, can go to live somewhere that suits you better."

"But what if no society suits me?"

"In that case, you're an exception, and, as an exception is an isolated individual, an isolated individual can do nothing against the mass."

"Well, what did I say? There I am, enslaved for life."

"If you're a unique exception, yes; but if there are others who think as you do, what prevents you from founding a colony?"

"What prevents us? Everyone, and even our own interests."

"I'm no longer following you. Let's see, what do you think is stopping you? Does not the liberty of those you reject ensure your own liberty? And as for general interests, do they cease because associates separate themselves? If some organization doesn't please, another is founded—does commerce lose its impetus in consequence? The human race is the great trademark, and peoples and groups are simply the various shareholders who each exploit life as they think best."

"But friend Verdin, there really are good and evil, and if people were allowed to act as they please, they'd do evil."

"My dear Théodose, there is above all, liberty; there is above all, humankind, against which human beings can do nothing. As you said just now, if I want to do you good, you can claim to do me harm, and that would be as just, for as soon as I touch you, you can touch me."

"It's necessary to let everything alone, then."

"It's necessary to let nothing alone, otherwise one loses one's liberty; but liberty stops at not tolerating those among us who want to absorb us; if you want to impose your manner of being on me, I, in order to reject it, exclude you. What could be more equitable?"

"But where shall I go, if there is no society anywhere in which I can be happy?"

"Well, as I say, associate with those of the same mind and live in peace, without worrying about whether other people live differently."

"But where can one go to live, overly naïve Verdin?"

"Wherever you happen to be—anywhere; there's no shortage of unoccupied space on earth."

"And who will give you that space?"

"Who will refuse it to you?"

"The government, the owner."

"Does uncultivated land belong to anyone?"

"You're very primitive or very limited, my dear Verdin, it you don't know the first thing about regulations. Let's see, doesn't the earth belong to the rich?"

"The earth belongs to labor, that's what I know, friend Théodose, and among us, everything that is not under cultivation belongs to anyone who wants to occupy it."

"Among you? But are you like not everyone else?"

"We're not, in fact, like your people, if they're as you say," replied Verdin, severely. "We don't want being to be an object of recreation or work, and if we neither can nor want to touch others, at least we don't suffer any parasite or despot who might absorb us. Among us, everyone who wants someone else marries, and anyone who wants a family recognizes our laws or goes elsewhere and founds others."

"And your high morality adapts to the fact that alongside you there are beings who live in brutal cynicism and debauchery?"

"Big words often replace thought in you, friend Theodore. My high prudence, which you have forgotten, informs me that one establishes nothing by force. I therefore allow the vicious to exercise their vices, and my high morality is there to receive them if it pleases them to return. Don't worry, the vicious in association become disgusted with one another in a short time."

"It would be better if there were harmony."

"And why do you want someone else to submit to you, but not to submit to someone else? The 'I want' is only really possible for oneself. I want people to love one another, so I love them—that is all I can do. If you want harmony, adopt the wishes of others."

"That's truly superb!" said Théodose, with a slightly mocking expression. "And that's how you act in your society?"

"Yes."

"In ours it's not quite the same, but that ought not to bother you, since ours isn't here."

"It still sickens me to hear it said that humans live like animals, which take one another and leave, and the strongest of which eat the weakest. If we expel such creatures when they want to live like that among us, we cannot approve of them when people simply talk to us about them; after our exclusion there is still our scorn."

"What rage to vent on others. Because one doesn't live like you, one is despicable?"

"Be equally scornful of us, if you wish. What stops you?"

"What would be the point?"

"Only he who is conscious of his rights perseveres in their maintenance, friend Théodose; progress is not made by the stars. It's because some attempt eternally to improve others that the human species improves. Is there any means more worthy than criticism? Your liberty and mine are respected; I find your actions bad, and I simply say so; if they seem good to you, you persist, and I persist in criticizing."

"But my poor Verdin, there are social conditions among us of which you're unaware. Thus, poverty often prevents people from marrying."

"That's the greatest of misfortunes, and you owe it to the rich."

"In that case, it's the rich who are the cause of all evil?"

"That's not so far from the truth. If there are people excluded from everything, it follows that there are others who have excluded them. Think: what can one man do? Nothing more than the work of one man. So, if one possesses a product that has necessitated the work of several, it is because he has taken their share, either by trickery or force, and you can see that the deprived are the inevitable consequence of the over-supplied."

"You're communists!"

"Yes, certainly; since it's the mass that produce, it cannot be appropriate that only a few profit. The profit must legitimately be shared between all those who have produced it. Can it be, by chance, that you have not yet understood that outside communism, there can only be appropriators of labor and hoarders of profit, Communism is the only justice."

"That's a dream. Is it possible that everyone could have an equal share? Can one even know how many individuals enter into the founding of a fortune? One couldn't calculate it."

"So you don't know about associations? That's something that simplifies the mechanisms."

"A fine invention! One is regimented—and that's liberty?"

"No, no, my dear Théodose, it's necessary to be consistent. Do you believe that it's liberty when a worker is forced to surrender his necessity to another, for whom it becomes a superfluity?"

"We'll never agree—let's leave it there."

"So be it—but I still want to say a few more words. You say that one isn't free in an association. Nothing changes, however, in one's habitual functions; work, under one name or another, is still work, and the association always exists; whether a proprietor employs the workers for himself alone or whether the same workers work for one another, it's still an association; there's merely the question of remuneration that is no longer the same. With the hoarder of profit, which is ownership, one receives what is granted; with the simple association of communism, one receives one's share. One of ten receives a tenth, and so on; it's a question of arithmetic. And if I wanted to go on, I'd say that since work is a human being's reason for being, there is nothing that can ever deprive him of it, and the only way for a human being to be free is to obtain a profit from that work. Now, only association provides that profit, so only association delivers freedom. The hoarders of profit are speculators on the human species, communists the liberators of the human species."

"I'm only astonished by one thing, my dear Verdin, which is that, given your enthusiasm for association, you don't mix your nourishment. Why do you leave the wine separate, and each food likewise? In your place, I'd make all of it into a socialistic pâté."

"That is, in fact, what you and I do, my dear Théodose. Your stomach receives the dishes that suit it either for the purpose of construction or pleasure, and those various foods make up an entire nourishment, from which your entire body profits. That's how association proceeds, and I'm delighted that you've offered me that example. In any case, you can't be unaware that everything is association: the individual is an association of limbs, marriage an association of a man and a woman, government an association of wills, suffrage an association of votes, the army an association of soldiers, a factory an association of workers, a bank an association of employees, nature an association of elements, and man and nature, the one living in the other, summarize the great association that is creation. Thus, association is the very principle of being, and nothing exists except by association."

"I can see," said Théodose, with affectation, "that you think me a monster; everything in my way of being horrifies you. You doubtless regret having saved my life."

"Oh!" said Verdin, with a gesture of profound commiseration. "Why do you say that? Is that really what you think? Far from regretting having saved you, I'm doubly glad. Our adversaries have the right to all our care; it's necessary that we win them over. We don't take you for a monster at all, but we can't agree with you, since your ideas seem false to us. In any case, if I was cruel just now when I spoke about the unmarried, it's because I didn't know that there was poverty where you come from. If you're poor, my dear Théodose, no recrimination bears upon you; a poor man is a victim, and a victim can never be criticized."

During this response on Verdin's part, Théodose hesitated to declare his wealth, but deep-rooted prejudice carried him away. "I'm rich," he said, proudly. Then, thinking back to his shipwreck, he added: "In fact, I've lost a great deal…but after all, I still have enough left."

Verdin nodded his head approvingly.

"If I had only been able to save my strongbox," Théodose went on. He did not say any more, not daring, for reasons of delicacy, to ask whether it had been found.

"But if that's the box you were holding in your hand, it has been brought here. It's there, with the big trunk that contains your effects."

"Ah!" said Théodose, rising to his feet with an explosion of joy. "What luck!" Then the idea crossed his mind that since the trunk had been opened, the box might have been opened, too—and then, well, who could tell?

Thus, it was in a very different tone that he said to Verdin: "The box has doubtless been opened?"

"No," said Verdin, almost astonished.

"The trunk was opened," Théodose pointed out, by way of explanation.

"The trunk was opened because it was isolated there, and in order to carry away one object rather than another, it was necessary at least to know what it contained. As you were clutching the box in your hand, though, it was no concern of ours what was inside it. If you had been dead, yes—but you were alive, and that was a different matter."

"That's true," said Théodose, slightly disconcerted. "I didn't think of that."

"Would you like to take it?" asked Verdin. "We can also carry the trunk into your room; there are clothes like yours in it; they might be useful to you." So saying, Verdin stood up. Théodose followed his host and, on seeing his precious strongbox intact, he thought he might weep with joy. Then, perceiving at the same time that the trunk was his own, the contentment he felt was so immense that he did not know which was the more agreeable—to have recovered his money or his means of adornment.

Immediately, Théodose, offering his excuses to Verdin, who had helped him to transport the trunk, shut himself in his room, and in the blink of an eye he had repaired the faults in his attire.

Théodose would be introduced into the town in a decent manner. Henceforth, everything about him reverted to its normal appearance; he was properly dressed, he had money; doubtless these people were very extraordinary, but what did that matter to Théodose? He could pay his way, so he was free. Thus, his physiognomy had become radiant again, and it was with an entirely casual aplomb that, on going back into the room where Verdin and his wife were waiting for him, he offered his arm to the latter.

"If you're walking with Nisia," said Verdin, "take this large parasol; it won't be too big for the two of you."

The proffered parasol was a true masterpiece of taste and elegance, but it was quite ludicrous from a Parisian point of view, so Théodose sketched a gesture of ill-humor and refusal—but French gallantry won him over, and he decided in favor of the lady, even though he was deeply resentful.

Chapter V
The Presentation

On emerging from the house, which was situated on top of a hill from which one could see the valley below, framed to either side by thickly-wooded mountains, with the sea in the distance, Théodose, Verdin and Nisia, his wife, set off along a shady path that descended into the valley.

It was morning, but the heat in that torrid climate commenced, so to speak, with the day—and in any case, what was perfectly tolerable for the natives of the region was a scourge for an inhabitant of a cooler country. So Théodose began to sweat and pant; he was stifling in his clothes, and dared not stir.

Finally, they reached the valley, but Théodose did not enjoy the landscape; he was entirely focused on his discomfort, and was beginning to envy Verdin and his light garment. If he had been known in the country he would have loosened his clothing a little, but a presentation! What impression would that make? No, he wanted to show himself to these people in all his dignity—so he melted in his garments.

Until then, the parasol had been unnecessary, and Théodose was wondering vaguely whether it would be necessary to make use of it. In that preoccupation, it was no longer the ridiculousness of the object that troubled him, but the heat that he would suffer under the sun. The precaution of a shelter indicated a danger, and Théodose thought about the sun. While he was thinking about it, he found it.

"We don't have far to go," said Nisia. "We're going to the forest that you can see there, and the heat is still quite mild."

Théodose wanted to reply, but he had eaten well, which had necessitated drinking well, and the poor man, fat, stuffed and tightly-strapped, was closer to apoplexy than anything else. So, on those words from the lady, he was only able to gaze at the route ahead. Opening the parasol, he advanced, breathless, mute, immobile in his warmth, his eyes fixed on the goal—which he could not even bring into focus, exhausted as he was.

Gradually, however, the shade became cooler. Soon, a watercourse that traced its bright line sinuously beneath the trees gave a little more mildness to the atmosphere. From one minute to the next, Théodose was recovering from his distress—except that he was soaked; his shirt was twisted and his trousers, like his jacket, had darker tints in places. In brief, Théodose felt half-submerged.

That disastrous condition caused him to establish comparisons with the costume in use in the region; he was not yet ready to adopt it, but he understood it. His self-assurance had diminished in proportion to the disturbance of the correctness of his attire. Théodose had given up on the idea of a triumphant entrance; he was more fearful than hopeful.

Soon, the three individuals, who had followed the stream, heard a confused sound of voices. A few strides further on, they found themselves at the entrance to an immense clearing, the middle of which, hollowed out in a basin, received the water of a spring and spread it out in a large thread that was lost to sight some distance away.

The scene presented by the clearing was animated by groups and isolated individuals, suspended from the branches, wading in the water, running, playing, sitting, lying down or arguing, some clad in blue, some in pink, in gray, in red, in gold or in green—all imaginable shades, in sum—combined infinitely by an incessant movement, in a clear but soft light, in the midst of fresh verdure crowding in clumps at ground level and sheltered at a prodigious height by a dome of foliage with interlaced tints. Little holes like pinpricks allowed the sky to be glimpsed—which seen thus, resembled a myriad of stars. Such a scene was as unexpected as the thought, also impossible to render visually, for the effect was that of an ungraspable mobility. It was necessary to see it, and Théodose, who was looking at it, stood there dazzled.

The people nearest to the place where Verdin, his wife and Théodose had emerged perceived them immediately. Running to meet them, they shook hands with the husband and nodded their heads as a sign of greeting to Théodose. At the same time, the movement of the first few having been perceived by others, everyone immediately began to group together, and a general silence seemed to interrogate the newcomers.

"My friends," said Verdin, taking Théodose's hand, "this is the voyager that the tempest has confided to us. He's from the country that is so dear to us."

Scarcely had these words been pronounced when a murmur of voices filled the air. Exclamations burst forth from the grave faces of the speakers; it was like the continuous but irregular sound of waves rising and falling.

Then one man emerged from the ranks and, turning toward the audience, raised his hand. Immediately, everyone fell silent. Turning toward Théodose and his guides, the man spoke:

"Verdin, I shall speak on behalf of everyone here, and they will ratify it if I have spoken well. You know that for us, every man is a brother, unless that man refuses of his own accord. The voyager is thus among his own people; his quality as a Frenchman, great as it might be in our eyes, is still inferior to his quality as a human being. As our peer, whoever he might be, he would have been received in the same way; as a Frenchman, he will only gain by seeing the gratitude and esteem that we have for his compatriots. I, therefore, as a man, offer my hand to you, as a man."

Stepping forward in a calm and dignified manner, the orator extended his hand toward Théodose. The latter took it, and shook it vigorously in both of his, stammering a few unintelligible words.

Without letting go of Théodose's hand, the orator had turned toward the audience as if to be judged. All of them, in response to the movement, replied with bursts of applause.

"Now, friends," said Verdin, "I ask in my turn, on behalf of the three of us, to take coffee."

Unanimous laughter greeted that sally; then, everyone making room, the trio was surrounded, and guided gently and affectionately to a corner of the clearing. There, beneath trees and bushes pruned into the form of an arbor, a well-furnished circular bench had been cut out in the earth, along with a carpet of thick grass. The enclosure was vast and the opening, very broad, permitted everything that was happening in the clearing to be seen.

In the middle of the redoubt, immense silver coffee pots were set on warming-plates resting on the ground, with a quantity of cups of the same metal. Enormous sugar bowls, still part of the same service, were overflowing with sugar, and various bottles covered with wicker with labels on their flanks were carefully laid down among the utensils.

Having arrived at the banquet, Verdin, Nisia and Théodose were invited to sit down first; then the oldest individuals took their places alongside them, while all the young people remained outside. Then youths and young women began to distribute cups, saucers and spoons. Having done that, some picked up coffee pots and others sugar bowls, and while some served in the arbor, others served at the entrance. The interior, less crowded than the exterior, being rapidly finished, the distributors came together to satisfy everyone at the doorway, and the operation was soon concluded. It goes without saying that although the distributors were the last to be served, they were not forgotten.

"My friends," said the man who had welcomed Théodose on behalf of the inhabitants, "let us drink to peace, concord and amity! We often talk about such things; today we have put them into practice; let us therefore name those virtues before our new friend, in order that he might learn that he has a right to expect them from us."

"To peace, concord and amity!" repeated all the voices, enthusiastically—and with that, everyone started to stir their coffees, and there was laughter, because one person was scalded and another spilled it. The oldest were amused by the sight of the youngest, and the youngest amused one another.

When the coffee had been drunk and the judgment it merited pronounced on its confection, some went this way and some that, peering at the labels on the bottles and each naming aloud the liqueur they had chosen for themselves. After having poured it, they passed the bottle to anyone who requested it. The latter did the same, until no one was any longer asking and the last put it back in its place.

Youth is lively, and had soon drunk its fill; there was a hectic stampede, some running after others. Everyone took their cups, washed them in the spring and deposited them on a white marble tabletop set out for that purpose.

Chapter VI
An Encounter

Soon, the entrance to the arbor was completely deserted; only one woman had stayed. She was sitting to one side on a small prominence. The attitude and physiognomy of the woman were a composite of ennui, disdain and preciosity. She might have been forty or forty-five years old, and was strong in her stature and her stance, except that the skin had the faded appearance of something withered, and the features seemed drawn, denuded as they were of the sheen that makes the charm and splendor of a face. She was like a fruit of good quality but overripe. In a word, she was a woman past her prime.

Nisia, who perceived her, interrupted her own conversation and addressed her.

"What, Madame Brunel," she said, getting to her feet, "you're here all alone? Come with us, then—but why aren't you sitting here, as usual? There's plenty of room." She led the woman into the middle of the arbor as she spoke. "You see, we have a few young people with us who haven't deserted us."

"I know full well that you would have found my age more than adequate to come in here," said Madame Brunel, in a bitter tone, "but just because I'm old, it doesn't prevent me from being timid. It's probably ridiculous, but I can't change myself, unfortunately." While saying that, Madame Brunel lowered her eyes, pursed her lips and put on an ingenuous expression.

"I've never considered what you just said, Madame," Nisia replied, with a simple kindness. "You sit here often, and it astonished me that you were outside today."

Madame Brunel replied, timidly: "I'm only blaming my own stupidity, Madame, for what has happened. There was a solemnity today, and"—her embarrassment increased and she kept her eyes lowered—"I didn't want to insinuate myself and to be seen. I always keep to one side, and unless I'm forced to come forward, as you did just now, Madame, I never do it of my own accord."

"But you could come and sit down like anyone else," said Nisia, slightly astonished, "and no one would have paid any more attention to you than anyone else. Why do you think you'd be noticed?"

"It is the case, in fact," articulated Madame Brunel, half suffocated by resentment, "that I pass unnoticed here, I must confess!"

During this conversation Théodose studied Madame Brunel. He knew the type, but he was astonished to find a specimen among these people.

In society, there is a certain kind of woman who retains until decrepitude an affectation of timidity and reserve that makes them somewhat reminiscent of elderly nuns. Add to that a certain very particular expression, by which they seem perpetually fearful of receiving a declaration, which always makes one wonder whether one ought to make one, and if, by chance, some idiot exploits their ridiculousness, they attribute the gallant result to the effect produced by their person. Such was Madame Brunel.

"By your accent, Madame," said Théodose, who felt at ease with such a person, "one would think that you were French?"

"So I am," Madame Brunel replied, radiantly. "I'm even a Parisienne." She raised her eyes to look at Théodose and immediately lowered them again.

"Then we're compatriots," replied Théodose, delighted.

"That's charming," Madame Brunel went on, with an infantile gaiety. "Well, Monsieur de Paris"—she simpered at Théodose as she called him that, looking at him this time—"a similar fate has brought us here."

"Have you been here long, Madame?"

"About a month, I believe."

At that moment, a few instrumental chords vibrated in the air, the different tones attempting unison. Then, the chord having been found, the performance began. At first, each intonation extended its departure, one on one direction, another in another, but soon, like scattered travelers rallying to the same route, all the notes were grouped into a sheaf, and powerfully and simply elevated a rhythm, like one immense, magisterial voice. The grave motif gradually achieved the plenitude of its force; gradually, the harmony invaded space and seemed to pass beyond the clouds.

Everyone in the arbor was attentive and subjugated. The body remained in place, forgotten by the mind, lost in the pursuit of the ideal.

After a long prologue, the cadence made a kind of pause, and a soloist, pure and vibrant, with a pearly sheen, designed the softest, most gracious and most immense song that the human ear had ever heard. It was crimson enveloped by gauze; it was brass muted by wood; it was strength sculpted by grace. The instrument was no longer singing, but it was still audible, and the final reprise by the chorus was, for the audience, the murmur that lulls but does not awaken.

Then, in the midst of that cast spell, a voice commenced; it repeated the tune that the soloist had played, but more marvelously still by virtue of the attraction that comes from life alone really speaking to life, putting a thought into the wave in which every imagination was wandering, and everyone followed it, believing that they thought the same.

It sang: "The liana of the desert enlaces space; the bird circles in the atmosphere like the wind; the sea rolls its waves and chases the land into the distance; the earth grows its forests, its grasslands and its crops; the star competes with other stars; the moon says 'The night is mine!' and the sun replies 'I am king of the globe,' and I say to all: 'The king of all is me.'

"My ax traces a path through the liana; I battle the eagle in its aerie and destroy its nest; I float over the waves; on the earth I command; the mountain would be hollowed out if I said 'the valley'; in the moonlight, I dream of my youth; in the fires of the sun I am animated, and I see. Do they give me life? No, it is in me that they breathe, in my being contained, and my life is life! The unknown is for me but a marker in space; beyond that which is, I seek that which is; there at the limits of the world I kick over the traces, and I, humankind, lose myself in my immensity."

The voice drowned in the distance gently folded itself away, the accompaniment fading along with the voice; the silence of immobility asserted itself, and for a few seconds, the people seemed to be listening to the sound of the foliage, barely stirred by a light wind.

Then, suddenly, as if with a start, everyone recovered themselves. They were there, they had listened, they knew it now, and they applauded because they were glad.

"Who was singing, then, and who wrote the words?" said Verdin, as he rose to his feet.

At the same time, he heard: "Vive Ulmé! Vive Néry! Vive Laor!" Perceiving that everyone in the clearing was heading toward the arbor, he remained standing in the same place.

Indeed, the entire group was coming, all together, each member with an instrument in hand and all of them animated by the fire of labor or attention.

At the entrance to the arbor they stopped, as one. Only one young man of twenty or twenty-two advanced into the interior, and took the hands of two old people sitting side by side.

"Grandfather and grandmother," he said, "I ask you for my life."

Immediately, the old couple got up, and the grandfather, speaking while his wife listened, said affectionately to the youth who was still holding his hand: "What do you want, Ulmé?"

"Nise for my wife," replied the one addressed as Ulmé.

Without making any reply, the two old people, with their grandson between them, took two steps toward Verdin, and

Ulmé's grandfather said, gravely and simply: "Verdin and Nisia, Ulmé requests Nise, your daughter, for his wife."

"Let Nise reply," said Verdin, looking at Nisia, his wife, who had stood up beside him and was nodding in agreement.

Nise, brought forward by her sister and another young woman, emerged from the ranks, which parted to let them through, and, after kissing the hands of her father and mother, said with modesty and dignity: "If you love Ulmé, I will love him." Tears of emotion streaked her lovely face.

"It is us who will love him, if you love him," said Nisia, her mother, weeping herself over the head of the child that was bowed before her.

"Well then, love him," replied Nise, uniting the two parental hands beneath her lips.

"My son," said Verdin to Ulmé, "embrace the one who will be your wife, and you, Nise, my dear child"—he kissed her as he spoke—"embrace your new parents."

Ulmé placed his lips on Nise's forehead with respectful tenderness, and she hugged the old couple affectionately in her arms. Verdin and Nisia embraced them in their turn.

Then the joyful acclamations burst forth; everyone was invited to the wedding, which, in accordance with the custom of the land, would take place ten days after the request.

"Ulmé," asked Verdin, "was it you who wrote the words?"

"I wrote the words," Ulmé replied. "Néry wrote the music, and Laor sang."

"Laor is a charmer," replied Verdin. "He keeps what he attracts, and whoever hears him can no longer escape him. But Laor is Néry's voice; if Laor attracts and binds, it is with the power of Néry. Néry has fashioned the marvelous form, Laor makes it live by giving it a voice."

At these words the crowd quivered with joy, and during that response, Verdin went on: "The harmony is the repose, and to all of you who have cradled us and absorbed us into you, thanks and glory."

While the applause thanked him for these words of praise, Verdin gazed at Ulmé profoundly. "Ulmé," he said, as if thinking aloud, "always think; thought is discovery; and discovery is treasure found."

With a prompt movement, Ulmé came to take Verdin's hand, and to rest his penetrating gaze upon him, frankly but without boldness. "Father," he said—and stopped. The two men had understood one another.

"Glory to Ulmé," said some who had not found that it was sufficient, and all those carried away repeated: "Glory to Ulmé."

Then the young people left again for the center of the clearing.

This time, the inhabitants of the arbor, stirred by the general animation, got to their feet, helping one another up, and followed the noise of the crowd, chatting. Ulmé's song was the subject of the conversation; everyone thought the young man very promising, and were happy to see him marrying Nise, who was also an amiable and very intelligent girl.

Madame Brunel and Théodose had relaxed into a superb mutism; they occupied themselves with one another with an utterly impertinent indifference, Madame Brunel adjusting her hair and Théodose looking this way and that, not appearing to be interested in anything.

"Well, what did you think of it?" said someone who happened to be beside him to Théodose. Said with enthusiasm, it was a kind of provocation of praise.

"It's original," Théodose replied, in a cold and disdainful tone, "but the regulation didn't give the author much trouble. It's not verse. What is it?"

The person to whom Théodose was replying had a simple and good nature. He understood that Théodose's intention was mischievous, but he did not know how to reply. Verdin, who had overheard, came to his rescue."

"Théodose," he said, "do you think it indispensable that every work should be enclosed in the same frame? What does the form of a portrait matter if the portrait is good? Similarly, what does the manner in which something is said matter, if what is said is good?"

"There's always less talent in suppressing difficulties than overcoming them," replied Madame Brunel, in a sarcastic tone.

"In versification, Madame, there are difficulties that can only be overcome by suppressing beauties, because regulation distorts and measures ideas, and the poet who sacrifices to regulation is always more a mechanic than an artist."[6]

"Well," said Madame Brunel, in a most impertinent manner, "that's truly peculiar. So, forming the ends of lines without rhymes is called talent, and our poets are machines? What do you think, Monsieur de Paris?"

Théodose was about to support his compatriot, but Verdin did not give him time.

"Madame," he said to Madame Brunel, in a dignified fashion, "you must have understood me, but you reply in a very particular manner that does not encourage discussion. My idea is that regulation is a hindrance even for genius, and that it would soar even higher if they were set aside. But for modest talents, rules are the annulment of the possible, for if genius is always genius no matter what, simple capacities are suppressed entirely if something hinders them. Now, between depriving ourselves of those capacities or the rules, we prefer to keep the capacities, and that's why we readily accept the setting aside of the rules."

"Oh, at your ease—no one is disputing the prize with you," said Madame Brunel, irritated, "but I don't know what name to give to your compositions, for they're surely neither verse nor prose."

---

[6] This advocacy of free verse was unusual for the time; it would be more than ten years before some of the leading members of the Symbolist Movement, including Gustave Kahn, took up that advocacy more loudly, occasionally practicing what they preached.

No one replied, and everyone drew away in search of more agreeable company, leaving Théodose and Madame Brunel aside.

"It's truly curious," said the latter, in a low voice. "I've never seen anything like it."

"It's a fact that it's impossible," said Théodose in the same tone. "It's truly laughable." And both of them, appearing to mop their faces, laughed into their handkerchiefs.

A beautiful young woman carrying a large tray laden with refreshments paused in front of the two French people. They strove to recover their seriousness, each taking a cup. They were the same ones in which the coffee had been served, into which some kind of sorbet had been poured this time.

That beverage, iced and truly delicious, made Théodose and Madame Brunel feel a little better.

"Fortunately, their cuisine isn't as eccentric as their ideas," said Théodose.

"Oh, I put such scant stock in nourishment," riposted Madame Brunel, in a precious manner, "that it's not a compensation for me."

Théodose bowed, finding nothing to say.

While the two individuals were chatting, the group raised the question of departure. It was agreed that after a stroll through the forest they would return to the dwellings by a different route.

Immediately, while the young men unhitched a nonchalantly-crouching camel and harnessed it to a light cart that served to carry the provisions, the young women washed the various utensils in the spring, replacing the bottles in crates designed for that purpose, and, when everything was deposited in the cart, two elders climbed up and slowly directed the rig along broad pathways, while the young people dispersed in the thickets.

Verdin and Nisia, not daring to leave Théodose, in spite of his lack of sociability, made the sacrifice of approaching to keep him company. As Madame Brunel was still careful to remain close to Théodose, the four individuals, not knowing what to say to one another, began walking side by side, aimlessly and without connection—and hence without any pleasure.

The forest was a masterpiece of nature, but the masterpiece was familiar to Verdin and Nisia; as for Théodose, he was bored, and Madame Brunel was only thinking about one thing, which was that no one was paying any attention to her except Théodose—so she was occupied with Théodose, and that was all.

The frightened birds fluttered away from them, deploying the most varied colors, and the impossible foliage combined the most eccentric gaps, but in vain; Verdin and Nisia were accustomed to them and looked on placidly, while their companions were uninterested, absorbed as they were in their own concerns.

Madame Brunel would have preferred to be left alone with Théodose, but Théodose was no more interested in Madame Brunel than the others, so their walk was one of the more monotonous.

After walking for some time, they began to encounter a few habitations, and the further they went the closer the successive houses were to one another, dividing the woods up into square gardens. Soon, there were streets instead of pathways and everyone hastened to the cart and took possession of the parasols that had been relegated to it.

Verdin and Nisia sheltered under the same one, leaving Théodose to protect Madame Brunel. The latter, glad of the opportunity, took her place beside Théodose with some embarrassment. Although much better than the morning, since he was now, so to speak, doing it on an empty stomach, Théodose remembered only too well what he had endured, and the prospect of a new trek under the sun was sufficient to render him peevish. So, without paying any attention to his companion, he advanced side by side with her, trying to sleep to pass the time.

Along the road, individuals quit the company in succession as they came close to their domiciles. The Verdin family and Madame Brunel lived further away, so everyone, in turn, bid them farewell, and when Madame Brunel had to take her leave, she saluted Théodose, like the others, even more coldly than was her habit. Théodose, however, profoundly indifferent to anything but his own temperature, bowed without knowing exactly how, nor whom, he was saluting. Scarcely had Madame Brunel reached the threshold of her dwelling when, returning round on the pretext of closing the door, she saw that Théodose was already far away.

A few minutes later, the Verdin family was back at home. In the blink of an eye a light meal was served, and everyone was refreshed.

"We're going to take a siesta," said Verdin. "It's the time of day when it's impossible to do anything." Indicating the room in which his guest had already slept, he added: "This room is yours, my dear Théodose. If you need anything, everything is there, and you can always call us."

Théodose thanked him. The two young women and their parents went up to their rooms, and Théodose went into his.

He was so overwhelmed, even though the dwellings were designed in such a way as to avoid the heat, that Théodose lay down on his bed, and all noise within the house ceased.

Chapter VII
Money and Work

For a few hours, it seemed that no human beings existed in the vicinity. Only the occasional monotonous birdcall was heard; one might have through the region uninhabited, and even deprived of quadrupeds, for under the influence of the mid-day heat, everything became torpid.

Gradually, however, the sun declined in its course; here and there, with bleating in the background, the birds began to stir, the distant forest emitted its particular sounds, and the torpor was shaken off. Beginning with the animals, the animation gradually spread to humans, and the menagerie woke up to the resounding cry of the cockerel, waking up the surroundings, and thus life gained ground.

Théodose opened his eyes, sought once again to take account of things, and, suddenly remembering, looked at a magnificent clock set on a shelf opposite his bed to see what time it was.

It was four o'clock. He had gone to bed at one o'clock in the afternoon, so he had slept for three hours. At any rate, he felt well rested.

Getting up immediately, he recommenced his toilette for the third time, but with less care—or, rather, with no other aim but that of being decent, for, instead of it being him, Théodose, who had astonished these people, it was him who had to bow down before their striking superiority.

Not knowing whether his hosts were up and about, he opened the door quietly and, not seeing anyone in the dining room, tried to go out into the garden. The only locks were a simple latch and an internal bolt. Théodose went out without making any noise, but he had scarcely taken two steps when he realized that all his precautions had been a pure waste of time.

Verdin was weeding in the garden and the two young women were going back and forth across the interior courtyard from a door leading to the kitchen.

All of them greeted him affectionately, and the mother, having said that she was preparing dinner, invited him to visit the habitation in the meantime.

The courtyard surrounding the house was separated from the garden by a delicate and tightly knit trellis. The courtyard was populated by birds of various species; compartments isolated young broods or incompatible kinds; appropriate constructions, but made with a remarkable elegance, served simultaneously as shelters for the livestock and ornamentations of the property.

Théodose admired the various species, all outside at that hour, occupied in feeding; then he went to join Verdin in the garden.

Immediately behind the trellis grew a few tall trees with dense foliage, which permitted the family to remain in the open whenever it suited them, though simultaneously shading the courtyard and the house.

Beyond those trees, the garden—which is to say, the cultivation—extended. Nothing was more beautiful, better cared for or better organized than that enclosure; whimsy rubbed shoulders with utility there, the most exuberant flowers blooming amid the most appetizing fruits; there was both nourishment and adornment in their greatest richness, as one sees flowers and dishes on the table at the same time on feast days.

"This is a magnificent garden," said Théodose. "What beauty, what richness—it's superb! But how hard it must be to have to work in such a hot country."

"One makes arrangements in consequence," Verdin replied. "People work almost exclusively in the morning and evening."

"Undoubtedly," replied Théodose. "And they must be well-paid."

"One is indeed well-paid," said Verdin, "for what the earth produces is marvelous."

"Oh, yes, that I can see," said Théodose, "but I'm talking about the worker."

"The worker is me," said Verdin, "so it's me that the earth pays."

"What—you cultivate this garden yourself?" Théodose looked at Verdin: his appearance, his physiognomy and his clothing.

"Yes, it's me," replied Verdin, contemplating him in his turn. "Does that astonish you?"

"You're a gardener, then?" asked Théodose, without answering the question.

"I'm an agriculturalist by profession," Verdin replied, "but my garden is my relaxation and my study."

Théodose was surprised to hear it.

"Father," said one of the young women, who had just arrived beside them, "Maman is waiting for us for dinner."

"Let's go dine, then, Mademoiselle Nise," said Verdin affectionately. Leaving his work, he followed his children. "Do you feel hungry, friend Théodose?" he asked.

"Not as much as this morning," the latter replied.

"That's understandable. You're like us; it's our first meal that's the best. One eats well enough in the evening, however."

"The evening? You mean now?" Théodose asked, addressing his host in a familiar fashion, in accordance with his mental disposition.

"No, the evening is before going to bed, at about ten o'clock. You'll see when you come back from the play."

"Are we going to a play, then?" asked Théodose.

"Yes," said Verdin, "but if you find the prospect tedious, you know, you may abstain."

"Not at all," exclaimed Théodose. "On the contrary, I'm delighted."

While conversing, they had reached the tall trees. The table was set up there, and while the mother invited Théodose to take his place and the two young women sat down, Verdin, who had been into the kitchen momentarily to wash his hands, took his place in his turn, and they began eating.

Naturally, Nise's marriage was the topic of conversation. Théodose, wishing to remain on good terms with his hosts, no longer dared express astonishment, fearing that he might offend them. He listened, and put on a semblance of approval.

"I'm very happy about their marriage," said the father. "Ulmé has a real talent, and he's also good-natured."

"Yes," Théodose replied, "but it's a good thing he's here. If you knew how many frustrations and disappointments would await him everywhere else..."

"Oh," said Verdin, with an intonation of denial, "I don't believe that his artistry could ever be unrecognized."

"Do you think so?" said Théodose. "Well, my dear Verdin, more often than not, one dies of starvation with that kind of talent."

"What, one dies of starvation?" repeated Verdin. "But first of all, one eats one's produce, and unless it fails...and as that's impossible, I don't see..."

"One eats one's produce?" said, Théodose, bewildered. "With what do you write, then?"

"We don't understand," said Verdin. "Explain it to us. I said, I believe, that Ulmé is a talented agriculturalist. Well, can a man who makes nourishment for others ever lack something for himself? Is that what you believed?"

"No—that Ulmé was an author."

"You mean a purely mental worker? There are none of those among us, friend. The body needs activity, and everyone ought to use that law of activity to the profit of all, for it is the employment of the totality of strength that results in the brief duration of individuals tasks, and, in consequence, the liberty of all.

"By virtue of the general execution of a labor indispensable to everyone, a third of the day, at the most, is necessary for the work of society, or the State, as you understand it; the rest of the time belongs to the individual, and thus, everyone aiding communal life, everyone benefits from the work of all and receives in addition time for themselves, which is the facility of development.

"Here, the profession chosen is almost always a derivative of the faculties. Ulmé, naturally inclined toward study and contemplation, has chosen the profession of cultivation, which is the one most favorable to thinking. A calculator generally becomes an architect, a shipbuilder or technologist, a botanist a woodcutter, in order to remain incessantly in rapport with the nature he studies—and thus, although work is obligatory, it is rather, by virtue of the liberty of choice, a simple natural matter of individual development. Marsile, who welcomed you on behalf of the inhabitants, is a blacksmith; he has an energetic nature that likes rude work. The man who played that magnificent flute solo is a weaver, that profession leaving him the suppleness of the fingers so necessary to a musician. Laor, whom you heard singing, is a carpenter. The play you're going to see this evening is by a fisherman—and so on."

"Perhaps it's the incapable who enjoy luxury among you?" asked Théodose, who was no longer surprised by anything.

"It's almost everyone," replied Verdin. "Luxury is recreation; those who amuse themselves do so in their own time, and as everyone traffics with one another, there's no one who isn't provided with those pleasant pastimes. Look, my daughters excel in embroidering tunics; in exchanged they're given those beautiful medallions, those earrings and those admirable plumes of rare birds."

"But those medallions and earrings are made of gold," objected Théodose.

"So what?" Verdin retorted.

"That makes those objects very valuable!" Théodose explained, in a rather uncertain tone.

"Bah!" said Verdin. "What does the raw material matter? Anyone can obtain it. It's only the work that gives it value, and thus there's exchange, work for work."

"Anyone can obtain gold, here?" asked Théodose, softly, as if he were scarcely astonished.

"Of course. Why do you think that would apply less to gold than anything else? Work belongs to the person who does it, materials belong to those who want to work them—everyone knows that, and I don't know why you're talking about it."

"Does one always know what one's saying?" said Théodose, negligently. "It's so hot that I'm dumbfounded."

"My poor Théodose, you won't be able to leave us for another twenty days."

Théodose learned about his departure before even having experienced any anxiety about his sojourn; that was a great relief to him. So, entirely happy and comfortable with what surrounded him and the prospect of soon going away, he experience the contentment that comes after a danger has been averted, when one appreciates the wellbeing of a tranquil condition.

"I shall think about you for a long time," he said.

"Poor Théodose," said Nisia. "We must astonish you a great deal, but it doesn't matter; you'll hold us in esteem because we're honest." She took his hand, and added: "And we hold you in esteem because your homeland has shaped you more than you have shaped yourself. Here, nature is so beautiful that it's necessary to follow her; the sap impels you, one must do as the plant does, while there, where it is necessary to drag oneself along, there is more merit for less distance traveled."

Théodose, moved, raised Nisia's hand to his lips and squeezed it affectionately.

"What do you expect?" he said, responding to his intimate thought. "Perhaps you're right, but it's still impossible where I come from; people would only laugh at it. Alas!"

"Come," said Verdin, "let's not be sad because there are unenlightened countries. There are gray days, but the sun always returns. Well, peoples are the same; sooner or later, they'll understand."

"Yes, in truth," Théodose riposted, "Verdin's right. It's not our fault if life is short and it takes humankind a long time to make a forward step."

"Yes," said Verdin, "it's the fault of everyone, individually. If everyone who senses that something is just, but thinks it inapplicable or uncomprehended by others, applied it, without worrying about himself, thousands of people would be astonished to encounter the same progress in themselves. Instead of that, though, everyone, because he is alone, because, in sum, there is only one of him, believes that he's of no importance, as if every majority and every force were not made of grouped individuals—and all of them, making up humankind, remain where they are, naively astonished that humankind is not making progress. But since humankind is you, me, and the next man, no matter who, if you want humankind to make progress, then make progress! There's no other possible means.

"People want to advance but remain stationary, without thinking that, stopped by the inertia of others, their own inertia is similarly stopping the others in their turn. An ironic simplicity! A man desires the wellbeing of humankind; that wellbeing depends on everyone doing his part, but no one does it, and yet everyone expects wellbeing to arrive! People are not yet conscious that, as members of the human race, their individual actions, paltry as they are, necessarily, for the whole, begin with a single moving fiber within the human body, and the entirety feels it."

"Bah!" said Théodose, in a bantering tone. "What would philosophers do if humankind were perfect?"

"They wouldn't bore their fellows as I'm boring you," replied Verdin, in the same tone, "but they'd still offer you this good wine, as I'm offering it to you. To the happy return to your homeland, friend!"

"How is it that I'll be able to return?" asked Théodose. "Do ships call here?"

"No, but we trade with neighboring countries, and every two months or so, we go there to make exchanges, or someone comes to us. You'll be handed on to the nearest tribe, which will pass you on to the next, and so on, until you arrive where ships regularly drop anchor, and you'll embark."

"It won't trouble the inhabitants to take me from one country to another?" asked Théodose, alarmed by the prospect of that journey.

"Are you anxious on our account and fearful that something might happen to you among us?" asked Verdin.

"Oh no!" replied Théodose, swiftly.

"Well, our neighbors are absolutely the same. Your journey will be a genuine pleasure trip, unless our mores annoy you to the point of making you angry...."

"Oh, my dear Verdin, you're putting words in my mouth! That's not our way of doing things, but it doesn't shock me."

Verdin smiled indulgently. "Poor old Théodose," he said, with gentle humor. Then, after a pause, he added: "We need to get ready to go. Théodose, see if you need anything, while the children and their mother see to themselves. We're going to the theater. It's six o'clock; we'll return at ten. People don't go to bed late here, because the mornings are indispensable for work."

"That's perfectly understandable," said Théodose. While making that reply, however, he was thinking about something else.

In every country, no matter which, one pays. Now, it would have been agreeable to Théodose to offer his hosts some compensation in exchange for the cares they were lavishing upon him—except that, if everyone could obtain gold on the isle of Utopia, Théodose said to himself, reasonably, his money ought to be worthless here, and he did not know how to obtain clarification on that matter.

In order to be prepared for any eventuality, however, he went to his room on some pretext, and equipped himself with a certain sum of money.

Chapter VIII
Master Zénon

The two young women soon came downstairs, clad in splendid costumes. Their silken tunics, one sky blue and the other bright pink, lined with tulle of the same hue, graciously festooned with dainty garlands of roses and cornflowers, made them look like pagan goddesses.

The mother, dressed in a long white cashmere tunic, simply decorated at the edges with golden embroidery, and coiffed with a light tiara of pearls, was between her two children, replete with the calm and serene beauty that seems to be the blossoming of a rich creation arrived at its full development; one might have thought her a symbol of the Harvest escorted by Spring. Upright without stiffness, self-confident without boldness, she walked with ease in her authority, like someone accustomed to sovereignty.

Théodose still felt an impulse to bow, but the altogether natural grace of Nisia stopped that respectful dread short. As soon as he was close to her, his ideas changed. There was strength there, but that strength was not oppressive; on the contrary, it was helpful, which meant that soon one no longer gave it a thought.

Verdin kissed them all, and, joyful in spite of the fact that all that splendor must be familiar to him, he gazed at them radiantly.

"What monsters!" he said, putting his arms around the three of them.

"On that beautiful reception," said the mother, laughing, "let's depart with confidence, my daughters."

Théodose searched for a compliment and ought to have found one, but he no longer knew what to say; he no longer knew anything, and remained silent.

As in the morning, they went down into the valley—except at this hour the air was cooler, and it was a charming stroll. The habitations, similarly distanced from one another but constructed according to whim with regard to architecture and placement, formed an entirely picturesque ensemble. The broad roads traced in straight lines were planted with trees on the edge of the sidewalk. Some houses rose up at the back of a garden, while others were adjacent to the street. It was a city in terms of the quantity of habitations, a rural area in terms of the unevenness of the plan traced by the individual initiative of each.

After a few turnings, Théodose stopped in amazement in front of a railway station; the whistle of steam pierced the air with its blasts. The train was getting ready to depart.

"What!" said Théodose. "You have railways!"

"Didn't I tell you that one of our people had brought back the scientific inventions of your homeland?"

"Yes," said Théodose, who could not get over his astonishment regardless.

At the same time, a large number of inhabitants were arriving, all richly clad. Scarcely had they entered when the Verdin family was joined by Ulmé, who was there in the company of a man about fifty years old.

"Greetings, Master Zénon," said Verdin to the later, in a respectful tone.

"Greetings, my dear Verdin," Master Zénon replied.

"You see in Master Zénon one of our schoolmasters," Verdin said to Théodose. "Almost all the young people here have been taught by him. He's Ulmé's master, Laor's, and mine."

"Monsieur," said Master Zénon to Théodose, "I would have liked to join the local people to welcome you, but unfortunately I had a sick pupil, and I wanted to find out for myself how he had spent the night. Now that he's out of danger, I'm tranquil, so I accompanied my dear Ulmé in order to present all my sympathies to you."

Théodose bowed and, not knowing what to say, was trying to find something when the signal for departure got him out of the predicament and everyone boarded the train.

Master Zénon having sat down next to Théodose, the latter had recommenced racking his brains, when Master Zénon got in ahead of him.

"There's no finer profession is there, Monsieur, than that of educating youth; we have the esteem and the affection of parents, and what a recompense it is if our pupils become generous and valiant citizens."

"Yes," said Théodose, "but in order for one to be able to say reasonably; 'I have formed a man,' it's necessary to keep the child until he becomes a man."

"That's exactly what we do, and you think very wisely," said Master Zénon.

"You have some who make complete studies, but so few..."

"All of them, without exception; how could one exclude any of them?"

"All your children learn until they are of age?"

"Can any of them be outside humanity? People are inevitably alike, and by virtue of that fact, are treated alike."

"So you teach children until...?"

"The age of nineteen."

"Very good! Then the family no longer counts; it's the professor that replaces it! And what if I, more jealous in my capacity as a father, wanted to keep my child at home?"

"As you please—except that your child will need to pass the public examinations like all the rest."

"And if it pleases me to give my child doctrines other than yours?"

"A professor only teaches science, which does not vary, and morality, which does not vary either; in brief, he only makes demonstrations of fact. One and one always making two, humans and nature are equivalent, since neither has any reason for being without the other, and humans, no matter what or where they are, are always human, and inevitably have the same rights—in technical terms, humans necessarily have human rights. Those are fundamental principles that no one can deny, and which families that keep children at home are necessarily called to teach them."

"But if my ideas were opposed...if I didn't want...my children belong to me, when all is said and done."

"Your children belong to humankind, and you are only the person in charge of them; you must account to society for the parts of itself that it has entrusted to your care. It cannot be appropriate for people to leave other people to be brought up as masters or slaves, for it is not only the dignity but the security of the human species that would be imperiled by that: as a master, he would attempt to enslave his fellows; as a slave, he would assist others to enslave them.

"A human must learn what a human being is, and what he, the individual, ought to be; as a representative of the human species, he ought not to conceive any idea of superiority or inferiority, even if he differs from others of his kind in some faculty or distinction. That which is distinct cannot be worth more or less; taste might make a choice, but the fundamental value is the same among all distinct things, given that they each of them inevitably constitutes a unity.

"It is only in one line or one way of being that one can say that something extends further than something else, which determines that imitators do not count or are always inferior, but imitators disappear when free rein is given to everyone."

Théodose had had his fill of the pedagogue, but dared not dispense with making some kind of sign of approval. He was no longer listening, and was waiting impatiently for the conversation to end.

"You see," Master Zénon went on, the silence of his interlocutor leaving the field free, "by teaching a child to respect humans above all else, at the same time as he respects others, knowing himself to be human, he will demand the same respect for himself—and everything depends on that."

"But at what age," said Théodose suddenly, a criticism having sprung to mind, "do your young people learn a profession?"

"From infancy, so to speak," replied Master Zénon. "In the immense buildings of the school there are workshops of every trade, and the child attaches himself to the one that is his natural preference. At ten one begins to employ him; if he loses his appetite for it, he is required to make another choice, and you'll understand that by the age of nineteen, it's impossible for him not to be a good worker."

"Can a father no longer teach his own trade to his son?" asked Théodose, ironically.

"A father can teach him anything he wishes in his own time, but during his work for the social association, he must occupy himself entirely with his work. The workers occupied in the school building are there in the capacity of teachers, but they're employed more in demonstration than execution— which is to say that they enable the child to work rather than working themselves. If every member of society were occupied in shaping apprentices, the brief working time of each would not be adequate; it is therefore a great advantage for the parents, and, in consequence, for society, that children learn their professions from teachers; that way, a single individual is sufficient to shape a legion of children; and as the hours of recreation correspond to the father's free time, the father can complete the child as he wishes."

"And when the child is a good worker, able to earn a living" asked Théodose, "is he free to leave?"

"No," replied Master Zénon, sharply. "The child cannot leave until the age of nineteen for a boy, or eighteen for a girl. All of them are good workers by then, and their work serves to maintain the school, so there is no need for any input except an initial outlay. That rule is invariable for two reasons of general utility: firstly, the maintenance of the school, which is a matter of primary utility in the State; secondly the surveillance of youth, which would cease if the young people left those they are accustomed to obeying. Now, we oblige all children until the final day, without exception, independently of manual labor, to undertake daily exercises in gymnastics, swimming, equitation and, for boys, the handling of weapons.

In that manner, boys and girls are shielded from mental follies, and it is unheard of for them not to wait appropriately for the epoch of their marriage, fixed, if they wish, for the day of their leaving school, which is the day of their independence."

"As I understand it," said Théodose, still ironically, "children are separated from parents, and live communally outside any family."

"What!" said Master Zénon. "I told you just now that the children return to their families during recreation times. In the morning and the evening, there is a total of six hours of school; three for instruction and three for exercise and manual labor; is that too many? Is the child, in consequence, removed from the family? The father has four hours of work to do himself, so the child has only two hours of direct supervision, and that's not much time in which to build a model individual."

"It's just, you see, that I like family life," said Théodose, with a tender expression.

"So do we!" retorted Master Zénon. "That's why we raise our children in this manner. By ensuring that they are active and instructing them, we preserve them from the vices that ignorance and idleness engender, and at the same time we preserve families. For no boy or girl can go astray without making their family, by repercussion, an accomplice or a victim."

"And then," Théodose continued, as if he had not heard, "it's nice to see children sitting at the paternal table."

"But where do you think they eat?" asked Zénon, slightly astonished by the comment and thrown off-balance.

"I thought they lived entirely at school?" said Théodose.

"You astonish me," said Zénon. "I can't imagine where you got that idea. It seems that you don't want to understand. When you desire something, you go where you ought to find it, and you come back. Well, the child goes to obtain instruction, and when the task is finished, he comes back. Why would he stay if there is nothing more to do?"

"Perhaps in order that he does not deviate from the path marked out for him."

"Quite the contrary—no path is marked out for him; he is the one who must trace it; his education only enables him to follow it. We professors are only concerned with the mechanism—which is to say, the establishment of principles of science and morality; the parents form the heart. That education is only done by example."

The train had just stopped; the Verdin family rose to their feet in order to get off. Théodose uttered a sigh of relief and, dropping back on the pretext of looking at something, moved away, glad to lose sight of his companions, so weary was he of Master Zénon's obsessions. Fortunately, the latter was not going to the theater; he had only come to wish Théodose welcome, and at the station exit he took his leave.

Théodose replied to him graciously, in his joy at getting rid of him, and as light and sprightly as a man relieved of a burden, started joking agreeably, encouraged by the good grace with which people listened to him. In brief, there was a reaction; he overflowed with enthusiasm, so bored had he been.

Chapter IX
A Singular Play

A short distance away, they reached the theater. It was a marvel of sculpture; the perimeter wall displayed a magnificent bas-relief of lovely arches closing their vaults in a dome. The large doors, a veritable masterpiece of woodcarving, opened on to mosaic steps. Nothing had been neglected; art and richness had furnished the materials of the edifice. Inside, there was the same careful execution: two superimposed galleries were supported by a wrought iron structure of incredible delicacy; the iron had been gilded, and variously colored marble colonettes decorated the white and gold background of the auditorium at intervals.

A frank, full light illuminated the redoubt so well that the spectator, coming from outside, where dusk was beginning to fall, thought for a moment that he had rediscovered midday in that corner. The seats in the stalls and the galleries were ample armchairs made of a kind of perforated rush matting, and were all exactly alike. One went in; one chose one's place; the first to arrive began, and those coming after made what arrangements they could. Nobody was preoccupied with it; all cheerfully sat down anywhere, firstly because they only had to arrive a little sooner another time, and secondly because the theater was small enough and low enough that one could see and hear from anywhere.

At the same time as the Verdin family came in, Madame Brunel, in the company of another lady, made her appearance at the opposite side. Whether out of coldness or reflection, the people sat down some way apart, as if they had not seen one another or did not know one another well enough to come together. Madame Brunel was wearing a floral-patterned costume; the style was adequate, but the lapels and pendants had a certain flamboyance that clashed somewhat with the lady's age; one might have thought her a Junoesque matron dressed

69

as a sprightly grisette. The contrast attracted the eye, however, and as Madame Brunel intended, everyone looked to see whether she really was young or old. The attention gained, the effect was produced; as for the interpretation the heroine put upon it, that was naturally to her advantage, as it usually is.

The auditorium filled up in a matter of minutes. Théodose was told that those who had not been able to get seats would go to other theaters, given that there were enough for the inhabitants to be able to relax there whenever it suited them, which was doubly advantageous because, by virtue of the multiplicity of stages, there was a more considerable outlet for the authors.

The performance began. The splendid scenery left nothing for Théodose to desire; by virtue of a spiteful sentiment, our voyager hoped to make up for that in the style of the play, but as soon as the first words were spoken he listened, no longer under that impression but in a kind of rage that forced him, in a way, to admit that there was no weakness for which one could reasonably criticize these annoyingly meritorious people.

The first act was perfect. The protagonist of the play, taken from European books imported into the colony, was a king captured and imprisoned far from his homeland. There, in his prison, he prays to his god; someone who hears him observes judiciously the god in question has no power in the matter, since, in spite of the prayers addressed to him by his believers, their enemies have been victorious. The imprisoned king thunders splendid words—worship, religion, salvation, the designs of Providence—and becomes decrepit along with those vivifying things, while his son, captured at the same him as him, is raised separately, in accordance with the simple and vulgar laws of nature.

Every month, the child comes to see his father; he was six years old when fortune or his god failed him; now he is twenty; he is a young man of clear judgment, who loves his father as one loves an unfortunate madman. Informed about the customs of different peoples, as well as the fundamental laws of the human species, he has a strong sense of what humanity is, and is astonished by the picture of base creatures of servility or arrogance, while, by comparison, he admires true humankind, so beautiful in its pure simplicity.

"All that exists in men what is made to exist there," says his aged jailer to the king. "The society in which you have lived has made you a subordinate of a fetish and a despot to humans, and that owes so much to society and so little to any Providence that of your son, born to be in his turn a worshipper and a dominator, we have made a human being. The thought of the finished and superior man is guided by nature, but the thought of the human child is primarily guided by humans; it is for that reason that you were separated. Twisted to the warp of those who have applied themselves to you, you would, by virtue of your very nature—which is to say, unconsciously—have twisted the being to whom you were applied. Now, your son is formed, and you are free." (End of Act One)

Théodose became bored while waiting for the play to resume. Ulmé and the two young women were chatting; Verdin and Nisia were sitting in silence. He turned his gaze elsewhere, catching sight of Madame Brunel, whom her neighbors had temporarily abandoned, and who seemed to be self-absorbed with a false air of indifference. Théodose decided to go and say hello to her. That was all the easier to do because some of the spectators had already left their seats in order to chat with others.

Théodose approached Madame Brunel in the most ceremonious fashion, and the latter, in an equally formal tone, replied to the studied greeting. Théodose, like all those who live incessantly in contact with what is known as "high society," was instinctively familiar with the imperceptible nuances by which one obtains success. He knew how shocking the negligence of his conduct that morning must have been for a woman like Madame Brunel, so he put an accentuated deference into his conduct toward her.

The procedure was successful. Madame Brunel, won over by that respectful opening, gradually abandoned her attitude of sovereign inaccessibility, and soon, entirely gracious in the face of that simulacrum of abasement before an idol, she descended from her pedestal, and the conversation took on a terrestrial tone.

"Sit here," she said, indicating one of the empty seats beside her. "That's done here—everyone returns to their own place when the curtain rises. Well, what do you think of the play? These people have nothing human about them—in truth, they're all heroes, but too much heroism becomes alarming."

"Only a woman can translate the finest and most accurate thoughts like that," replied Théodose, gallantly. "I was searching for my impression; you've just translated it. Indeed, all these people are automata of grandeur; they're molded, and, admiring themselves, they remain immutable in exchange for being bored, for it's not possible that they're enjoying themselves."

"I confess that, for myself, I honor that merit highly, but I don't lay claim to it," replied Madame Brunel. "I even find it slightly ridiculous; it's always seemed humorous to me that puritans affect to disdain that which constitutes life. How does it advance them to imagine that the world is vicious? To become unsociable, that's all? Well, my God, leave vices to others and only pay attention to yourselves. No one is funnier than these reformers. To hear them, everything is bad! Even if it were, what business would it be of theirs?"

"It's a fact, Madame, that one cannot be more mistaken than to occupy oneself with someone else's way of being. If it pleases us to have a court, lords and titles, and to render homage to all of that, what does it matter to others? Everyone lives as they please, and it's perfectly inappropriate and even ludicrous for these purists to want to guide us."

"Obviously—we don't oblige them to adopt our ideas; let them leave us alone," said Madame Brunel, sententiously.

"You have, Madame, a dazzling intelligence, which leaves me nothing further to say. Might I be permitted to see you tomorrow? The dazzle will still be the same, but perhaps I'll become accustomed to it, and if I'm able to spend a little time in your drawing room, I shall be able to believe that I'm back in Paris, in the hearth of distinction and elegance."

"In truth, Monsieur," said Madame Brunel, lowering her eyes emotionally, "the singularity of our situation obliges us to break with many conventions. We've undoubtedly only been acquainted very briefly, but it seems to me that the circumstances…in sum, Monsieur, I shan't refuse. If my society can assist you in tolerating the tedium, it would be overscrupulous of me to be too reserved. You will be welcome, Monsieur."

On those words, Théodose got to his feet and bowed deeply, and then went to resume his place. The signal having been given, everyone else was doing the same.

Two further acts unfurled the comparison of the true man and the protagonist of the play.

The king is withered by the regret of no longer being anything but a man; the king's son develops his being on a daily basis in accordance with his natural aspirations. He marries for love, works at the métier of his choice, acts in accordance with his ideas, loving humanity and honoring nature—which is to say, loving himself and honoring his reason for being. For him, a human being, no matter who—one or another, like this or like that, in this corner or that peak—is simply what he is himself: a human being. Only nature counts for him, since she is the only thing that figures in being with humankind. She makes him; she is the source upon which he draws; she is, in sum, his equal, while a man cannot number himself with men, a unity not being susceptible to addition to itself.

Being, or life, cannot be evaluated or counted, only existing by virtue of being divided into fractions—humankind and nature, and two unique fractions being, inevitably, the one that the other lacks in order to make itself Whole, Humankind and Nature, attributes and fractions of one another, inevitably count one another or know one another by means of the other, given that humans cannot exist without being juxtaposed with nature, which cannot be thus juxtaposed without sensing the difference between them; hence, addition, number, consciousness of number, which is Being. Thus the primordial unity exists.

An extraordinary thesis for the man-king, and, in consequence, exclamations, contortions, somersaults on the part of the poor puppet, who soon stops arguing, exhausted as he is by fatigue. Here and there, against that severe backcloth, a few charming scenes, very useful and agreeable enough.

Such was the play.

At the end of the second act, Théodose did not go back to talk to Madame Brunel. Verdin and Nisia were chatting to him, and he dared not leave them. Fortunately, the conversation was sufficiently insignificant, and did not bore him overmuch.

The play finished at approximately ten o'clock. They took the train again, and on returning to the house the young women set out a light meal. Théodose found some appetite for what was served to him; in any case, the table surrounded by the three women, so beautiful and so nicely dressed, had something seductive about it, which might have kept him there all night—but the Verdin family, after an appropriate interval, rose from their seats politely, and, obliged to go to bed, our Parisian returned to his room.

Chapter X
Utopian Government

Not knowing what else to do, Théodose had gone to bed and passed the details of the day through his mind; digestion having soon weighed him down, however, he was astonished the next morning to remember that he had not stayed awake for long.

The clock marked seven o'clock; he could not hear any sound in the house, and concluded that no one was up. While waiting, he imagined in advance how he was going to spend his time. He had promised to go and see Madame Brunel. Would the family Verdin still be occupied with him? Would he get bored during the twenty days that he had to spend on the island?

They were worthy subjects of meditation. Théodose spent a good hour doing so, and then, suddenly, an idea caused him to get up. He perceived the sun shining as it had the day before and, steered by the memory of its heat, went to pick up the loincloth that Verdin had offered him. As if unconsciously, he put it on, wrapping it around his hips, and, thus dressed, looked at himself in the mirror.

The effect was shattering. Théodose immediately changed his mind and tore off that impossible girdle as quickly as possible. Impatience hindered him, and he was frightened by his own appearance: with his fat swelling openly everywhere, rounding him out, that flabby individual, the product of an idle existence, had something sickening about him. It seemed to Théodose that he was looking at some kickboxing Herpin, his form damaged by long repose.[7]

---

[7] Herpin is not uncommon as a French surname; it is unlikely that the reference is to Théodore Herpin, the neurologist famous in the mid-19th century for his studies of epilepsy, but no other obvious candidate stands out in the historical record.

Eventually, the accursed loincloth yielded. In the blink of an eye Théodose had donned a shirt and trousers; then, anxious about his appearance, he looked at himself again. Nothing had happened; only he had seen him, but he swore not to try again and accepted mentally that he would die rather than make that athlete visible.

With that, he proceeded with an investigation of his wardrobe; it was very complete. As a good housekeeper he thought about getting his shirts bleached, and paused momentarily over the question of starch. Was it known here? If not, it would be annoying, because soft linen does not hang well.

His thoughts followed another path; he looked at his wads of banknotes, turned, swiveled, and decided to get dressed. The little utensils emerged from their boxes. Théodose had had one day of negligence, which was no small matter for such a careful man. The time spent in the embellishment of his person took him to nine o'clock. A few discreet raps on his door interrupted him at the very moment that he was observing that his costume was perfect.

He hastened to open the door; it was Verdin.

"Oh, but you're already dressed!" said the latter. "Come and eat, friend. I knocked gently for fear that you might still be asleep."

"No, no," said Théodose, and told him what he had been doing, omitting the incident of the loincloth.

"My dear Théodose, as soon as you wake up you can come and go in the house. The climate obliges us to get up very early. I had already left at four o'clock; now my work is finished, and I'm free until tomorrow. It's true that the middle of the day doesn't count, since one can't do anything, but the afternoon and evening compensate us."

"I congratulate you on that organization," said Théodose. "And do women work too?"

"Those who are not married, yes; they have to earn their living in order to be free; but a housewife is considered to have the heaviest task of all, for she's occupied with the making of linen, clothes, bleaching and the cares of the household and the cooking, so she is honored above others."

"And what is the salary of women?"

"There are no salaries for women, or for men. Everyone does their work, and having thus paid the duty of labor, all share in the products. Social work is organized in such a way as to produce in abundance and broad comfort: clothing, furniture, tools, instruments, machines, everything is made well and beautiful, but things intended purely for ostentation have no established state corporation because the sole justification for obligatory labor is the diminution of the work of everyone, and that work would not be diminished if some people were employed in superfluities.

"Society rightly obliges the individual to play his part in what makes life and makes it good, because everyone needs the useful in order to live, and everyone must do useful work; no one can refuse to carry out his task on the pretext that it is unnecessary, by virtue of the fact that a man who lives with civilized beings has ceased to have the right to live as a savage. Equally, however, society does not have the right to employ the individual to satisfy the caprices of a few.

"The work necessary to existence is obligatory for all, given that everything that lives must naturally maintain that which enables it to live; human life is not simply a matter of ensuring life, however, but of disposing it in a suitable manner; one therefore does not give life to humans if one does not give them time to themselves, and as that time is the source of caprice, of fantasy, of ideas, it follows that the manner of organization in question, far from destroying luxury, on the contrary, renders it general. Independent humans dream of beautiful things and execute what they imagine, since they have the means to do so, all the more so as, with the pleasure of displaying their talent or industry, they combine the benefits of bartering the surplus of their endeavor for someone else's surplus.

"There are, in consequence, few people who do not accept the occupation of their leisure hours in order to possess some work of art or superfluity that charms them—except that, instead of the poor workers who, we are told, accept in return for a meager morsel of bread to spend their entire lives, some in cutting diamonds into a thousand facets, polishing pearls, mounting superb clusters, while others weave lace, confect embroideries and decorations. Here these things are only made by people who enjoy it. In spite of that, our production extends from the simplest taste to the most immense beauty, because all human nature is to some degree artistic, and here, where no one is impeded in their own talents, and every diverse nature can donate the totality of its strength, that results in a vast quantity of very various works, all as complete as can be."

"I understand, of course," said Théodose. "There's even a sort of competition that must give rise to progress, because, not having to do these things under pressure, everyone employs all their faculties in order to win acclaim."

"That's right—so we have many masterpieces."

"But I've seen food shops," said Théodose. "Since you don't have salaries, how do you organize commerce?"

"They're not shops; they're storehouses, and those who supervise them accomplish their share of work in that fashion. We eat meat, vegetables and fruits, and a family no longer has to set aside an enormous room for those who have to travel several leagues in quest of a few yams or a melon. This is how the system works. A few people slaughter the quantity of livestock necessary for consumption, and others deliver the butchered meat to the public. Travelers come to collect fruits and vegetables, bring them to the city, and wardens working regular shifts supervise the depots. There's no need for formality; as there are deliveries every day and everyone has whatever they request, no one has any thought of accumulating unnecessary provisions, since they have no one to whom to give them and there will be fresh supplies the following day, and it's the same for everyone."

"How are your railways and theaters maintained?"

"By individual labor. The men employed in maneuvering or maintenance on the railway accomplish their tasks by that service in the same fashion as the boot maker accomplishes his. As the railway functions for more than four hours a day, there is no double service for the men involved, but double the number of men providing the service. While those serve us by means of that labor, we confect the rest of life for them, and thus, exchanging our labor among ourselves, everything here is ours—which is to say that everything is free: the railway trains are for anyone who wishes to take them; there are no other formalities.

"For the theater, we establish a distinction; its construction and the operation of its machinery are defined as national work, but the plays and the actors are matters of individual initiative; if there were no one who liked to write and no one who liked to act, we would have no performances—but, far from it, as you must suspect, we have plenty of authors and actors, and a certain talent is needed to distinguish oneself among that number."

"You've also mentioned trade with neighboring countries," said Théodose. "What do you exchange?"

"A calculated surplus of work is done with a view to that negotiation, and all that individual initiative accomplishes, which is at least as much."

"And with four hours of obligatory work per person, you have enough?"

"Yes, ample."

"It's very little."

"But there are so many arms. Remember that, everyone being associated, all administration disappears; hence, no more fictitious work, no more wasted effort; and then, I repeat, after the obligatory work, individuals occupy their time in accordance with their whims, and you know how industrious people are in exercises that please them."

"And what happens when people fall ill?"

"Some people accomplish, as a supplement, the task of nursing, and so on, each taking turns."

"But what do you do about people who have only one child, and people who have ten, in spite of any distinction of fortune?"

"You haven't understood, my dear Théodose; work is not based in such a manner as only to maintain those who work, but the society that they form, and that society is the whole formed by the healthy, children, old people and invalids. The healthy individual has been a child and has been sustained, so the healthy person has a duty in his turn to sustain children; the old person has worked throughout his healthy life and is worn out; thus, in advance, the healthy individual must sustain the old in order to be sustained in his turn.

"There remain the infirm, whom it is necessary either to slaughter like defective livestock or to surround with care like a suffering individual; now, what man, thinking of himself, would want humans to be treated as animals? Thus, the healthy, the source and principle of society, must sustain the society.

"If one family is more or less numerous than another, that is of no importance; society takes an annual census of its number, and the social labor is based on that calculation; if there are ten children in one family and one in another, that neither increases not diminishes the sum total of children, and everyone's children have the right to be raised by everyone, because children are the strength to come, the perpetuity of being; it is not possible for the group, which only continues through those beings, to let those who have engendered them die in penury. If that were so, the situation of the father of a family would be that of a gardener who, after having exhausted himself enabling the earth to produce, sees his crop harvested at the very moment when it is ready to be harvested.

"Whoever has watered, trained and pruned a tree, or furnished the tools necessary to its cultivation, can claim its fruits; but what right has someone who has simply watched him do it, pray? You see, therefore, that a society that does not participate in raising children has no legitimate rights over any man, since all of them are merely children grown up—which

80

is to say, become men. Such a society would merely be a den of beasts in which the strong and the weak are trying eternally to devour one another.

"There, in fact, the children formed with the anguish, blood and flesh of the father and mother are merely prey that everyone tracks, to prepare feasts, while the prey that escape wait in the shadows for an opportunity to rid themselves of the fratricidal hunter. But tell me, friend—is there any such thing on earth? Can you imagine it?"

"I don't concern myself with politics," said Théodose, smugly. Then, seeing that Verdin was looking at him in a rather inquisitorial fashion, he hastened to add: "I understand very well that life among you is accomplished communally, but you must have some people who don't do manual labor—your lawyers, for example, your advocates."

"We have, friend Théodose, a few vast intellects who employ their free time in enlightening us with judicious writings, clear and based on facts—they are the arbiters of law, the advocates of humankind: if there is anyone to be judged, they are the ones whom people seek out, but they do not make a profession of it and do not wait in their seats for some guilty person to be presented in order to justify their utility. In any case, the entire nation judges, given that no one can be especially dedicated to judgment, by virtue of the fact that one cannot increase conscience by training or decree.

"Everyone judges in accordance with what he sees, as everyone gazes in accordance with what he is looking at; justice is only valuable in proportion to the amelioration of humanity. The verdict of all does not constitute justice either, for the accused might surpass his century and only be guilty of not being understood, but the justice of one or several then caries the risk for the accused of being found innocent or guilty according to whether the judges are more or less superior.

"The judgment of all ensures that a man is at least dependent on society, whereas the judgment of a few would place him under the dependence of an individual who might even be his enemy. In brief, the judgment of all constitutes the judgment of humankind, while the judgment of a few is simply the judgment of those individuals."

"But what do you do to reach an understanding, to govern yourselves?"

"We have open meetings in which anything is discussed that enters the human brain: new ideas, philosophy, literature and arts. New ideas require reforms, philosophy leads to progress, literature and the arts soften the harshness of character; you can see, therefore, that by occupying ourselves with those things, we carry out administration, justice and civilization, and that if a fault in the machinery or vice in an individual presents itself, the case being foreseen and debated in advance before all, the conduct to adopt is easy for everyone. In addition, there are enough appropriate places for the people to be convened on the field of general deliberation if any matter of urgency crops up. That's the whole of our government."

"And these meetings are obligatory?"

"No, but everyone, men and women alike, goes to them, because there's a great charm in hearing fine talk and talking oneself. I say fine talk because the habit of judging gives everyone a clear sight of questions, and the habit of speaking in public an equally great facility in removing confusion and analyzing the fundamentals, so that only good and just things are proposed. And then, as human beings are not pure mind, but have material bodies, we have to look after the body in order to ensure that it does not draw the mind astray; for that reason, we have made our meeting halls splendid places; everyone is comfortably seated there at wooden tables in the company of all sorts of refreshments. They nibble delicacies, and in the long intervals that routinely separate the speeches, the people in the auditorium discuss matters at their ease. It's a manner of being idle that combines the useful with the agreeable."

"It's a true land of Cockayne!"

"No, it's the land of Utopia."

"But why the name of Utopia?"

"Because in reading your books, we saw that in your homeland, every truth was called a utopia, from which we concluded that 'utopia' signified 'truth,' and, wanting to qualify our isle as truthful, we called it the Isle of Utopia."

Théodose bit his lip and made no reply.

The meal was over, and everyone got up. Our Parisian announced his project of going to see Madame Brunel; he was given directions regarding the route. It was, in any case, not far away. Our man immediately put on his coat, picked up his hat and gloves, for form's sake, wished the family a good siesta, and set out thoughtfully for the residence of his compatriot.

Chapter XI
A Remarkable Tête-à-Tête

Fortunately, in order to reach Madame Brunel's dwelling, it was possible to avoid the sun, so Théodose made the journey almost without noticing it; he was deep in thought. It only took a few minutes to reach the house; he lifted the door-knocker gently. After a brief wait, the door opened noiselessly. Madame Brunel appeared, coquettishly made up, bowing preciously, as usual; Théodose did the same, and, one following the other, they went ceremoniously along the corridor, and re-saluted one another solemnly when they arrived in the drawing room. Madame Brunel moved a chair forward, and Théodose sat down on it.

"Madame," Théodose commenced, with the measured intonation and slow speech of people of good society, "I fear that I might have troubled your repose by presenting myself during the period of the siesta, but I was equally fearful of being accompanied by my savage horde, whom I have escaped like a prisoner—and, like a prisoner I have come to your house as an assault rather than a visit. My situation is some slight excuse, is it not, Madame? Without too much audacity, might I hope that it will justify me?"

"I take great pleasure in relieving you of any anxiety on that score," said Madame Brunel, affably. "I never sleep during the day. The widowed lady with whom I have been lodged is resting at the moment, but that manner of living doesn't suit me; I prefer to read, embroider or write. It's true that I don't work in the morning, as she does."

"You could work, Madame, and it would be the same. These people have the brute in them; as soon as they're fatigued or have nothing to do, they sleep! As if that leisure could not be more appropriately employed in chatting or playing games. Oh, Madame, to whom can you compare yourself?"

"To very attractive individuals," said Madame Brunel, delicately, "For they're almost all beautiful."

"Yes, but without grace, without charm. My cook, although beautiful, does not exist for me. It's the distinction, the elegance and the delicacy of a woman that makes her beautiful! Talk to me about Venus working with her hands, eating, drinking and sleeping under the sweat of labor or strong digestion, and that Venus would seem ever-ready to replace the exquisite weapon of disdain with the pointed thrust of the Amazon. We men like the suavity and the impressionability that make women sensitive, but we have a horror of female athletes."

"Ha ha ha!" said Madame Brunel, deliriously relaxed, "That's one way of putting the world to rights! If a woman said a quarter of what you've said, she'd be accused of jealousy, but I accuse you of being too demanding, for they're truly good."

Yes, thought Théodose, privately, *they're truly good and you're rather absurd, but I'm a long way from home, and these women, raised quite differently from ours, are not for me. The society of these men being no more practicable, if I want to maintain a pastime, it's absolutely necessary for me to capture the good graces of this coquette, and the only means of pleasing these narrow and ridiculous minds is to incense them.*

Thus, half laughing at himself and half at Madame Brunel, he replied with a convinced and discontented expression: "As you wish, Madame, but the women here don't please me." He paused, and then went on: "Then again, I have reasons for that, which you might not have yourself." So saying, he looked at Madame Brunel in a certain manner; she blushed and lowered her eyes.

Well, that got her, our man thought. *It doesn't take much for that type!*

With that, entirely confident of his skill in playing the role, he relaxed in his chair and sketched a conquering appearance.

"What do you think of Nisia?" said Madame Brunel suddenly, becoming embarrassed by the silence. She said it with an appearance of detachment.

"She's an honest woman," Théodose replied, coldly.

"They all are here," sniggered the coquette, as if it were a sarcasm. "And it could scarcely be otherwise, for no man pays court to a woman except to marry her; they only love by contract! You mentioned seduction just now, Monsieur de Paris; I advise you to plant it in this country if you want it to flourish, for it's entirely unknown thus far."

"Where you have passed, Madame, what could I do thereafter?"

"A woman doesn't have the means that a man has; we're made to defend ourselves, you to attack."

"I beg your pardon, Madame: when we attack, it's a riposte. Beauty dazzles us, that which dazzles dominates; now, when we deliver a assault upon beauty, it is, as you see, only a case of legitimate defense."

Madame Brunel raised her elbow slowly, placed it on the arm of her chair, deposited her chin in her hand, and then remained in that pose, her eyes gazing vaguely in front of her, while a smile of refined coquetry, simultaneously disdainful, creased her face and gave her an expression of supreme affectedness.

Théodose observed her, adding up the score and counting himself all the more a hero because he was bringing so many superb batteries into play. *Very good*, he thought. *Complete success.*

Aloud, he said: "How beautiful you are, Madame! I'm well aware that you're laughing at me. Be cruel, it's your right—but for myself, I can only admire you."

"Great God!" said Madame Brunel, drawling with an extreme nonchalance and giving her voice the most mocking intonation. "Cruel words count for little in the mouth of a man. You tell me that I'm beautiful, and now you're indignant because I'm not radiant under that praise!"

"You're right, Madame, but one would so much like the person that excites one to experience a sweet echo of emotion."

"One would doubtless like many things," Madame Brunel said, continuing in the same tone, "but it's sometimes necessary to do without that which one likes."

"Yes, Madame," articulated Théodose, with a sigh.

"But look," Madame Brunel exclaimed, radiant at the adoration she saw at her feet, and changing tack, "you're here and I haven't yet asked you how you're finding life with the Verdin family. Are you comfortable there?"

"Very, as regards the necessities of life," replied Théodose, in a melancholy tone.

"It's necessary not to think about prestige and sentiment," said Madame Brunel, in a teasingly sermonizing tone. "You won't find them among these people. They care for you, they pamper you; don't ask for any more—you won't be understood. A little ennui is soon past; I've been living here for a month, myself, with that society!"

"I pity you, Madame!"

"Not at all; I'm used to it—and when I think of my sensibility of old, I'm almost tempted to find myself ridiculous," said Madame Brunel, with an infantile ingenuousness.

Théodose had a sudden desire to laugh; he changed his posture in order to animate the situation, passed his handkerchief over his face, and then, as if astonished, looked attentively at a picture facing him.

"That picture is pretty, isn't it?" said Madame Brunel, slightly put out.

"More than pretty, it's beautiful; I've never seen a seascape like it." As if attracted by admiration, Théodose stood up, adjusted his lorgnon and went to stand in front of the canvas. "Excellent, perfect," he murmured. As he said it he thought about the effect that his words would produce and the deployment of his fine stature.

The entire gallery, composed of excellent works, was passed in review. If some pretty face was represented,

Théodose removed his lorgnon—which, as everyone knows, is more often than not an affectation of infirmity decreed by good taste.

In the meantime, Madame Brunel studied herself in a mirror, smoothed out a crease, modified a lock of hair and, always trying out new postures, explained negligently to Théodose that the works he was admiring were by the elder son of the widowed mistress of the house. The son was dead; his social profession had been that of a shepherd.

"You must know," the coquette added, laughing in bursts and measuring the effect of a coral bracelet on her arm, "that everyone here has to do some coarse labor. So, another son that remains to the lady in question is a fisherman; he's the author of yesterday evening's famous play."

"It would play well among the Trappists, that drama," said Théodose, in the manner of a discontented connoisseur. He came back to sit down and continued: "By the way, if you knew how bored I was during the journey to the theater; I was sitting beside a pedagogue of the worst sort. No, you can't imagine what I endured."

"To whom are you talking?" exclaimed Madame Brunel "Know then, Monsieur de Paris, that when I came here, it was the same for me. I was subjected to impossible and interminable demonstrations. Fortunately, they grew weary of it, and now they leave me alone."

"I didn't see you at the railway station, Madame; you were probably in first class?"

"There is no first class," said Madame Brunel, in a tone of profound scorn. "Know, Monsieur de Paris, that equality reigns here and that it's against the law to have delicacies. First class! You can't think so. Doesn't anyone have the same right as you to a good seat?"

"It's the same at the theater," agreed Théodose, with no less bitterness. "Have you ever seen a lack of discrimination for fortune or rank? It's true that they're all rich and all well-educated, but what a country! There's no charm, no supremacy, no glory—why do they live?"

"I ask myself the same thing," added Madame Brunel, with vivacity. "Emotions must be rare among them, for where would they get them from? As soon as they love, they marry, and afterwards, never any passions, despair or dreams! However little sentiment one has, it's stifled among these vulgar creatures. When one thinks that no glamour is possible, and no prestige—that they've leveled out everything, in sum…!"

"If they've leveled everything, Madame, they haven't calculated the unexpected. That there's no first class at the club, no box of honor at the theater, no high table, no throne for royalty, what does it matter? Royalty dominates of its own accord; its elevation is innate. Here or there, Madame, you will always reign by grace and distinction; to be ignorant of royalty, Madame, it would be necessary not to have seen you."

Producing these words with the gallant and skeptical air of a seducer sure of pleasing, Théodose stood up.

"Are you leaving?" said Madame Brunel, swiftly—and then stopped, in confusion.

"In order not to abuse the precious privilege that is offered to me, Madame, and to merit that it might be accorded to me often." Théodose said that with an exquisite, but impertinently confident grace.

"Come back whenever you please," murmured Madame Brunel softly, and stood up. "I wouldn't want to steal you from the Verdin family," she continued, "but as there are four days of work and one of rest, it's only natural that on the days when they can't occupy themselves with you, you'll be free."

"Damn!" said Théodose. "They certainly keep the Sabbath holy! Four days of very little work and a fifth to rest."

"To rest," said Madame Brunel, pulling an ironic face. "If one can call that rest, for they're always making something. But even so, it's a day of rest, since there's no obligatory work. You arrived on the island on one of those days."

"I'm no longer astonished that they were so splendid."

Madame Brunel and Théodose were standing up; Madame Brunel did not dare ask Théodose to sit down again; Théodose hesitated between finding a pretext to stay longer and going away. He was beginning to feel a desire to sleep; the expenditure of mental energy immediately after eating, combined with the influence of his hour, had wearied him, and as he felt that becoming cold after his gallantry would have had a disastrous effect, he judged it preferable to retire. Certainly, the society of Madame Brunel did not fill him with enthusiasm, but the conversation of any of the inhabitants made him angry, and our man of the world much preferred being bored in a flirtation to arguing over something commonsensical.

After these reflections, made within the blink of an eye, he bowed and held out his hand to Madame Brunel—who, indecisive, opened hers without budging. He took possession of the hand gently, raised it to his lips, and, almost walking backwards, made his farewells.

Madame Brunel returned to the drawing room alone, sat down in the same chair and talked to herself in the mirror as she had talked before, smiled at herself, delighted herself, and seduced herself. Light and radiant, she ran to a little desk, opened it, and, having taken out a rather voluminous notebook, looked at it as if meditating. Then, moving swiftly to a chair, she sat down, turned the pages, reread the last lines written there and wrote thereafter:

My dear Emma, you've already had the great incident of the arrival on the island of Monsieur de Paris, but today my journal will be augmented by a much greater event. How can I say it straight out? What words can I employ? Anyway, my God, is it my fault? You've always understood me, haven't you? Monsieur de Paris has come and he's caught. I've questioned Nise, and so I know that he's a bachelor; I'm a widow. Well, no, it's not what you imagine; I'm not thinking of abdicating my liberty, but I'm so proud when I see that, at my age, I can still triumph over other women that I'm forced to admire myself. Oh, my dear, if you'd seen him! He's ensorcelled. It's almost ridiculous to heap passion on passion, and if it weren't to you, I'd surely never dare say it; can one believe that I can't go anywhere, have a conversation, without being as-

sailed by tributes, while I see very pretty women, who even
dress very freely, who are never pursued?

Madame Brunel paused momentarily there, and an aura of glory invaded her physiognomy.

"*Oh*," she resumed, dictating to herself aloud, "*what distinction, my dear, how perfect he is! He would shine in any company in Paris; imagine what he must be here; but I alone understand him; he senses that, so he loves me. He loves me!*"

Madame Brunel followed that word; in order to see nothing but him, she closed her eyes and gently leaned back against the black of her armchair. A few moments later she dropped her pen, without thinking about picking it up again. The words had drawn the lady all the way to the clouds.

In the meantime, Théodose went back indoors and went to bed, only thinking about one thing: that he was beginning to get bored.

Chapter XII
A Marriage on the Isle of Utopia

Eating well, sleeping often and walking a great deal, however, Théodose attained each subsequent day more easily than he had anticipated. Having learned the evening after visiting Madame Brunel that she was a widow, he had judged it prudent to relent his haste, and the beautiful lady, who attributed that reserve to a timidity fearful of true love, strove to make the supposed martyr understand that he was not so disdained. So, while believing that she only appeared to be according a few kindnesses, she obliged him, so to speak, to take her to museums, libraries or any other sort of excursion.

One evening, at table, Verdin said to Théodose: "Nise's wedding is tomorrow; if you'd like to be there, you'll be very welcome. You're our guest, and a guest is a part of the family."

"I'll go with pleasure," Théodose replied.

The next day, at six o'clock, Verdin, who was familiar with his guest's habits, came to wake him.

"It's not until eight o'clock," he said, "but I didn't want you to be obliged to hurry in order to get ready."

"Thank you," said Théodose. "I'll get up."

"In the meantime," said Verdin, "I'll fill two glasses with the excellent white wine that you like. There's nothing like it for chasing away the heaviness of sleep."

Théodose smiled, and a few moments later the two men were clinking glasses, affectionately wishing one another good health.

"Well, until later," said Théodose going back to his room.

"Until later," Verdin replied.

When Théodose was ready, he looked for a way to pass the time; he dared not go down into the garden for fear of dampening his clothes with dew. He did not like reading, so no hands were ever better cared for than his; for half an hour he shaped, filed and polished his fingernails.

A confusing noise that he could hear in the distance came closer; through the small window, Théodose perceived a large and resplendent crowd. Everyone was approaching at an even pace, and a short distance from the dwelling a loud fanfare made everything vibrate so much that one might have thought that inert objects were being brought to life by the musical turbulence.

At the door, the march and the music ceased; as if in response to a command, everyone remained silent and still. Then, detaching himself from that complete rigidity, a young man came forward. Théodose recognized Ulmé.

Ulmé crossed the threshold, traversed the courtyard, came up the steps of the entryway, disappeared inside, and reappeared a few seconds later holding Nise by the hand. Fanfares and acclamations resounded then, loud enough to make the ethereal vault quiver.

The two superb individuals, clad in splendid white, isolated on the steps before their fellows, who were contemplating them, seemed a magisterial apparition of life, a personification of the immeasurable majesty of human beings. Hand in hand, modest and tranquil, they went down, and their simplicity, sculpted in striking relief, stood out against the backcloth of triumphant detonation.

Behind them, Verdin and Nisia, accompanied by Théodose, descended in their turn; then Ulmé's grandparents came to meet them, and the two families embraced effusively. That was like a signal; the musicians ceased playing, and the members of the audience threw their arms around one another, as if, in marrying one of their number, they were all marrying a sister or a daughter.

After a moment of benevolent expansion, the cortege got ready to depart. Nise took her place between her father and mother, and Ulmé between the two old people; the orchestra struck up a lively march, and they all filed away, two by two, in an immense ribbon, more varied than a prism and no less dazzling.

After a fairly short journey, they arrived in front of a magnificent edifice almost hidden in the midst of centenarian trees, clumps of bushes and lawns. It was an immense round hall raised up on large white marble flagstones; the elevated dome was supported by admirably sculpted columns. There was no enclosure; between all the columns one could see from outside what was happening within.

In the center of the hall stood a high, broad stage surrounded by a balustrade of silvery metal; that stage served as a pedestal for a table, made of marble like the rest of the edifice. On that table there was an enormous solid silver box, carved with the greatest artistry, and in front of it, a unique set, a marvelous armchair of the same metal as the box, with filigree cushions worked as delicately as fabric.

When the wedding party arrived at the foot of the staircase, the music stopped, the file gathered into a group, and, the two families having come in, everyone followed the into the hall. The armchair was occupied by a venerable old man who stood up to welcome the audience.

Everyone bowed respectfully, and the future spouses, accompanied by their parents, climbed up to the platform. The old men opened the silver box; it contained a parchment book. The book was opened in its turn, and in the midst of general attention, the old man spoke.

"My children, this book, conserved from generation to generation, is the solemn attestation of the affection of one human being for another; that voluntary and public attestation closes, under penalty of a loss of honor, the road to another choice, at the same time as it renders sacred—which is to say, isolated from all covetousness—the two beings who, being exchanged in the same donation, can no longer give themselves to anyone, let alone be stolen. If, before engaging yourselves, you reflect and drawback, you are wise; if, unconvinced, you persist, you are criminal, and remorse and misfortune await you.

"Do not think that, so close to the end and in front of everyone, it would be shameful to step back; it is only on the edge of the precipice that one can judge its depth, and those who accompany you, on seeing you turn back, will congratulate you for not having wanted to draw anyone with you when you are not sure of the descent. So, my children, mediate one last time, and do not forget that there is as much glory in taming an impulse that you know cannot be durable as in accomplishing, sure of yourselves, the duty of all life."

The old man stopped talking in order that nothing should trouble the absolute calm. The audience was pale; on the platform, the children and the parents were weeping silently. Nisia looked at her daughter; the child threw her arms around her neck and sobbed. The old couple seized the hands of Ulmé—who, his cheeks covered with large tears, withdrew into himself in order not to explode. But the mother detached her daughter, who was hugging her. "My children," she said, "let the noble words of this old man and your dignity as human beings guide you. Free, everything is yours, because you are your own; but a person who is free must always be noble in their actions."

"Nise," Ulmé suddenly exclaimed, turning to the young woman, "do you doubt yourself?"

"No," she said, holding out her hand to him, and both of them, smiling and weeping, took their places before the book.

"*I, Nise, daughter of Verdin and Nisia, accept for a husband, Ulmé,*" dictated the old man. "Write, my child, and read aloud what you have written."

Nise wrote, finished by indicating her age and the date, and then read clearly and distinctly. Then it was Ulmé's turn, and when both of them had signed, the parents added their approvals; after them came the old couple—and the book was enclosed once again in its metal envelope.

"My children," the old man went on, "the peace of every hearth ensures the public peace, so virtuous spouses are therefore doing civic work, and the nation is grateful to them. Ulmé and Nise, you are spouses; the nation is counting on you."

The two young people took the old man's hands and kissed them respectfully; he drew them together and hugged them. "Go, our son," he said, "continue our task; we can do no more than look to you; maintain and ameliorate incessantly that which we have founded, in order that the old will not have the grief of surviving their destroyed work, and thus, from generation to generation, the wellbeing of humankind will be eternalized in our homeland."

With these words, the old man extended his hands to the parents; everyone shook them with affectionate deference. "Dear friends," he added, "Go now to rejoice; society, too, rejoices at this union."

Then the family descended from the stage, but the old man remained there until the hour determined for the interval of marriages. Everyone went out, all turning round and bowing as they did so.

The band, which had taken the lead, acclaimed the regathering and preparation for departure with a joyful tune. This time the married couple went ahead, and, carried away, the violins and fifes became so delirious that it would have been necessary to be deprived of all elasticity not to feel the urge to launch oneself forward, dancing—so everyone marched quickly, for the simple pleasure of following the impulsion.

Thus drawn, some singing and others agitating, that beautiful, valiant society deployed its admirable forms with an ease that gave it perfect grace, while the natural severity of its power was softened by the most fantastic, sparkling and colorful ornamentation. That society resembled a joyful troop escaped from Olympus, frolicking at its ease without worrying about mortals.

The wings of gaiety had soon transported them to the place of the feast. In the middle of the forest, a palace whose gardens were only limited by the woods adjoined to the oases, and the oases succeeding the woods, received the guests. There, in one of the immense rooms illuminated by gigantic windows, a magical service enthused the sense of sight, while a succulent odor inebriated the sense of smell. Veritably famished, everyone, in the midst of the hubbub, invited a companion to the table, and everyone set down, immediately getting up again in order to make a toast to the nation and its perpetuity, which is marriage.

The sun had been darting its rays over the forest when the wedding party sat down at table under the shade of its trees, and it was disappearing meekly into the waves when the guests got up again, sated. Singing, music and dancing had served to rest weary minds.

A certain nonchalance had replaced the morning's vivacity; after a few negotiations, they set out *en route*, casually, by way of sinuous and bushy pathways. The most advanced hailed the laggards from time to time, but the latter, with perfect tranquility, allowed themselves to be hailed and did not hasten their leaden pace by an inch.

It was a veritable blossoming of satisfaction, for no one had any idea of tensing a single fiber as they went on and on. If the weight of an arm drew it to hang down alongside the body, one let it hang; if the whim took one to jump up in the air, one jumped; caprice presided as master, and, some jostling and others trailing, some swinging from tree to tree and some executing a dance step, the society arrived, all members in their own fashions, at the edge of a large pond. Elegant gondolas were awaiting their desire at the bank.

Immediately, there was a joyful embarkation of the troop, with no anxiety, since they could all swim like fish, followed by departure and pursuit, with the oarsmen sweating as each gondola tried to pull ahead of the others.

Soon, that pleasure loses its charm, and is abandoned, and the decision is made to go back, by other routes; in any case, beneath the innumerable interlaced branches, it is rapidly getting dark; without hurrying, they depart again, but do not pause. The road is long; darkness gradually veils objects; some close their eyes for fear of looking into the thickening darkness; others search it boldly, hoping to discover some new appearance of life; it seems that the obscurity is an enigma, of which the timid are frightened, while the audacious expand in that setting, and the tranquil harmonize with the influence that surrounds them, slowly singing some sweet melody.

Mischievous youth finds itself too well-behaved and seeks amusement in frightening sleeping birds; dreamers dream about the spheres from which the great shadows come, and—O disenchantment!—others simply talk about hastening their steps because they are hungry.

Proceeding in the same fashion, and thinking so differently, the company arrives within sight of the palace. Illuminated globes of glass have been set out here and there in the trees and hedges, profusely in some places and parsimoniously in others, producing vigorously emphatic reliefs in equal depths. Everyone prefers to sit down outside; immediately, the young go in search of liqueurs or pastries; rounds of drinks are poured; they drink, they eat, they drink again, and the desire takes them to go and bury themselves amid that foliage, so coquettishly luminous, so shady, and so eccentric.

Singularity floats momentarily around real things, and the delighted being follows every capricious appearance; imagination has conquered reason, going according to its whim, and creating a pleasing transformation in every object. While some flee the light and take pleasure in seeming to plunge into darkness, others glide noiselessly through the bright foliage; some disappear slowly into profound blackness; elsewhere, from an opaque backcloth, resplendent apparitions suddenly emerge; from every bush, every thicket and every tree trunk, a being surges; one might think that the forest is populated by mysterious and multiple creatures.

That rosy plume, so gracious to behold, gradually melts as it draws away vaguely into a the figure of a strange bird extending its wings over the head of an uncertain individual; that beautiful girl, so amply curvaceous, so fresh and so vivacious, is transformed in her distant march into a diaphanous vapor; eventually, depending on whether the illumination brightens or the shadow deepens, the aspect changes and the same person glimpsed in twenty different places seems, although always the same, twenty times renewed.

Théodose, who has passed through all the phases of the celebration, no longer knows exactly where he is; he thinks that he is in the Elysian gardens, among divinities or shades, and when someone offers him something to drink, and he takes them for Hebe or Ganymede, he dares not refuse— which ends up with him completely losing his mind. He is lying idly between two illuminated bushes, and there, gracious phantasmagorias go back and forth before his half-closed eyes. One form, however, stops in front of him. Théodose looks, and recognizes Madame Brunel, but he confuses Madame Brunel with Olympus, and is only astonished to encounter a mortal in this place.

"What beauty!" he says to her.

"Oh!" says the lady, simpering.

"The mind is confused here." Théodose continues. "I don't know whether I'm asleep or dreaming."

"I dare say, for sure, that you're under an illusion," the lady says, believing that the word beauty was applied to her.

"Illusion!" repeated Théodose, angrily. "Don't destroy the charm, Nymph! Are you the evil spirit of this place?"

"What evil spirit?" exclaims Madame Brunel, bewildered.

"Don't vex me, Nymph," says Théodose, with a weary gesture.

"It's the veritable delights of Capua here," says the supposed Nymph, ironically.

"Capua!" repeats Théodose, mechanically.

"Yes, Capua!" repeats the lady in her turn. "Does Monsieur not understand the language of the gods?"

"You have wit, Nymph."

"It's not forbidden," she says, with a satisfied smile.

"No, but as it isn't dictated by law either, one must be grateful to people who sometimes have it," Théodose ripostes, mockingly. He is resentful of the Nymph.

"One can see, in fact, that it's not obligatory," she says, and draws away.

Théodose searches for the meaning of that comment, but it escapes him among a thousand other ideas colliding in his head; then a group surrounds him and drags him away; he marches in its midst; he arrives at a place where there is a bed, lies down on it fully clothed, and neither thinks nor sees anymore.

Chapter XIII
The Women of the Isle of Utopia

The entire island follows Théodose's example. A few isolated bursts of voices can still be heard, but they soon become more rare and fade away entirely. Then, clear and well-defined, the occasional guttural cry resounds at intervals and in all directions, alternating with hoarse sounds—but that savage song is part of nature, so the accustomed ear does not grasp the sounds, and sleep is untroubled by them.

It is the moment when a new existence is about to agitate. Thousands of creatures emerge from crevices and lairs, run through the forest, crawl along the ground, shapeless swarms almost without changing place, leaping in agile fashion and gazing with eyes of fire, moving slowly, stifling the sound. It is the second degree of life, which succeeds the weary first, until the first reappears and sends its inferior counterpart back into the shadows.

Half bold and half anxious, each one goes in search of its prey; a few bones broken in the silence cause those nearby to prick up their ears, but the sound is monotonous and the next victim coveted by the rude jaws resumes grazing tranquilly.

Diminished by a few, and the remainder sated, the nocturnal population begins to frolic; little muzzles sniff the morning scents in every gust of wind; the night bird, seeing the dawn, begins to stumble; the insect comes and goes as if to shake off its wings, and the snake glides gently toward its refuge.

To that gradual retreat, new actors succeed, waking up and chirping at the appearing day. The idlest, irritated by the racket, sing to make them quiet, and others even stronger thunder in their turn. Without budging from the branch for fear of losing breath, each one adds fury to the chorus, and the most formidable confusion salutes the last rabbit returning to the warren.

In Verdin's poultry yard, the various species compete to exceed one another in the shrillness of their cries: the hens sing without restrain the glory of their eggs, and the ducks quack scornfully. Théodose is annoyed by that, even though he is still asleep, but his slumber is dominated by the noise, and from one falsetto to the next, a particularly shrill call eventually wakes him up.

He thinks about the previous day, and sulkily and wearily takes off his clothes in which he has slept; then, slightly restored by ample cleansings, he goes in search of Verdin, but only encounters Nisia, who explains to him that Verdin has gone to work, but that he will return.

"What!" said Théodose. "He can work the day after a feast like that?"

"But such feasts are habitual," said Nisia. "In any case, yesterday was the rest day, we got up late, in anticipation of the fatigue. We went to bed at the usual time; you can see that the order of things has not been much disturbed."

"It was only ten o'clock, then?"

"Half past ten when you went into your room. If my husband is tired, he won't be working soon. You know that as soon as the four hours is complete, he's his own master."

"Oh well! I'm worn out, even though I've only just gotten up. I'm wondering how it's possible that Verdin has already done his day's work."

"It's quite natural," said Nisia, with a thin smile. "These feasts are so commonplace here that we don't get carried away, whereas those who are new let themselves go, and exhaust themselves mentally and physically."

Théodose thought about what had happened to him and nodded his head as a sign of acquiescence.

Nisia continued: "As everyone at Verdin's workplace was at the feast, they decided to start work an hour later; that's usual when there's a wedding; that way, no one is indisposed. We'll be dining today at eleven instead of ten."

Verdin came in at that moment. "Friend," he said, extending his hand to Théodose, "come with us to eat the leftovers of the feast. I'll change clothes, and we can go."

Théodose allowed himself to be led. He rediscovered the same magnificence of service, except that the guests were far less numerous and the dishes much less varied. Excellent pâtés has been concocted; *hors-d'oeuvres* were spread all over the table, and the dessert also had a certain appearance; the whole was consolidated by an infusion of convenient roasts.

Without intending to, Théodose cheered up, all the more so because he was sitting beside a middle-aged woman of an attractive humor who chatted to him joyfully while seeming not to take any account of his expression. Memories and anecdotes abounded in her conversation, all of it cheerful, lively and agreeably narrated. Insensibly, Théodose acquired a taste for dialogue and soon began to question her.

"I wasn't able to determine, during yesterday's ceremony, whether marriage is indissoluble?" he said, at one moment.

"Indissoluble!" repeated his neighbor, emphatically, and repeated it again: "Indissoluble, the union of two beings— when the individual is only bound to himself because the arm cannot be detached from the shoulder or the hand separated from the wrist, you want an association that is only voluntary, and which would occasion no injury in being divided, to be indissoluble! But think—nothing is indissoluble in this world; whatever cannot be disaggregated by one thing can be by another. That's all."

"Then people divorce here as they wish?"

"They divorce on the same principle that they marry. Marriage is the pure and simple accord of two wills; when that accord ceases, the marriage is, of necessity, dissolved. Don't you feel that to oppose divorce would be to marry people against their will? And who, then, can dispose of a person other than himself?"

"What I've been told," said Théodose, mildly, "is that it's with a view to putting a brake on passions."

"Oh, you're making fun of me," said the lady, amiably. "It's applying a material brake that not only exasperates but gives birth to passions. Have you ever seen a frisky horse attached to a leading rein? It's annoyed, it pulls this way and that, and it breaks the halter regardless. There it goes, lost to sight. On the contrary, leave the horse at liberty and it looks all around, but, not being restrained, hardly moves away. It's the same with people. My dear voyager, be sure that the human species is like the rest of creation; it modifies itself according to the environment in which it lives. If a child is formed by virtuous parents, but develops in a corrupt society, there will be an equilibrium between the good and the evil, because the society will alternately defer to what the family has created. Here, people do not go astray because society is the mainstay of everyone. What is taught to one is taught to all; what one is required to practice, all are required to practice; so no one thinks of abstracting himself from the general rule. We teach respect for marriage, as we teach respect for parents, and the one is established like the other, without laws or penalties, by the simple fact that respect is natural and we have cultivated it."

"That's fine," said Théodose, gravely. He added, with a certain embarrassment: "I might be abusing your kindness, but tell me, have you no religion? I haven't seen any altar to the Supreme Being."

Théodose's neighbor looked at him frankly and benevolently, and replied affectionately: "Nothing exists for us but Nature and human beings. Our religion is respect for humankind, because it's only the amelioration of humankind that can bring about amelioration in the order of things. Nature fills infinity and we venerate Nature, but we equalize ourselves with her because the consciousness of her Being is within us, and the consciousness of what exists must necessarily precede the organization of what exists. Thus, by the grandeur of Nature we judge our own grandeur."

As she spoke, the native woman's visage was transfigured; an extraordinary nobility and authority was suddenly reflected. Immediately recovering her usual simple expression, however, she smiled and continued: "If you hadn't seen the play the other day, I might hope to convince you by explaining a rule of arithmetic, but I can see that a brain habituated to error can no longer envisage the truth at a stroke. If the matter interests you, I can give you the principles of Creation to study; it's a very small calculation, as simple as one plus one makes two, but by virtue of its very simplicity, it escapes many, like those beautiful discoveries by which one is quite astonished, when one knows them, that one has not imagined before."

Théodose thanked her, although mocking her privately, thus imitating the intelligence of those who laugh at discoveries until they are applied and functioning.

"What are your principal laws?" asked the lady in her turn.

"Our laws!" said Théodose, astonished. "I know them well enough to follow them, but I'd have great difficulty formulating them."

"Is that possible? Here, as soon as one begins to reason, that's what you learn. The first law is that every human being has a self, and that in consequence, one must only want for others what one would want for oneself. The second law is that to punish instead of ameliorating is only to value what the guilty party values, for burying a criminal in order to be rid of him is as if a physician were to kill a patient in order not to have to care for him. Now, physicians who refuse their aid to the suffering, and just individuals who condemn the perverse, are merely executioners who beat or condemn the man in order to avoid healing the wound. The third law..."

"You have a good memory Madame," Théodose interrupted, "but I'm fearful of tiring you."

"And I of putting you to sleep," the excellent person riposted, affectionately.

"Oh, you're mistaken, Madame; the proof is that I'm going to ask you who made these laws?"

"Everyone—and everyone approves them, rectifies them and improves them..."

"You have no leaders, no representatives?"

"At the head of each labor section there's an accountant who calculates the conditions of employment, the materials employed, the number of workers in the section; that accountant serves for a month, and then cedes his role to another, and everyone takes on the role in turn. Those positions serve to establish the quantity of operations performed and to divide out the labor when one industry has too few or another too many. The calculations are presented at the meeting; everyone can check their exactitude, so there is no possibility of any trickery, and everyone employs the same system. Whatever rectification you want to make, you propose it squarely, it's discussed, and the plurality admits or rejects it. If you think you're right and haven't been understood, you write down your ideas; those who think they're false write their refutation, and thus judgment is formed."

After a moment's reflection, Théodose said: "Women here are probably considered equal to men?"

"Women everywhere are the mothers and daughters of men. As mothers, they create men, as daughters, they're created by them. You can see that, engendered and engendering by turns, every human being is merely a link in the chain of the species, and that the blood of the first flows in the veins of the last, as in all. How can you expect the same blood to be inferior and superior at the same time? That is as absurd or ignorant as to venture to make a distinction between the blood at the feet and the head of the same individual."

"That's exactly what I said to myself, Madame, and I only mentioned it in order to be more convinced."

"What! You needed to be convinced?"

"Oh, no, Madame, it's just that..." Théodose was cornered; he did not know how to get out of it. Luckily, at that moment, someone passed him a cup of coffee. He hastened to put it down in front of his neighbor, declaiming enthusiastically upon the taste of coffee drunk hot, and then embarked on a

106

digression regarding the hygienic merits of the excellent beverage, its usage in Paris, etc., etc. The lady seemed charmed; she asked Théodose if he took it often, and he said yes, given that Nisia made it deliciously.

"But now I think of it," he added, "I'll be departing without knowing their names. I've always meant to ask, but something or other caused me to forget."

"Their names are Verdin and Nisia."

"What, no family name? There's no possibility of illustration?"

"You mean there's no possibility of usurpation—it's necessary to become illustrious oneself."

"The woman could at least take her husband's name."

"Why should the husband not take his wife's? Here, one associates, but one does not annihilate; everyone remains themselves."

Under the pretext of smoking, Théodose got up. Ulmé's grandparents, Verdin and Nisia decided to accompany the young household, who were talking about withdrawing. All of them having invited him to go with them, he accepted gladly. Ulmé, Nise and her sister took the lead, and the two families followed slowly.

The newlyweds' house was like all the others in terms of its dimensions, but, also like all the others, it was organized to the tastes of its inhabitants. This one was positioned between the courtyard and the garden, very simple but charming to behold by virtue of the elegance of its roof, the shape and disposition of its openings. A delicate bas-relief, winding around it like a garland, was its only ornamentation. Inside, on the ground floor, there was an immense reception room-cum-dining room, furnished with superb dressers, paintings and mirrors placed opposite one another, which reflected a succession of rooms. There was a piano, in the French style.

In that country, the place where one eats is the place where one lives, for it is at table that one learns to appreciate the arts; thus, the dining room is the receptacle of the beautiful and the artistic. The seats are comfortable armchairs in which one is not hot, and where the body can relax after the fatigue of a good meal, and then one listens to some song or declamation. Also on the ground floor is a room like the one Théodose occupies in Verdin's house, and then the large bathroom and a vast kitchen. On the first floor, there are three beautiful bedrooms and more bathrooms, all furnished in the same manner as the dining room.

Verdin explains to Théodose that every household had its own house; that if the spouses die leaving children not yet of age, and with the children then being taken in by the families, the houses revert to society, which renders them in turn to other newlyweds; that if parents leave children who are of age but not yet married, those children continue, if they wish, to live in the house; that if only one child remains, it can be obliged, if necessary, to share the dwelling with an orphan of the same sex, because such large dwellings cannot be sacrificed to a single individual; and that, finally, dwellings are constructed in accordance with anticipated population growth and that with each in turn being called to choose between a house left vacant, every couple can then exchange their own for one that suits them better, without prejudice to the voluntary changes that occupants may make at any time.

Ulmé's and Nise's house was, in any case, entirely to their taste.

"With that system," said Théodose, "One can, strictly speaking console oneself for not having a family heritage, although it's nevertheless very pleasant to leave one's property to one's children."

"It's very odd how you don't take account of the meaning of words," said Verdin. "You speak in contradictions, and seem to think that you're saying perfectly sensible things. If I've understood what a particular heritage is, you would only dare speak about it to pity those who admit it. Here, look at that tree; a thousand branches are growing there; suppose for a moment that, when its evolution was complete, those braches had the possibility of being transfused into another branch of their choice; you can easily imagine the monstrous aspect of the tree; some parts would soon acquire the contours of a barrel, while others would only have the paltriness of a liana, and once the laws of logic are violated, all solidity ceases. Sometimes the heavy parts threaten to break of their own accord, and sometimes the thin parts hang onto the stronger ones and risk dragging them down; there is no harmony, the tree is ever-ready to fall of break. Such is society, by virtue of the simple fact of family heritage.

"On the contrary, with natural or social heritage, the fortune acquired by the society returns to the whole society, as the branch growing on the tree communicates its sap to the entire tree. Then, too, the property of those who die is the natural prerogative of those who are arriving in the world, given that, superfluous to the others who lived before, it is indispensable to the newborn who would otherwise have nothing or would only have something levied on a part of the living—and that way, every birth would be a decrease in fortune; whereas, by making the wealth of the being who has passed the wealth of the being to come, births do not inflict any privation on families."

Théodose was scarcely listening; he could not get over the fact that everyone was lodged in regal fashion. When Verdin had stopped talking, he said: "I was thinking that it's very fortunate that you have railways, with a city of such great size."

"My friend," Verdin replied, "one progress occasions another; it is only because we have railways, and are able to transport whatever we want to wherever we please, that we can fill the land with our dwellings without isolating ourselves from one another, and it's by virtue of machines that we can obtain any wealth uninterruptedly with a sum of labor that would only provide the indispensable if we were employing our arms alone. That is how, by science and its application, humans can succeed in satisfying their needs and tastes more liberally every day, while diminishing their efforts."

Having toured the house, they sat down in the garden, and after resting and taking refreshment, the two families returned home.

Chapter XIV
The Return to France.
Théodose's Marriage.
The Last Shipwreck

A short time afterwards, the inhabitants of the neighboring islands arrived to make their exchanges; when they left, Théodose and Madame Brunel were handed over to them. The couple was ferried with all possible care from one place to another all the way to countries where ships dropped anchor. That journey lasted twenty days, and was nothing but one long party. Scarcely had they arrived when they had an opportunity to embark; the ship dropped them at the first port on its route, and there they embarked once again, this time for France.

The relationship between the two travelers became increasingly cool. Since the scene at the wedding, Madame Brunel had been piqued, and Théodose had not done anything to reconquer her good graces, making the lady bittersweet and Théodose indifferent.

The forty days he had spent amid traditions so new to him had made a deep impression on Théodose; his meditations during the crossing contributed to new speculations, and he formed the intent of marrying a poor young woman in order to realize the virtues of the isle of Utopia. Such a project was not calculated to bring him closer to Madame Brunel, the aged coquette, so their conversations became increasingly rare.

At the end of the voyage, Théodose offered his address to the lady and asked her to let him have hers, but did so with such glacial politeness that Madame Brunel, beside herself with spite, replied in the same tone that she would probably be changing residence, and that she would let him know her new address at a later date. Thus the conversation was terminated.

It was not without any motive that Théodose had conceived the project of marrying a poor young woman. About a year before, he had become infatuated with a charming child;

she was the daughter of his launderers; she often came alone. Théodose had attempted to corrupt her, but had been received scornfully; furious, but a thousand leagues from any thought of marrying, he had turned his gallantries elsewhere. Now, however, the memory of that young woman returned to him, and, finding her worthy to be his wife, not only was he no longer hesitant but also could not wait to make his pronunciation.

As soon as he could, he went to Meudon to visit his launderers, talked about this and that, and then, very embarrassed, he asked for a private conversation with the father and mother. In that tête-à-tête he spoke about humanity, said that he understood that those who had a fortune ought to use it to the profit of the disinherited, and concluded by asking for the hand of Laure, the eldest daughter of the household. The parents, who had worked for thirty years to achieve a very meager living, thought that they ought to express their gratitude, and said that they would consult the child.

"May I not know that decision immediately, or at least what I might hope?" asked Théodose.

The mother, slightly nonplussed, dared not refuse, and ten minutes later she reappeared accompanied by an admirable creature, tall, blonde, shapely and superbly alive.

It was perceptible that the young woman must ordinarily have had a relaxed and open expression, but at that moment, she could hardly have been more embarrassed; her beautiful fresh complexion had turned crimson.

With the ease that fortune brings, Théodose went to her and took her hand. "Mademoiselle," he said, "forgive my haste, but I would be so glad to take away a word of hope."

The young woman had undoubtedly been schooled by her mother, for she replied immediately: "Monsieur, I have no reason...." As she spoke, however, her voice trembled, and, the tears arriving in a flood, she was unable to continue.

Théodose took that for natural emotion, and, kissing the hand that he was still holding, he said: "I'm a brute. Forgive me, my dear child; I'll leave you. Be good!"

He took his leave and made an arrangement with the parents to return soon.

When he had gone, there was no talk of anything but the marriage. Laure had a brother and a sister who were still very young; the father and the mother often spoke about those children while working with the washerwomen; they told one another that if Laure accepted, they would have no more anxieties—because, they added, we might die, or one of us might, and what would become of the poor unfortunates then? We're getting old, and they're far from grown.

These remarks and others like them, which the washerwomen made to give pleasure to their employers, and endlessly repeated before Laure, made her understand that if she refused, her parents would accuse her of sacrificing the future of her family to a caprice. Furthermore, in her situation, she could not see any possibility of a union that would suit her, and, balancing one displeasure against another, she told herself that it was better, at least, to gain wealth thereby than to add poverty thereto. In any case, she was beautiful and intelligent, she desired to live, and poverty, as everyone knows, is merely a vegetative state. So the cruel certainty of a future without hope convinced her to choose what seemed to her to be the lesser evil, and she accepted.

Théodose, at the peak of joy, immediately send magnificent presents.

The poor child, stunned by those splendors, hesitated every day between possessing them and going back on her word, and was not yet certain on the morning whether she would say yes; she allowed herself to be dressed and then taken forth, still thinking that she might escape—but as no miracle occurred, the City Hall did not collapse, and no lightning bolt struck anyone, she dared not withdraw of her own accord, and signed.

Théodose immediately took his wife to the country. He owned a large property a long way from Paris, and he established himself there in order to live at this residence permanently.

For two years the novelty of the situation held Laure in suspense. She did not know whether she was happy or not, but as she got accustomed to it, she began to fall into stagnation. To distract herself she learned to ride, and went out on random excursions; that tired her out and prevented her from thinking. Théodose, debilitated by this disorderly youth, was not always able to accompany her, and resented the fact that she left him alone. From remarks that were initially mild, he progressed insensibly to reproaches; his temperament contributing, he became increasingly ill and, in consequence, increasingly peevish.

Laure's firm and sober character also contributed to exasperate the aged husband. When Théodose recriminated, Laure explained her reasons for action, and, having demonstrated that those reasons were entirely honest and just, she continued tranquilly.

In the meantime, a young widow and her mother came to live nearby. The two ladies soon made the acquaintance of Laure, who charmed them immediately; furthermore, the young widow, cheerful, amiable and intelligent, enchanted the poor bored wife no less. They visited Théodose, who received them too coldly for them to be decently able to come back, but Marianne, the young widow, urged Laure to come and share her recreations. Laure promised, and frequented her neighbors very assiduously; they often had company, and Laure attracted a good deal of attention because of her beauty—but she had such a true dignity that even the women honored her.

Théodose did not hesitate to consider himself a martyr; he told himself that he was a victim of his generosity, that his wife was nothing but an ingrate, that it was necessary to punish her severely to prove himself, and he meditated a great effect.

One evening, when Laure returned from an evening at Marianne's house, which she had left at ten o'clock, a domestic told her that Monsieur was waiting for her.

That day, as was her custom, Laure was wearing a white muslin dress and a rose in her hair. Nothing was prettier than she was thus. She went placidly into Théodose's room. The latter, at the sight of so much beauty, felt his jealous rage redoubled.

"Good evening, my love," she said. "I was afraid that you were ill."

"I am, in fact, very ill," said Théodose, gritting his jaw as he spoke. In a sudden burst of fury, he exclaimed: "I'm revolted by your audacity, Madame!"

"I urge you to calm down, my love, if you don't want to become seriously ill," said Laure, coldly, and sat down.

Théodose had half-risen from his armchair; he fell back into it, dazed by his wife's calmness.

As she saw that he was about to cry out again, she said, in a coldly dignified tone: "Let me speak, and you can pass judgment afterwards. In buying my youth with your fortune, you were not dispossessed; I understand that you have not become poor in consequence, but that, to the contrary, you have gained an element of distraction by the acquisition of a young person who pleased you. It is perfectly equitable that my youth should also be left to me; that is my contribution, to which I have associated you as you have associated me with ours; and my youth, buried and locked away, would no more be my youth than your treasure, if stolen, would be your treasure.

"Still young and advocating for that youth, I claim the right to continue to live as a young person, since you, rich and supported by that wealth, are continuing to live as a rich man. You understand, now, don't you, my love, that it's necessary for you to adapt to seeing me seek the distraction appropriate to my age, just as it's necessary for me to adapt to seeing you drink the excellent wines that are appropriate to your income."

Laure stopped speaking. Théodose, his eyes staring and his mouth open, was still listening.

"Oh, monster!" he vociferated, recovering his presence of mind with a start. "Perverse creature! I, who have made your happiness..."

"Yours, you mean!"

"And yours, I suppose."

"Mine? No. Happiness is harmony, and our union resembles a being whose head is withered while its body is barely formed. Is such a sinister dissonance harmony? Although the head might be senile enough to rejoice in that graft, can the vivacious body thus atrophied expand in delight? The best that can be attained is that it loses the power of thought. But what a picture, Monsieur! Is that not enough?"

"Yes, Madame, it's enough," said Théodose. "Oh," he continued, sobbing, "Oh, why did I marry?"

His sadness was so immense and so true that Laure ran to him; she kissed him on the forehead, moved by his suffering. Inert, sunk in his despair, he let her do it.

Suddenly, as if galvanized, he stood up, terrible and menacing.

"If I wanted my happiness, I also wanted yours, infamous woman! You were a wretch condemned to distress, perhaps ill-treatment, and I put you in a nest of wealth and adoration—and you can say that I have not made you happy?"

"No," said Laure, looking at Théodose with limpid eyes and letting her words fall one by one. "No. To make the happiness of a disinherited man, it is necessary to give him the means and to let him choose his happiness of his own will. To make my happiness—that of a poor girl condemned to spinsterhood or a coarse and brutal husband—it was necessary to give me the dowry that would have permitted me to marry the husband of my choice. Instead of that, you imposed yourself, at the price of your wealth." She pointed to their two faces reflected in the mirror and added, slowly: "Look. Have I not given as much as you?"

As she pronounced those words, Laure had a smile of infinite sadness.

Théodose looked, bewildered and unconscious. Finally, he shuddered. "Go away," he said. "I'm asking you for mercy." His head was bowed.

Laure waited for a few seconds; then, seeing him still in the same posture, she went out without saying another word.

The next day, the chambermaid told her that Monsieur was very ill, and that Joseph had been obliged to care for him all night, but that Monsieur had forbidden anyone to inform Madame.

Laure went to her husband immediately, but he did not recognize her. A few moments later, the physician declared that Théodose had a high fever.

The delirium lasted for a week; when the invalid came round, his breathing was very weak; the fever had undermined him. After recovering his reason he was obstinately taciturn; he did not say a word—not one. His gaze, discontented or indifferent, was his only manner of making himself known. He became weaker and weaker.

One night, it seemed to Laure that the sick man pronounced her name; swiftly, she leaned over the bed and listened, holding her breath. Théodose repeated it, and signaled with his eyes that she was not mistaken. The young woman moved closer.

"Laure," said Théodose. "in spite of my delirium I saw you caring for me like a child; you're a worthy creature and I deplore my fatal illusion... I was sincere, though... The fine enthusiasm...I wanted to imitate...! Poor automaton, I thought I could act as a man, and only mutilated as a madman... Humanity is a summit, and one only reaches it by degrees...I was down below, I drew to myself what was above me and thought to raise myself thus toward the summit... It's too late...!"

He stopped, and gazed ineffably at Laure, who was weeping.

"It was very beautiful, my child, the isle of Utopia... the isle of Truth!" he went on, piously. "For it was very true!"

Then, after a pause, he extended his hands toward his young wife. She squeezed them tenderly, but found nothing to say but: "My love."

She thought he was insane.

"Adieu, my child," Théodose murmured. "Forgive me, my daughter," he added as if in a sigh—and he died.

6 September 1872

THE WORLD TURNED UPSIDE DOWN

Incantation

O earth, do not shudder to the extent of causing mountains to fly hither and yon, and collide in space with precipitate worlds! O moon, do not flee in panic, dragging in your wake the myriads of stars! O sun, do not go forth, carried away by the turbulence of vertigo, to set ablaze on your route the universal ocean! Cataracts, beware of swallowing the infinity of summits beneath your indomitably unleashed waves! Globes that rotate, endlessly entangled with one another, do not go forth, rebounding with horror, to crush one another in frightful chaos! Thunderbolts and craters, detonations and tremors, do not go forth, hollowing out gulf after gulf, pulverizing and petrifying to the very last atom! All of you, in sum, who exist—earth, sea, air, fire, creation, nature, humankind—contain your agitation, moderate your alarm, overcome your terror, but prepare to be frightened! I am going to tell you the story of Célestine Chopin.

Chapter I
Célestine's Origin, Education, Life and Character

Célestine Chopin was a gamine of the Faubourg du Temple. Her mother, Mademoiselle Chopin, the issue of nomadic parents, had, so to speak, raised herself on her own. At eight years old she had been placed to earn her nourishment, and the rest of her career had been spent going from one factory to another. For education, argot; for mores, license; for horizons, hazard—such had been Mademoiselle Chopin's education.[8]

As she had become very beautiful, her life had been a composite of opulence and poverty. She had never made a fortune and had never had a stable situation, because, profoundly independent, she went forth following an idea or a caprice, not imagining anything beyond. It would have been astonishing, in talking to her, to dominate her by interest; it was not that she was romantic or delicate, it was simply that she did not know how to be bored, much less to constrain herself.

At rather distant intervals, she had brought three daughters into the world. The fathers were not exactly well known to the mother, so they were absolutely zero to the children, who never even imagined anything about them. They had had fathers, that much was certain, but as for knowing who they were, that was of no importance.

Célestine, the youngest of the three daughters, was fifteen years distanced from her sisters; they, who had become as

---

[8] Célestine's surname is not mentioned again after this paragraph, and has no need to be; the supplementation would be superfluous if it were not symbolic in some fashion. The name would inevitably have recalled the composer Frédéric Chopin, and the two things that everyone in France knew about him were that his music was divine and that George Sand had been his mistress.

beautiful as their mother, lived in much the same fashion, so that carelessness of all position and indifference to things established a kind of harmony in that family of sorts; they sustained it voluntarily and lived in good accord; above all, they were cheerful within it and indifferent to everything. If one of them left in the morning in a printed cotton dress and came back in the evening wearing velvet, no one asked for an explanation, and no action was followed by reflection. It ought to be said, too, that no event led to any moral alteration; there was always the same demeanor, the same individuality; if there was velvet, they felt its softness and its thickness, but the effect it produced stopped there.

Those three women, aiding one another, were not unhappy, and little Célestine, cherished by them after their fashion, was a doll with which they amused themselves all day long, dressing her up, teasing her and teaching her. The society admitted into the house completed that educational endeavor, and at eight years of age, Célestine could have rivaled an Opéra rat or a walk-on player at the Variétés in repartee.

At that age, it was decided to send her to school. Her instructresses wanted her to have the talents that demoiselles possessed; for themselves they cared as little about that as turning forty, but their idea was that it would be different for the little one, and that amused them.

"Célestine will be knowledgeable," they said. "It won't do her any good, but it will please us."

Célestine seconded their designs marvelously; she learned everything that anyone wished, wore clothes as if she had none on, and was all the more marvelous a masterpiece of form and beauty. At mealtimes, she often went to find her sisters at the factory; there, the bosses, the foremen, and the workers of both sexes edified the child that had already been loosely sketched by the contact with her family, so there could not have been a creature more disparate and more original than Célestine.

Superior in her endowments, she was the most perfect of young ladies at school, and among her family and its acquaintances the flightiest and most risqué hussy that it was possible to encounter. The reason for that was easily understandable; Célestine had one of those natures made to excel in everything; living in a low environment, she had grasped all the finesse of the genre, and elevated it, rendering it more cynical still by the piquancy of her wit and the prestige of her admirable person.

Her sisters, increasingly enthused, wanted her to learn drawing and music; in any case, Célestine sang like a nightingale—there was a future in that, no doubt about it. The Opéra and the theater were whirling in those heads thereafter. At fifteen, Célestine quit her studies and occupied herself solely with her singing; that was a new phase, the world of aspiring artistes, and an environment in which there was another idiom to master and different mores to learn.

With her perfect sagacity, Célestine succeeded in familiarizing herself with things without being found out; she took on the surface of whatever surrounded her and did not reveal her interior self. Thus she appeared as a dream, an incarnation of the art—hence, profound jealousy on the part of pupils, exalted admiration on the part of professors.

At any rate, Célestine justified all expectations; whether because the ensemble of beauty united in her added an immense force to her abilities, or because there really was nothing with which to find fault; she did not, in sum, seem inferior.

As people talked about her, Célestine soon had a following. Between the homages rendered to her and those that she saw offered to her sisters on a daily basis, there was all the difference of aristocratic refinement and plebeian informality, but Célestine, as supple as a snake, responded right away to whatever role was played out before her; treated as a queen, she immediately acted as a queen, so magisterially that her courtiers could not imagine that they might have approached her in any other way; then, with her family, leaving behind her aura and prestige as one takes off a costume after a performance, Célestine became an authentic brazen hussy again, a typical daughter of the faubourg.

Once the effervescence of early youth had passed, Célestine began to reflect; her ideas had been considerably broadened by her frequentation with the various classes of society, and at twenty-two, she had learned to know men at first glance, as a skillful mechanic is able to take account of any system at the first examination. Her manner of procedure was particular to her: never using any subterfuge, she got straight to the point, saying what she wanted clearly, always imposing her will and never yielding to anyone.

"You're ruining me, beautiful Célestine," said one of her servant cavaliers one day.

"My dear," she replied, disdainfully, "what's the purpose of your fortune? To amuse yourself. Now, could you ever procure a more regal feast than being loved by me? You can see, therefore, that you're making the best employment of your money that you could possibly make."

"One is no longer infatuated!" the piqued dandy riposted.

"Prove it by leaving me," said Célestine, mockingly.

The insult was sharp, and the favorite had a strong desire to go away, but Célestine appeared to him more beautiful than ever on that pedestal of arrogance, and, by virtue of a sudden change of mind, he felt that it was almost glorious to be touched by the iron hand that was crushing him. To remain was doubtless to be a slave, but by virtue of that fact, it was to count as something to be in proximity with the force; it was to be beaten, and that seemed to him to be an honor, for Célestine did not deign to martyrize everyone. As humble as a devotee in the presence of his God, the rebel knelt down, begged for mercy, and, having obtained it, hurled himself like a tornado in pursuit of his ruin.

Thus Célestine governed.

She had sung and acted in generic theaters; she would have been capable of achieving the most immense celebrity, but the entourage of suitors, incessant and relentless, the overabundant profusion that they heaped upon her, and the impossibility of the fantasy that they sowed beneath her feet, loosened the cords of her thought, and Célestine, carried away from enchantment to enchantment, no longer had the possibility of the rectitude of judgment that alone leads to genius.

Célestine could have played the part of the queen of love or some intoxicated goddess marvelously, in its purest sense, but it had become impossible for her to shed the morbidity that was dispiriting her life. Célestine was not the fiction of delirium, she was delirium personified.

That brain, by virtue of vibrating with overexcited notes, had lost its appetite for them. In the heights of the empyrean, Célestine suffered from spleen. She was then twenty-eight; she had exhausted the possible.

She decided to travel, not hoping for anything much, but tried it anyway. She departed for countries that were distant and hot, looking for something unexpected that might reanimate her depression, and wanting to leave all known horizons behind her. She disappeared without saying a word and embarked with a maidservant hired for the occasion.

The voyage did not charm her; that fiery imagination had more beauty within it than anything in nature, and she did not find anywhere the expression of the indefinite vagueness of which she dreamed without being able to make it precise. What she saw was magnificent, but what she aspired to was impossible, inconceivable and inaccessible. It was not a matter of beauty or ugliness; it required something superhuman to reanimate that creature, who, having become a statue by absorbing into herself everything that enabled life, was thus obliged to live internally, dying of her own ennui.

An event, however, came to cause her some agitation. Her ship was attacked by pirates. In the blink of an eye, the crew, too inferior in number, were taken prisoner, and the passengers were passed in review. At the sight of Célestine, a murmur of admiration went up. The corsair captain said that she was the most beautiful item in the cargo, and, immediately remembering that general booty had to be shared, ordered that Célestine be treated with all possible care, in order that the capital in question should not deteriorate, and that everyone could receive his share in good gold coin from some sultan or other—who, they knew, would give all the jewels in his kingdom to have such a superb item in his flock.

The fiery eyes of the pirates blazed at the sight of Célestine, but the bandits also looked at one another, the energy of every visage announcing a similar decision to its neighbor; without exchanging a word, they all understood and accepted that Célestine was reserved to be sold, because everyone had mutually affirmed that he would kill anyone who tried to appropriate her. That having been thought, it was done; such burning characters are as tenacious as they are prompt. Célestine was kept out of sight, and they set sail precipitately toward the realm of the sultan who was the most expansive in the matter of his harem. Her servant had orders, under threat of punishment, to look after her mistress' beauty.

As soon as they had disembarked, Célestine was taken to an isolated house and put into the hands of an old woman, but without being separated from her servant, for fear that the slightest annoyance might spoil the serenity of her physiognomy. Baths of all sorts, philters, oils, powders, opiates and downs were employed further to embellish—or, rather, fully to bring out—the unimaginable perfections of her body. Appropriate nourishment, amusements that provided recreation without fatigue, sleep, early morning walks—in sum, an existence of refined sensuality—rendered Célestine an unparalleled glamour.

Far from being sad, she adapted to that way of life, not resignedly but wholeheartedly, which allowed her to be stirred and molded without feeling the slightest impression. Thus, it required very little time to eradicate all but the most imperceptible trace of fatigue, and the pirates and the old woman never ceased ecstasizing over that masterpiece of character and beauty.

The captain resolved to make the most of this immense point with regard to the sultan, and, acting toward Célestine is a manner that was not his custom toward the other slaves, he told her that she was going to be presented to the sultan and asked her whether he might flatter himself that that condition was agreeable to her.

Célestine, reclining on her cushions, looked at the captain, smiled nonchalantly, and said half-heartedly that she would be pleased if he would spare her such ludicrous questions in the future.

"I'll explain to you one more time," she added, "that I consider men to be a stupid and insipid breed, so your sultan is of no consequence to me. Regulate your conduct on that basis, I beg you."

"What! You wouldn't have any preference if you were free?" asked the captain, profoundly astonished.

"Explain to me on what I could base my preference," Célestine replied, lazily. "As regards sentiment, I'm blasé; as regards men, they're all the same; and as regards those worthy to be loved, where are they to be found?"

The captain could not suppress a surge of anger. Célestine had said that in such a way that one sensed that her judgment was immutable, so he rebelled in his capacity as a man—but at the same time, he was stimulated by that disdain, and the woman he had thus far admired coldly he now coveted as a challenge; it seemed to him that to make that creature quiver would be the ultimate seething of life.

Lightning flashes passed through his head, but profit and his position interposed themselves like a cold shower; he felt that he would be vanquished if he hesitated for a second, and immediately, ordering Célestine to follow him, he set out for the sultan's residence.

Chapter II
Célestine and the Sultan.
Célestine's Strange Amusements.

There, in the most secret apartments, stripped of her garments, Célestine was exhibited to the expertise of the eunuchs. The latter immediately summoned the sultan, who, as soon as he had seen the magical creature, had no aspiration but to throw himself at the knees of that paradise of adoration. He made a sign to the eunuchs and they were obliged to count out the most insane sum to the corsair.

Célestine having asked for her maidservant, she was immediately granted to her.

The entire seraglio learned that a sun had set the master ablaze. Installed in an inaccessible place, Célestine had slaves of her own, and was served as an idol more than supreme. The old monarch would have invented the inconceivable if he could, simply to make that star of delights smile.

Never had such an annihilation been known to the slaves; everything to which the imagination could give birth, those unfortunates had to carry out, and without respite, day after day, from minute to minute and second to second—for, in order to make that statuesque face stir, the sultan would have pulverized the world, and himself. He was hanging from the fibers of that woman, and her slightest quivers were reverberated around her in ripples, bounds and crushings. She modulated life, and everyone echoed it in outbursts of strident joy or frightful howls.

Soon, Célestine no longer deigned to move a muscle in her face; strive as the sultan's folly might, nothing moved that splendid statue, and the poor sire was exasperated by despair. One day, however—O joy!—the statue was animated, and, passing her arm adorably around the old man's neck, she manifested the desire to see him disguised as an ostrich.

An old leaven of dignity caused his Turkish majesty's eyebrows to frown, but, Célestine already having removed her arm and extinguished her smile, the master-slave, trembling like a leaf and grimacing an expression of happiness, thanked the idol for deigning to demand something of him. Célestine replaced her arm and smiled even more delightfully, and the intoxicated sultan asked her to fix the day.

"Immediately, if possible," she replied.

"Oh, my divine!" he said, in exaltation.

On quitting her, the sultan launched himself forth with great haste, and summoned the costumer. Under threat of death, the disguise had to be executed and delivered the same day, by midnight.

For her part, Célestine had ordered that the costumer be brought secretly to her. There was no possible objection; death was everywhere; the slaves resigned themselves to it and succeeded in introducing the requested foreigner.

"I want the ostrich to be made," Célestine told him, "in such a way that the bird's head can be detached and, as it falls, will leave the head of the disguised individual visible. Go. This purse will be your reward if you carry out my order; death awaits you if you dare to ignore it."

As the costumer did not leave, she asked him what he was thinking about.

"About the system I need to employ to produce the effect that you require," he replied, "for if I execute it without explaining it to you, it might be a waste of effort."

"That's all right," said Célestine, and sent for pencils and paper. The artist drew his plan, and five minutes later he demonstrated by means of lines where the joint had to be located and the functioning of the connection.

Célestine approved; the costumer went to work. Then she, in order to wait, had herself rocked in a hammock to the sound of soft voices and muted instruments, in the midst of a cloud of incense.

At eleven o'clock, she was woken up; she had supper with the sultan, emptied cup after cup, and, at the end of the meal, demanded the costume. The sultan suggested, timidly, that she might be content to see him thus decked out in private, but Célestine, thumping the table like an angry bacchante, dismissed the old fool's feeble scruples, and then softened immediately, with her enchanting grace, and asked him how he could fear ridicule dissimulated in such a shelter.

The convinced sultan donned the plumage joyfully, and then, Célestine having put him on a leash, the doors suddenly opened and in the midst of the most splendid glamour, a thousand variegated individuals dazzled the view. At the same time, as prompt as thought, they spread out in a unique dance, to the resounding accompaniment of cymbals, bells, glug-glugs, tom-toms and boom-booms.

Then, one leading the other, the ostrichian Majesty and his wardress steered through the sinuosities of those inextricable prancings. At first, the guided ostrich advanced gravely, but soon, carried away by the strangeness of the song and the rhythm, the obliging fowl began to caper himself in a manner that no voyager would be able to describe.

Meanwhile, Célestine, at the peak of hilarity, took it into her head to ride that strange mount; immediately, without deliberation, she leapt astride her beast; there was an acceleration of pace in order to sustain the long neck and maintain equilibrium on the feet, and Célestine, thus perched, recommenced madly the tour of the assembly.

Having returned to her departure point she halted, demanded something to drink. She drank regally, and then threw the glass away and suddenly leapt off the ostrich, dragging the long neck forward as she descended. What remained depicted the body of a bird preceded by a man's head representing the sultan.

The amazement was as great among the assembly as in the monarch. A surge of anger seemed to render his power to him; he took a menacing step toward Célestine, but she, simulating the most profound astonishment, said: "Oh, my Lord, that was you? What grace toward your slave. You deigned to take the care to amuse her yourself!" She turned severely toward the crowd, and said: "On your knees! On your knees before the sultan of sultans!" With an insinuating softness, she continued: "Lord, how can you not be loved?" And she kissed his hand tenderly.

Everyone was on their knees, trembling with fear. The dejected sultan did not say anything; he wanted to turn round, but his sheath, which until then he had, so to speak, not felt, caused him at that moment to fly into a furious rage.

"Get me out of this ignoble thing," he said to Célestine, harshly, "and hurry, for..." And he growled.

"I shall never forget such a favor as long as I live," Célestine continued to proclaim. "I've seen a great deal, but nothing has moved me so much. What sentiment! What soul! What fire!" As she slowly detached the bird-monarch, she exclaimed emphatically: "How one is warmed at the hearth of such a heart!"

The sultan followed her with his eyes, while lending himself to the operation; he strove to disentangle irony from truth, but was impotent in that task.

"My dear Lord, how warm you must be," said the mocking woman, finally enabling the costume to fall.

Without further explanation, the sultan withdrew, and while the slaves went to bed, shivering with fear, Célestine laughed as she had not laughed for a long time.

The next day the sultan, although mortified, dared not say anything, and as the wearied Célestine had resumed her torpor, it was the master who asked the slave what might distract her, and even, after a moment, offered voluntarily to recommence the previous evening's performance.

"No," said Célestine, lazily, "that wouldn't amuse me anymore."

They both fell silent. Suddenly, Célestine sat up straight, sharp and petulant. "I want to see the Christian Hell," she said. "Have it represented for me."

The adherent of Mohammed hastened to condescend to that desire. In accordance with Célestine's ideas, costumes were made representing the vices in animal form. Leopards, snakes, goats, hyenas, monkeys, foxes and chameleons with human heads were to depict the various forms of society. This time, the sultan was exempted from any role. In the center of appropriately vast subterranean caverns, a formless swarm was made to move through the gloom and the mire, a hideous chaos of those animals with human faces, animated by musical instruments and voices chanting to a savage rhythm.

When that cloaca had exposed all its horrors, a troop of blissful devotees, hypocrites of wisdom, renegade philosophers and cynically pious journalists made their entrance with compunction, but soon, seeing the emptiness of their mummery and the aspect of the place, those unctuous individuals took off their masks and exceeded in great leaps and wild dances everything that Hell had to offer.

Then, appeared in their turn the people incensed by those false devotees, the hypocrites of virtue, the renegade philosophers and journalists available to the highest bidder. At first those canonized individuals tried to impose themselves by means of a benignly paternosterial attitude, but seeing their apostles hooting even more loudly than the damned, they too launched themselves into the general riot, and. heads here, arms there and legs in the air, moving, capering, stumbling and howling, the infernal band executed a round dance such as Satan had never beheld.

Passing back and forth with an ungraspable briskness, sometimes it was ascetic girls who were prancing a frantic jig with a few filthy beasts, sometimes satyrs with holy costumes and over-ripe complexions dislocating their joints in frantic contortions; sometimes, all of them caressed one another, stroked one another, and then suddenly fell backwards, wrenching and spitting. Hell itself, bewildered by such excess, would have stopped and applauded wildly.

Soon, the dancers, overexcited by the enthusiasm, dragged everyone into their circle; then, the founders of Hell, demons and reprobates alike, whirled joyously in a colossal and irresistible gallop, drawing Célestine with them.

Shortly thereafter, the inferno disappeared, leaving Célestine swooning with fatigue.

When she woke up, as she gave evidence of great satisfaction, a slave, in order to pay court to her, proposed the representation of Paradise. On hearing that, Célestine rudely threw her slipper at the impertinent individual and demanded to know why anyone dared to offer her something so insipid. Then, without waiting for a reply, she declared that the slave was mad and had him locked away in a lunatic asylum.

Meanwhile, that mode of life took its toll on the sultan; his health gradually declined; soon he had to take to his bed, and the physicians declared that he would not get up again.

A crazy, ludicrous idea immediately crossed Célestine's mind; she demanded to know how long the sultan's life might last.

"Two months, perhaps," was the reply she received.

Having received that information, she sent for a professor, and with an exaggerated ardor—as with everything she did when she took it into her head—she applied herself from morning till night studying the language of the country. Her sojourn with the corsair and in the seraglio had taught her, without her thinking about it, the most common locutions, so, as soon as she wanted to, she discovered in her memory a quantity of terms that she immediately translated. Her progress was incredible.

When she could jabber away about anything, she sent for the captain of the guard and, deploying her irresistible seduction, rendered the man madly infatuated with her. When she saw him thus disposed, she told him that the price she required for her person was so immense that it would be better not to talk about it any longer and that he had to forget her.

The unfortunate threw himself at her feet and even offered to murder the sultan, but Célestine refused to listen to him and sent him away.

As soon as he had gone, however, she summoned the young servant she had taken on when she left Paris. That daughter of hazard possessed infinite merit; devoid of ties and family, she had attached herself to Célestine and adored her as an idol rather than regarding her as an employer.

"Marthe," said Célestine, when the servant was before her, "I'm going to confide my plans to you because I believe you to be worthy of that confidence. In any case, if I'm mistaken, it will only be one fantasy less in my career, that's all. You're intelligent; a few words will suffice: I want to reign." With a marvelous smile, she added: "Not for long! My only means of arriving at the throne is to seduce the sultan's guard; with that and the time I have before me, I can render myself mistress of the realm. The captain is at my disposal, but a little artifice will deliver him to me even more fully. After having cast my spell upon him, I've sent him away; it's therefore necessary for you, under the appearance of letting him win you over, to introduce him to my apartments. That semblance of intrigue will render him even more insane, and I'll obtain anything I want from him. Go, and serve me if you wish."

The servant kissed the hand of her dear mistress, who smiled at her affectionately, and went out without saying a word.

On the evening of that same day, Marthe took Célestine to one side and told him that, the captain having run head first into the trap as easily as an innocent bird, the supposedly temeritous individual would arrive at her room at any time she cared to indicate."

"You're a pearl of diplomacy," said Célestine, laughing. "Hazard is a good purveyor; my daughter, I put my left hand over my right when I took you into my service. Thank you."

Things went as ordered. The captain thought that he was emerging clandestinely into the presence of his favorite, and the latter feigned amazement and anger as no great actress ever imagined. She appeared to soften, however, although keeping the supposed adventurer at a distance, and she agreed, in response to his crazed pleas, to tell him the fatal conditions that he demanded.

"I don't like verbiage," she said. "Open your ears and try not to be stupid. I want to reign for a month, but to reign

134

alone, absolutely, as a man. "Her gaze fixed upon the captain's frightened eyes, she added, emphatically: "In brief, I want to be the sultan. When that month is over, I'll return the throne to you, and you can, as a faithful servant, pass it on to whomever you please, and boast of having stolen it from me." Coldly, she concluded: "Well, what do you choose?"

The overwhelmed captain stared and tried to pull himself together; he wanted to say that he could not do it, but the magic of the woman and the fear of peril battled within him, and paralyzed him completely

"But how?" he said, finally, breathless with emotion.

"Does a woman have to inform a warrior, then?" Célestine replied, disdainfully. "Disarm the cohorts under some pretext; put together a troop of tatterdemalions; the large salaries suppressed for a month will pay your expenses amply, and the nation will even save money in the process."

"And if I promise you the throne," asked the captain, feverishly, "what will I get?"

"A promise in return for promise," replied Célestine, while tranquilly taking a small pistol from her pocket. "I'm buying a crown; in order to pay for it, it's at least necessary that I possess it."

"So I have no say in the bargain?" asked the captain, angrily.

"Oh, no sentimental banalities, I beg you," said Célestine, drawling sulkily.

"Well, then, no sentimental banalities," said the captain, launching himself toward Célestine—but she cocked her pistol phlegmatically.

"You or me," she said. "Decide."

The man stopped short, and, even more subjugated by that new allure, stepped back. Before disappearing, he swore that he would succeed.

Chapter III
Célestine's Government.
The First Decree: "Men must obey their wives."

The sultan languished for two more weeks. In the meantime, although the captain proposed the most impossible stratagems to Marthe, he was not admitted again to the presence of the favorite. He saw her before her servants, however, and with an unparalleled skill, she knew how to stoke up the volcano without awakening any suspicion.

Finally, the sultan died; the undermined power collapsed dully at the appointed hour; arms were removed from the janissaries and handed to excited cohorts; a general uprising devoid of any precise aim permitted Célestine to take possession of the government. Immense bribes immediately distributed to the people assured her of support from the beginning. The nobility, undone by that prodigality, were rendered impotent, and obliged to wait until the popular gratitude had calmed down; the wealthy caste, also too soft to put up any resistance by itself, yielded no less rapidly than the nobility, and everyone bowed down, smiling, awaiting an opportunity to overturn the master who never emerged from the royal enclosure.

Before the day's end, the leader of the conspiracy had Célestine solemnly crowned.

Rich feasts were held in the poor quarters of the city, and the imperial palace resounded from top to bottom with the thousand sounds of an orgy all night long.

Célestine, clad in imperial costume, presided splendidly over the banquet of honor. Success had multiplied her beauty tenfold, and the most profound carelessness gave her a certainty of action that surpassed the most regal appearances by a hundred leagues. Never had any dynastic despot imagined such heights, Célestine seemed to repose with plenitude upon the entire world, and seeing her so sure of herself, everyone doubted themselves but dared not doubt her or her power. Célestine was a veritable ruler.

Nahour, the captain of the guard, sitting opposite her at the same table, waited anxiously. No gaze or word favored him more than any other; rage was seething in his heart, but he contented himself nevertheless, as much out of hope as dread; he too trembled before the queen that he had made!

At dessert, when the fires of the drink circulating in the veins were agitating spirits madly, and joyful, furious, tender and savage explosions were going past one another like incendiary rockets, Célestine rose to her feet and lazily lifted her cup, full to the brim.

"Silence!" she said, in her siren voice, which she could extend or modulate at will. Immediately, everyone looked at her with the fearful respect that surrounds despots.

"Nahour," said Célestine, "I love audacity, and you are audacity itself; I declare you my trusted friend. Hear this, Nahour, my trusted friend! Here, where I rule, no other power counts; I am the will, the rest is merely the arm. It's yours, Nahour, who chose your sovereign in order to let her hand fall. Do you want it?" And with a divine gesture, she extended her arm toward the captain. At the same time, with the attitude of an enchanter, she added: "I drink to fortune, will you drink to it, too?"

Nahour seized his cup and leaned precipitately toward Célestine, but, not being able to reach her, he howled a triumphant toast, and, overturning everything in his passage, he launched himself in pursuit of the splendid woman, who, emitting a loud burst of laughter, disappeared slowly in the direction of her apartments.

It was like a signal; everyone collided with one another pell-mell, tables were broken, garments torn, and madness ran through the seraglio in a truly epileptic surge. The memory of hindrances provoked an inextinguishable thirst for excesses, and the dawn illuminated a few furious individuals still tearing around as if possessed, while inert masses snorted like seals in various corners.

Meanwhile, the city waited with curiosity to see whether any change would transpire. At the time of the council meeting, Célestine took her place on the throne, with the guards obedient to Nahour surrounding, as usual, the royal person. Everything was the same except for the depositary of power.

In the midst of the most profound silence, Célestine addressed a salute to her people, then made a sign, and the book of the law was brought to her. That voluminous dossier was shown to the assembly, and when that had been done, Célestine spoke.

"Dear children of Mohammed, I don't know your laws, and you probably don't know them either, but don't worry, I don't want to touch them. I presume that you find these edicts excellent, since you have kept them, and my presumption does not go so far as wanting to give you the better that is, it's said, the enemy of the good. Perhaps you don't understand what I mean, but that's how things usually are, because there are very few things that can be defined with certainty. By Allah, therefore, I respect your laws and adopt them for myself—by which I mean that I, a woman, order that henceforth, all women should be subject to the laws that rule men, while men must benefit in their turn from the laws that regulate women."

With that decree, the empress ended the audience.

The most confused rumors did the rounds. The men pricked up their ears, but the women dared not cry victory; they were fearful of a misunderstanding, an error—or, rather, a change of mind, for they were sure that they had heard correctly.

By the time of the morning meal, all the households were morose, Messieurs making grimaces and Mesdames unable to dissimulate expressions of abundant joy—and, unusually, behaving in an affable manner. Messieurs were all the more shocked by that, and shrugged their shoulders at everything, only opening their mouths to criticize what they were eating. The most delicious dishes were declared insipid.

"Women aren't even capable of preparing a good meal," sniggered the bearded oracles.

Mesdames listened imperturbably and calculated the vengeances that they would apply if the promulgation turned out to be true.

At midday it was announced, to the sound of trumpets, that the Empress was going to preside over marriages for one occasion, in order that the magistrates would be familiar with the new manner of applying the laws. The future spouses were therefore instructed to come to the throne room immediately.

For an hour, all newlyweds hastened to form a line, although people of high status said that they would be ashamed to get married in front of their tailor or shoemaker. People were not sure why, but one joker affirmed that it was because the rich feared being moved to pity, to the extent of being unable to help themselves returning to the poor the wealth that they had extorted from their production. Knowing their generosity, they wanted to avoid yielding to it, the worldly wise commentator explained. No one took any notice of him.

However, the scene around the vicinity of the palace became more and more joyful. All the windows were packed with spectators; the sidewalks were taken by storm. At every moment batches of carriages of every sort were arriving; comments were made to the people in the carriages as they passed by, and the coachmen and the public laughed at the gibes. As they got down onto the pavement the fathers, brothers and in-laws in company with the couples offered themselves copious libations in order to give themselves an appropriate aplomb; the mothers, sisters, wives and daughters nagged them to begin with, but finally joined in, matching them cup for cup without counting; this one was in honor of one, that one in honor of another...and they always had another, and never finished.

The jesters in the street, seeing that formidable influx, clucked as if to rally a flock of turkeys, and the street urchins replied to them by imitating the crowing of cockerels—but the most disastrous were a few strong lowlifes who, in order to show off their exploits, took to braying with a vigor capable of frightening a herd of elephants.

The more serious wedding parties, frightened by such a racket, were tempted to retrace their steps, but the first one to turn back was greeted with such jeers that, the coachmen having refused, none of them dared to confront such a charivari on foot.

As the solemn moment approached, everyone thought about taking their places, but then, as they all moved forward and tried to get in first, there was such a deafening shouting match that some, in order to make others quiet down, started throwing a hail of punches which fell at random on virginal brides, fathers-in-law and mothers-in-law trapped in the melee.

The combat suddenly ceased without anyone knowing why, and they recommenced arguing, but the meek brides, perceiving the pitiful state of their ornamentation, began to screech like peacocks, while weeping over their pitifully crumpled garlands, and pointing at the same time at their unworthily unkempt hair. Then, increasingly furious, they went bustling through the crowd, calling for their mothers and saying that they wanted to be taken away immediately.

The mothers abused the fathers and sent their daughters packing. The brawl was about to recommence when the palace door opened; then, a troop of guardsmen having shoved back the crowd pell-mell and issued an imperative order to sit down immediately, everyone sat down, more or less at random.

A few minutes later, Célestine made her appearance, surrounded by a brilliant cortege. Immediately noticing the strange accoutrement, flushed tones and singular organization of the audience, the Empress asked loudly whether it was really for marriages that the people had come.

A disorderly hubbub rose up in response to those words, but when the usher had rapped terribly to impose silence, the reply was made that the people were future spouses and their families who had come to swear eternal amity. A dull growl ran through the ranks again. Célestine smiled, the court sniggered, and the members of the audience showed one another their fists behind their backs.

"Mesdames et Messieurs," began the Empress, "I don't believe there's any need to make a speech about the amiable grace of the ceremony that has brought you here." (Murmurs.) "What can render the nobility to these hands extended toward one another in order to unite than the union of those hands itself? How could you be more delightfully moved than by your own emotion? Today, therefore, speech gives way modestly to action. Yes, I repeat, in order to penetrate you more fully with the ineffable sweetness of the bonds that you are about to contract, there is no means more effective than the application of those very bonds, so we shall not delay for another second the mutual exchange of your devotions, your abnegations and your beings."

The audience was having difficulty containing its anger; the usher took advantage of the pause to make the recalcitrants relent, and the Empress continued in these terms:

"There is in this code"—she put her hand on a monumental book set beside her—"an article relative to marriage; that phraseology is habitually read out, but since all of the value contained therein can be summarized in the word 'obedience,' I believe that formality to be quite unnecessary, since whoever swears obedience swears a third and a quarter, black and white, green and blue—in sum, everything that can be executed. Thus, a list, whatever it might contain, is always derisorily restricted. Obedience means everything; whoever says obedience does not need to say anything else.

"Before proceeding, however, permit me to address a word of praise to the future husbands present in this assembly. I am happy to observe that the laws made by men with a view to ensuring the rights of the species that constitutes the legal half of the human species are equitable, right and perfect— which is to say that they really have been made for creatures equal to men, since, turned upon men, they can be adapted without anyone thinking of being astonished. It is thus that virtue has its own reward, for today, man has decreed that woman will benefit from all his justice toward her.

141

"Ushers," the Empress concluded, "bring the couples forward in order of the benches; we shall receive in our hands the oaths of obedience of the husbands to their wives."

An audacious clucking greeted that order. In the midst of the effervescence, however, one voice said clearly: "Has anyone ever seen the like?"

"No," replied Célestine, agreeably, "no one ever has; that is why I am enabling it to be seen." Then she invited the recalcitrant to formulate his grievances. Immediately, silence fell; people turned to the person addressed; he was a middle-aged man.

"I have to say, Your Majesty," he exclaimed, without preamble, "that a man cannot obey his wife."

"Why not?" asked the sovereign, tranquilly.

"Because he doesn't want to," replied the orator, proudly.

"That's a very good argument," said Célestine, "and I congratulate you on that riposte; but what are you going to do in order to marry? The law is formal: it prescribes obedience."

"And I tell Your Majesty and all the skirts in the kingdom that marriage is abolished," riposted the boor, rudely.

Masculine bravos acclaimed that sally frantically. The guard, angered by the irreverence, began to draw their swords; then, knocking down and trampling the women without any further concern, the men ran away in disorder.

Those left behind vociferated against the runaways and Célestine. They were about to leave when the Empress gave a signal for the doors to be closed. By a great reinforcement of banging and shouting, she succeeded in obtaining silence, and rose to her feet as if in fury.

"Women," she said, is a powerful voice, "how can you be such cowards? What! Can't you see that those flat-footed louts have no other merit than that of beating you? Are you, then, debased to the point that you have no enthusiasm for liberty? The wretches have fled before you. What they want is a plaything! They have reduced you to the level of merchandise, and there are so few among you that have blood in your veins that you have all accepted that mannequin existence. What is the work that will resurrect you? Where is your heart, that it might be touched? Where is your anger, that it might be animated?

"Oh, if I could only infuse you with my audacity, if I could only electrify you, I would say: Women! Here is your revenge! What your masters have given themselves, you, mistresses in your turn, take for yourselves—believe me, it's good! That supreme right, devoid of appeal, impose it! That profligacy, so appetizing, offer it to yourselves! That indifference to the despair, the supplication, the heartbreak of the oppressed, adopt it, as they have! Smile and say: 'Poor creatures!' In truth, these men are too ridiculous; let them carve, turn, hollow out, build and make children and occupy themselves with nothing else. Go, little ones, go!"

The wives and daughters, already excited by spirituous liquor and entirely beside themselves because of the insulting abandonment of the men, gradually became excited beneath Célestine's flamboyant gaze and enthusiastic speech. "Yes, vengeance, vengeance!" they cried unanimously, when the heroine stopped speaking.

The latter, delighted, contemplated them proudly and said: "I shall organize a guard of women; those Amazons will be armed and will have all the prerogatives of warriors; high pay will give them the facility of an existence of delights. Whoever enrolls will be invited in turn to participate in our feasts and will be able to deliver themselves legally to the debauches previously reserved for the bearded species. Until now, men have thrown you the handkerchief; I have taken it from them and I offer it to you. Answer me: do you want it?"

At that interpellation there was an indescribable tumult in the hall. All the young women who had hoped to be married that day, and all the wives who divined what awaited them at home, hesitated, consulted one another and debated. The fumes of the wine, rage and the passions glimpsed had made furies of them; they insulted one another, but in the end, furiously carried away, they swore to replace men and demanded to start immediately.

Célestine made a sign; immediately, Amazon vestments and weapons were brought out. The court and the guard retired momentarily behind the curtains. A few moments later, a hurrah in the hall having announced that the transformation had been accomplished, the audience reappeared, and found itself facing the proudest and most gallant regiment that one could ever see.

"The virtues of a soldier are ferocity and gallantry," said Célestine, insinuatingly. "Don't be half-soldiers, Mesdames." The she added: "I'm holding a fête this evening; five hundred young male slaves have been sent to me; you shall choose—I abandon them to you; have no scruples; remember that you are men, and in that regard, restraint would be shameful. We are not founding anything, Mesdames, we are executing what we have been taught; that which honors men, the strong, can only honor women, the weak, more. A little while ago, you were no more than a morsel of flesh, a machine—and by what right? By force! Now, things are inverted; the man is on the ground, the woman is standing up. Let us crush, Mesdames, let us crush!"

As if electrified, the audience screamed in solemn oath: "Let us crush! Let us crush!"

Then they shook hands and embraced one another, and while Célestine returned to the interior apartments, the new regiment went forth into the city, crying victory and seeking out recruits.

Chapter IV
A Revolt.
The Enslavement of Men.
Old Faruknas.

Now, during the night, while the palace was feasting ri-
otously, a revolt broke out. Célestine was alerted in time to be
able to oppose a vigorous resistance to it. Before dawn the
peril had been averted. The rioters were calming down under
lock and key, waiting to be judged.

At the hour of awakening the leaders were summoned
before the sovereign. They were all the sons of wealthy families, of financiers and merchants. They expected death, and
put on a brave face.

Célestine simply said to them: "According to the intelligence governing men, I ought to have your heads cut off, but I
don't see any profit in that, and it's at least necessary only to
work for something that brings a return. If, again in accordance with masculine perspicacity, I simply put you in prison, I
confess that I'd be the loser by it. I'd need jailers to guard you,
edifices to shelter you; furthermore, you might move philosophers to pity—which undoubtedly isn't dangerous, but at
length, even the smallest blows might produce unfortunate
effects.

"I have, therefore, thought more sagely; I shall condemn
you to the proletariat and employ you in the mines. That way,
you'll reenter the general framework and not interest anyone,
because the proletariat is considered a naturally excellent
thing. You'll be brought out again when your sentence ends;
the wages for your work will be allocated as a benefit to the
workers in the mine, who will thus have every interest in making you work hard. They'll also nourish you out of those wages, and thus you'll obtain a benefit from pleasing them.

"I glimpse in this innovation fortunate results for the future; if the domination of the workers is harsh, brutal and sav-

age, in anticipation of a possible return to their yoke you might perhaps occupy yourselves with civilizing them as much as possible when your liberty is returned to you. By making those men more sociable, you would be preparing a gentler subordination for yourselves, in case new grievances reintegrate you into their company. And for me, it will result that every attempt to overthrow me will be an opportunity to enrich my people, and, in consequence, to consolidate my position."

She turned to her guards. "Carry out my orders," she said,

As soon as the prisoners had been led away and joined with those who were waiting in the dungeons, the whole troop was taken to the mineworkers, to whom the sovereign's wishes were explained. Such an unexpected benefit could only enter into rustic minds after many explanations, but they eventually understood, and thanked the Empress warmly for the gift that she had sent them.

When the parents of the condemned men learned about the mode of punishment they came to Célestine to protest, reminding her of the promise she had made not to touch the laws.

"What do you take me for?" the Empress asked, arrogantly. "Is it me that you expect to convince that men are in the habit of keeping their promises? Since I'm replacing them, is it any wonder that I no longer keep mine? If I'd acted honestly, I'd understand the justice of your reprimands, but since I'm adopting your system of phraseological virtue, everything leading me to act in accordance with your cynical duplicity, can you be brainless to the point of protesting against your own procedures? Go away—I'm beginning to think that it's a real song-and-dance that we're about to exercise in replacing men. What a pitiful role!"

"Well, be careful," replied one young man, boldly.

"Fine, my lad—you'll lose; you'll see how funny your image is; until now, you've only contemplated it from a height, but now, fully exposed, you can't imagine how much it changes. Anyway, I've only replied to you because you're young and quite good-looking; that's habit, but it's sufficient—and that's enough; show these numbskulls out."

"There's a reign that's making a fine start!" one of the group risked launching.

"You'll see many others," shouted Célestine. "You don't know yet, my dears, but we're going to reenact your own history before you, and it's a fine show. Get out!"

With that adieu, she disappeared.

The anger was great among seducers of women, but the prospect of the mines tempered their excitement, and like balloons deflating by letting out air, those puffed up with anger swore, raged and cursed so much that by the end of the day they were exhausted.

It was, however, necessary to dissimulate in the presence of women. Mesdames did not intend that Messieurs should be permitted to gossip about things that were not their concern. Politics was henceforth forbidden to men; they had only to occupy themselves now with silly things, and it was imprudent not to take account of the observations of the governing sex, because, at the slightest sign of emancipation, the tyrannical skirts called in the Amazons, who had grown in numbers to the point of becoming a State within a State, and at the slightest masculine misdemeanor they sent the recalcitrant trousers to the mines.

"Those aren't reprisals," a man once said to one of those beautiful despots, "for after all, we never restrained you physically."

"I believe that you did!" replied the lady, hotly. "We were continually restrained! We only received visitors if Monsieur permitted; we only went out when Monsieur allowed; we only wrote what Monsieur tolerated; we only worked as much as Monsieur ordained; and we only executed the movements that Monsieur commanded. What more could have been done to us under official lock-and-key? Go on, my dear—we were slaves, and to be a slave is not to be oneself. What does the manner in which one disposed of us matter, from the moment we were disposed? We could never do more for you what you have done for us, for we could never make you more than slaves, since to be a slave is to be suppressed. You're no longer men, Messieurs, you're women, so it's as women that you'll be treated—so much the worse for you if the system isn't good; it should have been made better; we've only taken it as it was."

"But in the end," he man insisted, "when laws are bad and vicious, great minds and generous hearts work and struggle to bring about reforms. If we've acted badly, repair our faults, surpass us, be great! Wouldn't that be vengeance enough?"

"Yes," said the housewife, "but in order to act nobly, it's first necessary to know what nobility is, and women know nothing about it, my dear. Look, I, who understand you, have never hidden the fact that in spite of just grievances, you make me feel pity, and I'd prefer to forgive you sincerely—but if I said that to my companions they'd tear me apart! Woman has become, thanks to your baseness, a base being in your image. Go and undo that now, then—you've bitten them, they're biting you; it's the law of talion; they know no other. I only have one consolation to give you: do you believe in miracles? No, well, my poor fellow, as the tree has grown, so it is; such as you have trained woman, so she is made: cowardly, rascally and, like you in her regard, your mortal enemy." On seeing him become thoughtful, she added: "There you go! I'm not bad at consolation am I?"

"That depends," said the man. "At least with you one doesn't conserve hope!"

"No hard feelings," added the woman, on the point of departure.

"It's me who's asking you for forgiveness," said her interlocutor, sadly, "for I'm a man, and if you're intelligent and generous, it's not because of my species that you've been able to achieve that."

As they were about to part, a woman came in and looked at the man angrily. At the same time, she questioned her companion, who was in haste to depart.

"I've caught you, Monsieur my husband!" said the newcomer, nodding her head in a significant manner. "How do you know him, Madame? What do you have to say to him, if you please?" And the harpy planted herself in front of the husband, terribly.

"Don't get angry, my dear wife. I can assure you that we were talking about utterly indifferent things."

"That's rich—one goes about chatting with loose women, and one thinks that that I might approve? I demand that you act more appropriately! You're forgetting that men must be reserved with women, who are now no longer the same. Once you gave us your tasks to perform, and we had to be good while you larked about; you locked us up to make us play the vestal in counterpart to Monsieur's libertinage. Which of us has to play the vestal now? Don't you know that, Monsieur? Is it necessary for me to oblige you to remember?"

"Do what you like—I don't care about your threats! What would you and your kind do without men? Idiots that you are."

"We'd do less, because we'd be less, and it's evident that, after us, the human race would end—but that's the only consequence of your perspicacious sally. You have, thank God, accustomed us to toil, durance and suffering—be reassured, we're battle-hardened to everything, having passed through your hands. It's a rude novitiate that you've designed there, you know! So we know the métier of despotism, because you haven't neglected anything in educating us, and we know how to bridle people!"

"La la, let's make peace, darling," said the husband, coaxing the tyrant. "Come on, damn it, we've had our good moments! Hasn't that pretty little face been able to lead her little husband by the nose whenever the pretty face wanted to?"

"Hum!" grumbled the pretty face, soothed for the moment. "Did it require baseness to manipulate you? You were so infatuated that there was no means of appealing to your reason. We were always play-acting. Look how superior we are—for once, if it was me who stood up to you as you've just done, how long would it have been before you sent me to the kitchen without wanting to listen to me any longer?"

The husband sighed; the wife fell silent. Then, after a pause, she said: "I'm dining in town with friends this evening—don't wait for me."

"But my dear wife, today is Saturday; I've been working hard all week, and for recompense you're going to let me eat alone—me, who, on the contrary, would like to spend my evening agreeably, since I don't have to get up early in the morning? What, to me, who is your companion, your only true friend, you prefer strangers? You're neglecting me—me, whom you love, me, who cares for you—for others who are only interested in you to amuse themselves and who'd replace you with anyone who came along! But my dear companion, don't close yourself off from my affection, which is the only one possible; remember that in order to be loved it's necessary to be everything to the one you love, and you can't be everything to everyone; those people love elsewhere and only give you a fraction of their hearts, while I, your husband, if you're amiable and loving, will cherish you without division, because by whom will I be loved, if not the person who lives with me? Don't you want to be loved, then, my wife?"

"In truth, my dear, I couldn't have put it better back in the old days—but it's all nonsense! It's asking too much for me to be your slave, and I can't always be behind your apron! A woman has other needs, other pleasures and other occupations than a man; it's necessary for you to conform to the laws of your sex. To you, private life, to us business, movement, agitation! A worthy father of a family ought to remain by his hearth and respect his wife, without deafening her with tearful recriminations! Well, it's settled; you go to bed; I've prepared your soup, you only have to warm it up. Oh, as for that, I don't want it to be said that I let you lack anything, for then you'd really have a right to complain! But you have enough to eat and drink; I don't refuse you decent clothes—the rest is childishness. *Au revoir*, my love, and good night."

In that fashion, most reasonable households were governed—but in the riotous classes there was nothing but rebukes, invective, reproaches and eternal threats. The poor men were at bay; absolute strangers to sleight of hand, they blundered and became confused and were caught a hundred times where a woman would not have been caught once.

Masculine mores could not, however, be reformed overnight, and many forceful vengeances were taken; the unfortunates were decimated like flies; it was incredible that they were not exterminated in a matter of days.

It must be said that, carried away by habit, those inconsequential beards followed hot on the heels of the first flirtatious mouse that crossed their path, so the wives aware in advance were always on the lookout and scarcely had to wait long to catch their prey. Pitilessly, as well-trained pupils, they exterminated mercilessly, and the weak among them dared not show themselves more merciful in order not to seem inadequate to the masculine role that they had taken on. There were even terrible ones who struck out on mere suspicion; those female Othellos became the joy and admiration of their sex.

In sum, there was nothing but one immolation after another, accomplished by the neophyte men with the pious fervor of the disciple who desires to receive ordination. Those women decreed to be men, piled sacrifice upon sacrifice in order to honor the masculine divinity that they represented, and the river could only carry away the bearded and hairy pious holocaust.

At the imperial palace Célestine maintained thousands of slave-men for show. At the slightest suspicion of indiscretion, a quick apprehension was made; the delinquent was tied up in a sack which was sealed and then thrown in the river. It was delightfully neat and brisk.

Before dying, the late sultan of ungentle memory had placed a large order for those exterminator sacks; he had not used them and Célestine found them on her accession to the throne. By virtue of drawing from the heap, it diminished; when it had nearly run out, the Empress summoned the usual entrepreneur of the expeditious funeral garb.

It was a horrible old woman named Faruknas, venomous and repulsive, who slavered her filthy praise over you in spite of your disgust. As soon as she arrived at the foot of the throne she threw herself on the ground and then looked up, her face abject, grimacing an ignoble smile.

"Great sovereign," she said, "glory to you for sending all that carrion into the mud. Men behave like brutes with all the creatures they encounter, not to mention that they keep victims at home for fear of lacking one. They treat us as filth and wallow pleasurably in our corruption; it is the case, therefore, that a man is a veritable sewer, and you are only developing his nature by obliging him to putrefy completely."

Célestine nodded her head, as if to express that there was nothing to add, that the indictment was complete.

"I need sacks," she said, "and I can see that you're disposed to get busy." She made a sign to the old woman bidding her to stand up, and asked: "Have you been working in this profession for a long time?"

Since my early childhood," the harpy replied. "We've always been sack-makers, mother and daughter; my mother made the one that was used on her." Blinking like an owl she added: "Personally, having always been ugly, I've avoided working on my own account."

"No one has ever asked for your hand?" said Célestine, in the nonchalantly ironic tone of the great talking to their menials.

The old women darted an oblique glance at the beautiful sovereign and replied boldly, in a viperfish hiss: "Might I ask why Your Majesty is interested in my person?"

"I don't know," Célestine replied, laughing. "Is that what I said?" Then, stretching her limbs and squirming in her armchair, she yawned, murmured, and then said full of effort: "I'm bored!" and fell back into somnolence.

In the meantime, the old woman withdrew.

Chapter V
The Development of Faruknas' Principles.
A Pagan Feast

Like mortals awaiting the awakening of a god, no one dared move around Célestine; they avoided breathing, everyone looking out for the slightest sign, simultaneously motionless and alert as they waited.

After a few minutes the divinity smiled and said, aloud: "It would be rather droll!"

Then, getting to her feet, she marched back and forth to rid herself of torpor, sent for the female viziers and secretaries who were in charge of the fine arts, and declared to them that she wanted to crown the most perfect works in the three genres of the purely literary, the simply poetic and the philosophical.

"The competition will take place in one of the reception rooms of my palace," she said. "Inform the academicians, vulgar authors and brewers of journalism, in order they may all come to dispute the prizes. I'll give them until eleven o'clock tomorrow to make the choice of their most esteemed work and transport it to the palace. It goes without saying that each one only has the right to a single entry. Until then, the books brought will be sorted; they'll be arranged in order of size. At eleven o'clock the doors will open, and the ceremony will commence at noon. There will be places for the friends who want to watch, until the hall is full. The prizes will be made known at the time of the ceremony. Go tell everyone to hurry and recommend the greatest respect." She added: "By the way, are my prisoners in the mines well-guarded? Is everything in order?"

"The people are saying prayers asking that the culpable be brought to them," was the reply. "Such joy has never been seen. The prisoners are a source of wellbeing, and it would be good, even in Your Majesty's interest, if there were new ones to replace those who finish their sentences."

"Nothing easier," said Célestine. "When necessary, we'll lock up the men of the cities at the slightest misdemeanor; as for those of rural areas, I expressly forbid you to touch them. The countryside is the seat of power; it's the means of circling the city tightly and curbing it to one's will; it's the body of the government. Only touch it in order to satisfy it."

Everyone bowed. Célestine sent word to Nahour that she was about to go incognito to a pleasure palace.

Accompanied at a distance by a few guards, Célestine, leaning on the arm of her maidservant, with her face well hidden by a thick mantilla, went through the city on foot. As it was summer, she had asked that she be taken by the longest route. She watched assemblies and listened to arguments, amused to see the poor husbands tugged by the beard and harshly treated in a fine fashion, not daring to breathe a word.

"That's where old Faruknas lives," one of her disguised guards whispered in her ear.

At that moment Célestine was in an old quarter, in front of a frightful building; an open ground floor window permitted the interior of the hovel to be seen.

Faruknas had just gotten home; she had probably been delayed gossiping. As she dropped an enormous bundle of fabric on the ground her shrill voice exclaimed: "And there's another load of work! We won't be scraping the bottom of the barrel with that she-devil! What a head, daughter, what a head! She's turned the world over—bang! Women were drowned, men will be drowned! A lot of women were drowned, even more men will be drowned. Things have to be done on a large scale. Oh, I never believed that Heaven would have such joy in store for me before dying!"

"It's very easy for you to talk," the daughter replied, bitterly, "but I'm thirty years old and haven't yet found a husband. I don't believe this system of destruction will make it any easier for me to procure one."

"You ought to blush, my girl, at the interest you take in that vile species."

"It's all very well for you to say that, Mother; haven't you been married?"

"Is it for you, my daughter, to reproach me for a union to which you owe the light of day?"

"And can you blame me, Mother, for wanting to imitate you?"

"You're a fool."

"And your Célestine's a good-for-nothing. Why is she interfering?"

"But after all, my girl, what reason do you have to weep for men? None of them has wanted you. Isn't it pleasant, in your neglect, to feel yourself avenged, and isn't it to that woman that you owe it?"

"I'd rather have been loved than be avenged."

"Be loved! Great God, can Célestine work miracles? Come on, my girl, that's never been seen, a man who loves."

"And yet you married my father."

"Your father and I filled one another with horror, we were so ugly," the old woman sniggered. "He was even worse than me. You take after him, my girl. Anyway, that ugliness obliged us to be faithful, and I believe that we were the only united couple. You see, my girl, in matters of beauty, the most beautiful is dethroned by the most piquant, the nonchalant by the lively, the lively by the petulant, the disdainful by the mischievous, the amiable by the capricious, frank laugher by simpering laughter, the sharp gaze by the languid gaze, but the apogee of ugliness isn't dethroned by anything, and that's its immutable advantage. So, while the so-called beauties spend their lives mutually stealing one another's men—who, for their parts, do nothing but preen their plumage in order to be stolen—while those ephemera flutter from white to blue, from blue to pink and from pink to blue, dreaming about the white, we, although coveting the butterfly folk, remain forcibly bound to one another, poor caterpillars that we are, and everyone flees from us except ourselves. It's less pleasant but it seems more virtuous; unfortunately, there's no profit in it, for those nicely-groomed, titivated and perfumed fools take it for granted that virtue smells rancid, and whoever scents something unpleasant is immediately disgusted. Let's be disgusting, then."

"Mother, you're a monster!"

"You'll get there, my girl. Like us, you've grown up on misery and ill treatment, all washed down with bile, and like us, you'll become bitter. We are, my girl, the detritus thrown on to the wayside of the human species; the older we get, the more fetid we become—that's the law, it's just a matter of getting old. But anyway, to get back to our drownings, don't you see that that's your only hope? Feminine hatred will permit you to amass a princely dowry by men of an unprecedented confection of vengeful sacks, and when we have such a dowry, don't worry, even if there's only one man left, he'll be yours…until you've married him!"

Old Faruknas softened her tone. "You don't know what the heart of a mother is," she went on. "Personally, I'd see the entire human race drowned and I'd be glad, so long as I can I furnish you a carriage and fill my pockets. But truly, you've made me too emotional; tell me, my daughter, do you still have any of that excellent rum? I feel myself getting weak, and that liquor, you know, does me good!"

"Look in the cupboard," said the daughter, sullenly, "And at least try to leave some for me."

Célestine had had enough; she drew away without having been noticed.

"That," she said to her entourage, "is the difference between cooking with garlic and cooking with sugar; it's always the same stew but it isn't the same sauce, and I find these spicy dishes have some charm after our usual sickening insipidities. Anyway, it's healthier, because one doesn't eat as much; it quickly becomes repulsive."

So saying, the little troop arrived without incident at the château. Everything had been prepared as if by enchantment; prodigality, pleasures and graces mounted an assault in order to charm the eccentric divinity that had arrived in the locale. Young women and young men clad in mythological costumes came to meet the amiable traveler; at the entrance of the portico, nymphs frolicked gently around Célestine, drawing her into an elegant pavilion, and there, having bathed her and doused her in perfume, they placed the girdle of Venus around her.

Thus ornamented, more beautiful than the most dazzling fictional portrait of the enchanting goddess, Célestine, surrounded by a ravishing cortege and supported by Graces, slowly climbed the steps of the portico and went into the palace. In the midst of azure and golden hues, precious stones, flowers and perfumes, Nahour, representing the god Mars, was reposing on his throne, while a troop of amours tried to charm him with a delicately figured dance.

All the second order divinities were standing up, forming a ring around the dance, interlaced with one another, their eyes searching, commenting mutely but in a laudatory fashion on the pleasant scene being acted out in front of them.

As Célestine approached the amours ran, or rather flew, toward her, and, lifting her up in spite of her efforts, they carried her triumphantly toward the god lying on the throne.

Mars, who had raised himself up in order to admire Venus, stood up completely as she drew close, leaving the place vacant; the amours deposited the goddess there.

Then Mars bent his knee before her, kissed her feet and remained slavishly on the steps of the throne. The dance recommenced, more seductively and more animatedly. All Olympus joined in a quadrille. Soon, the troop came back to abduct Mars and Venus, and, carried in those soft and rounded arms, they were deposited in the fantastic gardens, before a Homeric feast.

The nectar, which was flowing copiously, drove all the guests to ecstasy; there was beauty, gaiety and admirable cordiality. Royalty and subjects came together to love and laugh, and cups circulated from hand to hand, uniting all those lips in a single kiss. There was peace and there was grace reigning over a lost corner of the earth...

The night seemed too short, and the empyrean flew away with the fumes of the wine. The guests became sad and morose again, the gluttonous complained of fatigue, the connoisseurs despaired of new delicacies. In sum, the immortals of the evening woke up as the next day's invalids.

Chapter VI
Academic Scales and the Prizes
for Poetry, Literature and Philosophy

Célestine was never more bored than when she had shaken off her torpor for a while; however, when she was reminded that she had promised to award prizes in *belles-lettres*, she immediately pulled herself together and ordered that she be woken up at ten o'clock in order to have time to get dressed and eat a meal before midday.

On the morning of the day in question the city was encumbered from an early hour by parcels, as commissionaires ferried masterpieces from every quarter. The thickness and number of the volumes was marvelous to behold; the public was ecstatic on seeing those solid conceptions file past. Few of the works sent were paltry in appearance, although they thought that a few of them were rather flat—which is to say, thin—and the most disdainful astonishment mocked those meager productions as they went by. A few authors mingling with the crowd sucked up praise on the wing and tried to contain their joy beneath a sanctimonious hypocrisy.

"Oh, look at that big heap," people exclaimed to one another. "He's a scholar, that man who's done that!"

"It must be admitted that we have capable men," affirmed one grave individual, professorially.

"Was it truly taking the trouble to write for so little?" mocked a group before a slender pamphlet. "Tell me about that pile!"

"One can say a great deal in a few words, though," observed one young man.

A few people turned round, gazed stupidly at the speaker, then looked at one another, and, without having opened their mouths, returned to examining the porters' burdens. The young man slipped away timidly and went to stand somewhere else, but did not dare to utter another word.

At eleven o'clock the doors were opened to the authors. The first to arrive naturally took the best places, and then examined the interior of the hall. The works were lined up methodically, the stout first, the medium, the small and the pamphlets afterwards. Everyone who had used up four inkwells and a dozen reams of paper swelled with pride at the sight of his product.

One fat author overflowing with satisfaction turned to his neighbor, a meager and modest brochure, and said, without thinking: "What do you think of my work?"

"I think it's not as good as mine, since I'm competing with you for the prize," the other replied, with simplicity.

The braggart was confused, but then he shrugged his shoulders and turned to his other neighbor, but that one, a cantankerous old churl, was not calculated to help him get his confidence back, and in turn the distant reaches of the dense line was resigned to awaiting their triumphs silently.

As time went by, more authors came into the hall. As each one arrived, all heads turned and interrogated the new arrival. When it was a well-known personality, he was greeted by a sentiment of jealous dread; when it was an unknown, a disdainful attitude seemed to presage a ridiculous defeat for the inconsequent in question. Gradually, the hall filled up; the friends and relatives of the leading lights had taken so many places that there was not a single one for the comrades of authors devoid of success.

At a quarter to twelve the hall was crammed. Many members of the audience were gossiping and pontificating loudly enough to be heard; others, more thoughtful, were trying to take account of something that seemed to them to be prodigious—to wit, the fact that Célestine was about to have to judge a quantity of works such that it might reasonably require an entire lifetime merely to scan the procession of tomes. Now, as the Empress was young, new to the realm and only recently initiated into the language, how could she pronounce upon the merits of what she was absolutely incapable of knowing and understanding?

That was a major impossibility. However, forgetting—doubtless for this one time only—the laws of logic, the authors forged miraculous explanations at their ease; they told themselves that the divine woman, probably enthused by some work or other, wanted to crown the said work without paying any further attention to others; and as each of them esteemed his own verbiage above all superiority, each of them privately awarded the award to himself, and from then on no longer considered the convocation and piling up of the books as anything but a simulacrum of competition, a ceremony designed to raise the value of the prize to be given.

Self-absorbed in spite of almost general conversation, the competitors searched their memories for beautiful passages. The philosophers proved to themselves that Célestine must have a just intelligence; the litterateurs envisaged her as a booted beauty in need of distraction; and the poets, thinking about their savage harmonies as storms in the desert, or so purely beautiful that the Madonna would suckle her newborn thereon, told themselves that their region was the real homeland of Célestine, the beauty of beauties, the star of stars!

Social habitude ensured that the public, impressed as it was, was nevertheless calm in appearance, The closer the time came, however, the keener the emotion became, the chances of success were increasingly calculated, comparisons and rivalries accentuated, and then melted away, and no one imagined a contest except to declare himself the winner.

As midday chimed, the curtains were lifted. Célestine, dazzling in beauty and ornamentation, radiated over the assembly like a diamond in black hair. Preceded by her pages, she headed for the throne; immediately behind followed a eunuch bearing a set of scales. As Célestine sat down the scales were deposited at her feet on the steps of the throne. In great ceremony, the court filled the stage and the guards took up positions at the doors.

Then, in the midst of general attention, the Empress, scanning the assembly with her gaze, spoke in a harmonious tone of voice.

162

"We thank you, Messieurs, for having been kind enough to submit the best of yourselves to the judgment of a sex thus far declared by you to be incapable in everything and scarcely worthy to engender you. This, Messieurs, proves forever that value is only a question of displacement; we were worthless, you were completely worthy; a spin of the wheel and everything changes, you take our place and are worthless, since we, having replaced you, are now completely worthy! But let's get straight to the point.

"It pleases us today to occupy ourselves with your little essays; you amuse yourselves scribbling, we're told; there's no harm in that, and as long as you aren't wasting your time or forsaking the modesty appropriate to your nature, which is your greatest charm in the eyes of women, we don't see any inconvenience in letting you continue.

"We'll go further than that; wanting to be progressive, we encourage men in that activity, in order that they cannot say that the doors of development are closed to them. Yes, Messieurs, we desire to admit you to our ranks freely; we repudiate the prejudice of inferiority based on the natural rudeness and coarseness attributed to your sex and we shall strive to facilitate the means of proving it, of discovering whether you are, in fact, merely a rustic instrument of labor, or an intelligence comparable to ours.

"So, Messieurs, you can count on us; you shall always find us disposed to acclaim merit without preoccupation as to its origin. Persevere in the path already commenced, and ensure that this gathering, in which you are about to obtain from women, your judges, the prize for some talent, will be succeeded by other gatherings. Then, women will gradually become accustomed to considering you as their equals, society will cease to be disdainful of you, and it will be all the more necessary for you to attain complete perfection in order to be honored, for we ought to recognize that the idea of inferiority attached to men influences in a disastrous manner everything that emanates from them. Educated only to consider their fathers, brothers, husbands and sons as incapable creatures, women pick apart masculine works to the smallest word and only approve of them, when they are forced to do so, half-heartedly, whereas, woman to woman, they're disposed to indulgent applause.

"I am therefore honored, Messieurs, to be the initiator of the emancipation of men, by means of the inauguration of an open field offered to their faculties.

"Now, it's time to pass on to the object of the session; please be silent, Messieurs, and listen no less attentively—this concerns you. Dart a glance over the volumes that are stacked up here from floor to ceiling, and you will immediately understand that it would be much easier to be buried by these books than to read them. On the other hand, any difficulty only being removed by being toppled, I am only demonstrating to your eyes the immensity of the obstacle in order to enable you to appreciate the incomparable ingenuity of the expedient. In fact, having admitted that the thinnest work can contain as much truth, and certainly encloses much lees stupidity, that the stoutest, we have deduced, in accordance with that logic, that the prize ought to be awarded to the most emaciated work."

At these words there was an explosion of murmurs in the auditorium. The rage was increased by the insult of the speech previously heard; people wondered if they ought to stay, but the pride of an award, no matter under what title, retained the grimly wrathful competitors in their places. The fat authors darted Carib glances at the puerile and inept accumulators of a hundred pages; there was a danger of conflict. Forgetting all dignity, the constructors of quartos bellowed passably strange interpellations.

The general shouting eventually facilitated a moment's respite, however.

"Let's see," said Célestine. "Let's explain ourselves. I give the floor to this fanatic." She pointed at an ample compiler, and commanded, in an absolute tone: "Inform us of the verities that are in your book."

"It's a history," retorted the quarto, in a surly tone.

"History is only written to demonstrate one or several truths," said Célestine. "Otherwise, what use would it be? So show us the truths that you have deduced from history."

"But Madame..."

"Let's pass on," said Célestine, swiftly. "A verity doesn't take so long to state, and the verity in your case is that you don't know what a verity is, so there can't be any in your book." With that she added: "The books will be weighed."

The tumult recommenced, more loudly than before; anathemas, imprecations, audacious oaths and lethal sarcasms overlapped, with no regard for the majesty of the occasion.

Bells, signals, orders and commands having had no effect on the tempest, the guards raised trumpets to their lips and sounded such a fanfare that everyone ducked, as if the collapse of the edifice would indubitably follow.

Célestine had put her hands over her ears; in any case, it only required a second of that unimaginable chaos to stun the crowd to the point of rendering it incapable of the slightest articulation.

Then, in the midst of the general daze, the operation of weighing was undertaken. The prize having to be awarded to the least ponderous, the contest was only established between the smallest productions. Each result, declared aloud, was inscribed in a register. In literature and poetry the victorious figures hardly surpassed half a livre;[9] the victorious weight in philosophy only amounted to a few grams.

The greatest amazement still reigned in the auditorium. People stared at the scales, the books, and Célestine, but no one knew exactly what they were seeing, and did not even think of looking at one another—except that, from time to time, they interrogated the terrible trumpets suspended from the arms of the nonchalant guards.

---

[9] The *livre*, or metric pound, had various values at various times; in 1872, although officially abolished, it was still in common use, and amounted to 500 grams.

All those people seemed hallucinated; they frequently passed their hands over their faces as if to recover the clarity of their vision.

Célestine, having paraded her mild and affectionate gaze over the unfortunates, said to them, softening her voice for fear of frightening them: "We're going to announce the results, Messieurs. These will be the recompenses:

"For poetry, the winner will be allowed entry to nocturnal feasts at the palace and a purse of gold, for poets and folly go hand in hand, and as the general rule is that those singers of delights are vagabonds, the dream accomplished and the purse of gold seemed to us to be a suitably appropriate gift.

"For literature, the winner will be granted entry to the court on ordinary days and the right to wear on his person as many medals as the author judges appropriate to decorate the sum of his heroes.

"As for the victorious philosopher, we give him the right to decide whether the previous prizes ought to be awarded or refused, which seems to us to be the only worthy recompense that can be offered to wisdom."

The Empress concluded: "Such is our decision," but added, with grace: "We are too well aware, Messieurs, of your habitual self-effacement to emit the slightest doubt as to your approval."

Having listened to those words, pronounced slowly in a suave voice, the assembly wondered what conduct to adopt, but violence was far from its thoughts, for the recent shock had calmed it down completely.

The poets, ever enthusiastic, gave the signal for applause; the unprejudiced philosophers tranquilly applauded their own triumph, while the rest followed suit, and the coldest animation of all rang out in the academic ranks.

"These are the prizes," Célestine said, indicating two cushions by her side, on one of which was deposited a fat purse and an invitation card, and on the other, a pile of certificates with all the accessories, including crosses, crescents, medallions, plaques, semi-plaques and sashes. "Let philosophy speak through the voice of its interpreter," the Empress added, addressing the prize-winning philosopher, and indicating with her gaze that she was awaiting his response.

Immediately rising to his feet, the individual summoned, without coughing or requesting indulgence, said clearly in a level voice:

"Illustrious Queen, I honor your decision not because it has given me supremacy, for the merits that surround me know that philosophy is only worth as much as the truth it explains, and, truth being the inalienable domain offered to all, everyone who is listening to me can tell themselves that they would have been able to render themselves masters of it, as I have, perhaps even better than me, since they can only consider me as a workman who, by virtue of effort, has rendered himself something of an expert, but whom anyone might overtake and surpass if it pleased them to educate themselves in that kind of knowledge. My merit, therefore, is merely a matter of labor and cannot wound anyone, since anyone, by occupying himself with the same game, might become a worker no less skillful and no less understood.

"I shall, therefore, not decide in accordance with my own personality, which does not exist, but in accordance with the few verities that I have learned; it is those verities that I have tried to render functional, and if I apply them badly, it is because I do not understand the mechanism well enough. In consequence of that, attribute any fault to me, for, I can assure you, Messieurs, truth itself is always perfect—except that it's necessary to define it well in order to apply it, and that is a difficult task."

Having pronounced that exordium modestly, the orator struck a pose indicating that he was about to decide. An increased attention held the audience motionless.

Then, with an affectionate mildness, the philosopher said: "The prize accorded to poets is just, and is to prepare them for healthier works rather than to show them at closer range the follies inaccessible to their poverty. The unknown fashioned by them at the whim of their imagination charms them, subjugates them and often depraves them; when they are able to put their finger on the puerile ephemeral nature of those delights, they will be convinced that the beings that devote themselves to them are unworthy of generous commiseration, because, in order to play gods sated with enjoyment in the midst of the suffering of their fellows, it is necessary for those poor creatures to have abdicated or misconceived all intelligence and reason. The latter are the babies of the human species, or those fallen back into infancy, and I glorify the sovereign for having admitted the poets to these infantilisms or senilities; on seeing them at close range, genius will no longer be inspired by anything but an enfeebling pity and will surely return to a valiant and incomparable nature, the one and only source of all strength and all beauty."

A mixture of muffled groans and approval rippled through the ranks. The orator looked around as if to consult on the question of whether he ought to continue. Reiterated *shushes* having imposed silence, the philosopher continued:

"Whatever applies to poets applies in a more restricted fashion to litterateurs. The latter often have more desire, I believe, to rise above the pernicious illusions that form the minds of their readers—at least, I suppose so, on seeing them almost invariably making use of subject material such as supremacy, mastery and petty despotism without thinking any further as to whether those substances are harmful or efficacious, and in what way they might be useful.

"I therefore approve of the intelligent decision that permits litterateurs to familiarize themselves with those vulgar engines and, in consequence, to abandon them as old outmoded usages about which one wonders subsequently how their practice was ever possible.

"In speaking thus I am speaking in accordance with my conscience—which is to say, in accordance with the sum of verity I have acquired; if that judgment is in the view of the sovereign and it pleases the judge, I am glad, out of sympathy for my fellows."

On those last words, Célestine rose to her feet. "My brother," she said, nobly, "we humbly ask your pardon for having associated you with our joke. Let your generosity accept this reparation of the culpable; great as your indulgence might be, our regret will surpass it."

Célestine was standing up, her head bowed in all humility; she remained thus curbed momentarily, and then slowly straightening up and turning to her guards, she added gravely: "Have the prize of this evening's fête withdrawn from our brother. He would not come without his family, and his family is too numerous to be contained in all the palaces put together, because they are the disinherited. Farewell, my brother, and pardon me."

She bowed her head again while the philosopher, wiping away a tear, followed the guards, who escorted him respectfully.

When he had disappeared, Célestine straightened up. "Do you realize that that is a man, you others who are called Messieurs?" she said, insolently. "If you have gazed at the individual who has just gone out, you have had good fortune, for he is one, and I don't know where to find another."

A ripple of sniggering broke out that that remark, but, immediately spotting the terrible trumpets, the assembly reentered into silence as if by magic.

"I've had enough; this is becoming insipid!" said Célestine and retired, ordering that the prizes should be handed over and the hall evacuated.

There was no feast at the palace that evening. Célestine read, and chatted agreeably until midnight with a few intelligent people; in sum, it was a veritable family feast.

Chapter XII
Célestine gets up early.
The vizier.
Astonishing statements by the Empress
regarding men and orangutans.
Nahour.

While a host of slaves were busying themselves at day-break to prepare every minute of Célestine's idle existence, the latter, awakening for the first time in her life at the hour when she normally went to bed, was quite astonished by such an event, and summoned Marthe to discuss that singularity with her. The Empress' conversation felt the effects of the natural sleep that her body had had; she was amiable, cheerful and did not seem at all difficult to satisfy, at least for that morning.

Her maidservant thought that she had recovered, and made certain reflections on the subject.

"My child," Célestine interrupted, "When the tempest blows through the forest, the forest inclines its treetops, but when the wind drops, the forest becomes upright again; that's what has happened to me; wisdom has caused my vices to incline momentarily, but now the wisdom has passed, my vices have stood up straight again." And she started to laugh. "Let's see," she said, "don't you have some scandalous story with which to amuse me?"

"There's nothing remarkable to tell you, Madame. Mes-dames spent the evening at the club, the casino or the brothel; Messieurs, for fear of the mines, behaved modestly and worked, all the more so because Mesdames are spending enormously. Everything is the same, but upside down."

"There we go," said Célestine, scornfully. "That's it: imi-tation. No superiority in anything. Servility even in venge-ance; one causes suffering as one has suffered. Humans are a plaything as insipid as all the rest; if one wants to enjoy them, it's necessary to teach them to sing, because in themselves they're despairingly monotonous." She burst out laughing. "I believe they live by imitation; one makes a maneuver and the rest immediately follow suit. What pitiful nullity! Tell me, Marthe, do you know the history of the kings of France?"

"No, Madame."

"Not even that of Saint Louis?"

"None at all, Madame."

"Well, my child, King Saint Louis was remarkable because he rendered justice under an oak tree; I, too, want to render justice under an oak tree. I have my reasons for that variation, and then again, instead of a saint underneath it there'd be...bah!" She resumed, jokingly: "There's still be a saint underneath it; one doesn't look very closely before allocating people a place in the celestial amphitheater. Call my women, I want to get dressed. Warn the vizier in charge of justice, and send him in while I'm getting dressed."

Marthe lifted up a curtain and opened a door. Immediately, a swarm of beautiful young women, adorned with the most gracious costumes, invaded the imperial bedchamber. As lively as birds, some surrounded Célestine and helped her out of bed while others, on their knees, placed marvelous slippers to receive her delicate feet; yet others held out fine fabrics to envelop her, while a few, stationed in an embrasure, delicately modulated a light and lively symphony.

Célestine, enveloped in a silky shell fleecy with lace, was scarcely on her feet when a thick curtain slid on its golden rod and revealed a dressing room of such delightfully refined elegance that it seemed that a human ought to be transformed into a divinity merely by virtue of spending time there.

Surrounded by her satellites. Célestine went nonchalantly into the sumptuous redoubt; then the nearest of her women took off her envelope and, lifting her body, placed it in an exquisite bath.

As soon as the odor of the bath had soothed and refreshed the bather, the pretty and hurried servants lifted her out of the water and, having wrapped her up once against in sparkling satin, laid her down on cushions that yielded so softly to the form of the marvelous creature that one might have thought it a cloud adapting undulously to the contours of a goddess.

The symphony, which had not ceased to make itself heard, then took on a gently dreamy motif; all the women, crouching around the sleeper, maintained the most complete immobility. The perfumed atmosphere, the silence and the lulling rhythm had such an infinitely absorbing influence that it seemed that the torpid body gradually became incapable of movement.

A quarter of an hour passed thus. Those living individuals resembled the waking dreamers whose eyes are open to the world while their minds contemplate imaginary regions within themselves.

Célestine however, raised herself up onto one elbow; instantly, all of them shook off their torpor; they came back to life like resuscitated individuals chasing away their dormancy. Accustomed to comprehending at a gesture or a sign, all the slaves hastened in response to the sovereign's mute commands; a seat and a looking glass were placed beside her.

Leaning on arms eager to sustain her, Célestine rose from her cushions and took her place in an armchair, with her reflected image in front of her. Her admirable brown hair undulated a thousand times beneath the imperceptible teeth of the comb; the sweetest essences, natural flowers, pearls and gemstones were deployed for the magisterial work of coiffure.

No artiste responsible for that care ever recommenced the following day the masterpiece of the day before. Célestine, as incomparable as beauty itself, was beautiful in all aspects, so she left to the inspiration of her chambermaid the care of deciding the royalty of the day. Sometimes there were long curls that descended alongside her face and gave her a physiognomy of ravishing softness; sometimes the silky threads, swept up boldly to the summit of the head, displayed her splendor in an irresistible audacity; but Célestine always disdained to occupy herself with any detail; hazard and caprice decided.

If her glamour had ever been able to fail just once, she would not have accused the chambermaid or the hairdresser, but her beauty, and from then on she would have ceased to adorn herself, for a semi-sovereignty could not suit that spontaneous nature. Célestine wanted the crowd at her feet in the most immense disorder or framed in the most marvelous adornment; her person was the same, beautiful by virtue of its beauty, and making things resplendent, but not resplendent by reflection. She wanted to be the illuminating nucleus, but never the ray that receives, and hence free at whim to sparkle as she pleased.

While the chambermaid tried to sculpt a new physiognomy on that incomparable model, a short stout man, tottering on thin legs, his torso surmounted by an enormous head, caparisoned with a colossal turban, appeared in the frame of the half-closed curtains. He remained there, nailed to the parquet, as stiff and motionless as a dormant spinning-top. Célestine, alerted to his presence, turned her head slightly toward him. Immediately, the little man bounded and stretched, in order to plunge to the ground, but Célestine, amused by the grotesque, made a sign that prevented him from doing so, for fear that he might hurt himself.

"Come closer," she said, smiling with a frank gaiety. Then, without waiting, the young women, shoving the little man gently by the shoulders, back and elbows, brought him to within three paces of the sovereign.

There, he tried to drop flat again, but Célestine, contemplating him and laughing wholeheartedly, made a gesture, and the slaves maintained him upright. Astonished by this reception, contrary to custom and almost prohibited, the masculine individual darted a glance at Célestine, but the unfortunate individual, astounded by that sight, forgot everything, including himself, where he was and the rank held by the person he beheld, and stood there wide-eyed, staring at the apparition, his mouth paralyzed in an interesting opening, and the whole animated by an expression of such exaggerated covetousness that the Empress, herself surprised by the impression made by her beauty, started laughing until she could no longer sit still.

The women, seeing that excessive hilarity, understood that it would be currying favor to associate themselves with it, and the impudent cortege dissolved into such immoderate laughter that the bewildered vizier suddenly recovered his self-composure.

Célestine became serious again; all faces hastily refashioned a kind of gravity, and silence fell as if by enchantment.

"You're our servant at the Ministry of Justice?" asked Célestine.

"Yes, splendid sovereign," the vizier articulated, emotionally; he had never been able to hear the Empress' voice without feeling stirred from head to toe.

"Well," said Célestine, "have you anything interesting to report—any punishable cases that merit attention?" At the same time, with her coiffure concluded, she stood up; her women, having surrounded her, passed garments over her of an unimaginable richness and fantasy.

Then, the masculine official introduced into the sanctuary sometimes glimpsed a shoulder whose model, skin and delightful dimple would have made Apelles dream; at other moments it was a leg that Diana the huntress could never have gloried in, and the sage, dignified, strong, governing half of the human species—the masculine race, in sum—represented by that man in the midst of those women, no longer knew what he was doing, nor who he was, nor why he was; he lived, sensed, waited and received his impressions as inert matter receives the fluid that galvanizes it.

"Didn't you hear me?" repeated Célestine, turning toward the man she had questioned.

At that movement, all the women having scattered, the Empress, half-undressed by the strangest garments, blasted the imagination of the unfortunate male sex once again with her incomparable prestige.

Velvety black tones in her costume caused her flesh to project like an irradiation; her sculptural bearing and her superb figure seemed freely to be escaping her silken jacket, molded to the very asperities of the fibers. Célestine surged out of her envelope like a star from a cloud, and the dazzled eyes expected to see her emerge from it entirely.

That is what befell the valiant master of the world, man! He adored mentally, he prostrated himself, and he annihilated his will before the woman, that small worm, that insect, that futile excrescence!

But Célestine, profoundly indifferent, shook that master rudely with an imperative interpellation. Stamping her foot and raising her voice, she snapped: "I said, didn't you hear me?"

"Yes, yes, great majesty," the masculine individual stammered, "but...I...adorable sovereign...luster of the world...paradise of joys..."

"You're burbling," said Célestine. "Your paradise of joys was singularly clogged up before my arrival. Do you think, by chance, that the seraglio seemed to women to be a celestial abode? Pull yourself together, please, for your shabby species can't excite our minds. As homuscule[10] majesty has awarded itself women as prey to its whim, homuscule majesty is nothing to women but a mere orangutan whose appetite causes it to move in accordance with the will that can satisfy it." She looked the vizier up and down proudly, and added: "Man has always been the slave of the brutes he has made, and we have, in truth, nothing to demand of your species except to amuse ourselves momentarily."

"Has your majesty only summoned me in order to insult me?"

---

[10] The word *homuscule*, meaning little—or inferior—man, never reached the French dictionary; Rouzade was not the first to coin it, but was probably unaware of it previous use by Jules Barbey d'Aurevilly.

"Hey, signor man, you're forgetting yourself! I summoned you in order to talk business; instead of that you coo your stupid impertinences at me, and then your dignity is ruffled by the words it hears, and speaks of insult! Which of the two of us has insulted the other, pray? Do you think your amorous litanies are agreeable things to hear? How derisory! You beg to take offense—that's truly to labor under a delusion, and I would never have thought of it without your remark, but if I were under your dependency, I believe that you would have sent for me with premeditation and with no other objective but to insult me mortally—your eyes affirm the fact! We're more delicate, and when no force obliges us to do so, we have no interest in stray hairs!"

Célestine deployed her figure radiantly. "I'm beautiful, am I not, vizier? And your wisdom and noble superiority turn to regret the moment that beauty is not at your service. What do you expect, my dear: the ugly, the old, the young, the beautiful, the intelligent, the stupid—all of them are so abject, so prostrate before women that they no longer care to lower themselves or make any sign to conquer those cruel and proud little beasts. Forget, then, venerable beard, the insane visions of your austere sex, and console yourselves for this defeat with the sentiment of our complete disdain for the generality of your pitiful breed."

"Oh," said the vizier, with bile in his voice, "women have no soul."

"Women have no soul? I have no soul? But I have yours, imbecile! And all of us have at our discretion your soul and those of your peers. Your pleasant merchandise is only worth anything in our hands, for can you even sense your manly soul except when a woman embraces it? Idiot, idiot and triple idiot!"

The vizier's face was red; he was suffocating with rage. "Take him away," said Célestine. "These men seen in a cold light are truly astonishing." She shoved the respectable stock of Adam away forcefully, and went on: "Marthe, look in the dossier of our amusing half, no matter where, and read at hazard—the first idea you come across will be good enough."

"Madame, I can see here a case dealing with the crime of *lèse-majesté*; would you like me to read the article?"

"Yes, but only the fundamentals—skip the commentaries."

"Madame, it's a matter of a draper and a merchant of decorations, whose shops are adjacent. They had a quarrel, and it's alleged in the deposition of the decoration seller that the draper called his neighbor a supplier of fancy wrapping, a vendor of optical illusions and other invectives, each as incongruous as the next, after which the merchant of decorations, not irritated on his own behalf but on behalf of Your Majesty, to whom he supplies his merchandise, cried regicide. His regular clients supported him, and an entire legion of the beribboned and the medaled has come forward to confirm the denouncer's allegation. The affair is on the point of coming to court."

"That's exactly what we need," said Célestine. "Tell Nahour to send his guards to arrest the lawyers that were to appear in the case and all the relatives, friends and acquaintances of the two parties. Inform the people that they'll be set at liberty this evening, and announce to the people that I'm going to render justice in the place inhabited by the rival shopkeepers. Finally, have a stunted oak tree set up there, at the height of a man, arranged in such a manner that I can install myself beneath it solidly and comfortably. Then tell Nahour that I'll expect him for the morning meal."

Marthe left.

A few minutes later, Nahour, wearing his rich uniform, his fine figure and his vivacious thirty-five years nobly, presented himself before Célestine. As timid as a child, he bowed in adoration before the idol, but the latter had immediately taken his arm in a charming fashion.

"I'm in a good mood," she said, "and I want you to have the advantage of it." Then, chatting gaily, they drew away, preceded by slaves, toward the room where the meal was to be served.

Célestine had never been so communicative; her expansion rendered her irresistible.

Nahour could not eat; he was ecstatic. The longer the meal went on, however, the more legible a vague expression of anxiety on his face became. Finally, he could no longer hold back. "I daren't ask what you're going to do," he said. "I always tremble at each of your whims. What if there were a revolt? If I were to lose you...perhaps horribly...? All my blood is churning and, at the risk of displeasing you, I wish this terrible month was over."

"Nahour, you've lived too long for these puerile fears to seem well-founded to you, if you consider them coolly. People revolt against a light hand that they suppose to be incapable of reprisals, but they submit to an implacable tyrant, even if his cruelty is impossible to bear. Remember that it's necessary to be virtuous and enlightened to prefer death to degrading abasement. You're not unaware, my dear Nahour, that virtuous and sane individuals are so rare that, if they consented to it, one could raise huge sums by exhibiting them to universal astonishment."

"Alas, yes! How insane one becomes when one is in love! And I'm more than in love with you."

"Yes, in sum, you no longer know what you're doing or who you are. Nor do I, so I won't judge you."

"Vagueness is sometimes a good thing."

"Be polite enough, Nahour, not to underline my replies. Your deprecation obliges my eulogy, and it's then somewhat fastidious for me and of scant value to you."

"It's incredible how cruel you are, and yet one tolerates everything from you. How? Why?"

"Because my cruelty is simply your own thoughts separated from yourself. You call me cruel when I reveal you to your own eyes, but you submit to me because I know you, and you don't know me; you have to learn in my presence, and perhaps you hope to catch a glimpse of me. I'm the unknown that floats above your head, but which you can't penetrate—that's why, in spite of my rudeness and my asperity, I attract you."

"Where do you come from, Célestine?"

"From the great fatherland—from myself! You've lived in the reflection of others and have never learned on your own account what exists outside of you; in brief, you only have as much being as others have themselves. I, on the contrary, take my individuality from everything that exists; it follows, then, that I've become exceptional and that I astonish everyone around me, while everything is desperately monotonous to me. Now, that which astonishes attracts and subjugates—that's the secret. Come on, are you going to meditate now? My dear Nahour, don't turn me toward philosophy; I'm going to examine society at close range, and I wonder what it will look like under a microscope of wisdom. Will you give me the pleasure of accompanying me?"

"No, I'm too anxious, I tell you, when I see you among the crowd; all I can do might not be enough to keep you safe."

"Well then, until this evening," said Célestine, holding out her hands to him. "I'll entertain you with my story, for want of the spectacle."

Nahour pressed Célestine's two small hands in his, and, utterly nonplussed, utterly embarrassed, he tried to speak, while his supplicant gaze tried to make itself understood. "Célestine," he finally said, tenderly, "you don't care anymore about me than the others, since I'm only what they all are, but you…you… How I wish I could protect you! You will be careful, won't you?"

"I'll dazzle them," said Célestine, laughing adorably. "What do you expect them to do? Does one rebel against an idol? Remember that I only have men against me." So saying, she disengaged her hands with a prompt gesture, drew Nahour's head toward her and kissed him swiftly, and then escaped before the latter had time to think.

Chapter VIII
Célestine Renders Justice Under an Oak Tree.
Adultery and Mystery.
Man and Woman.

When Célestine, surrounded by her escort, arrived at the square where the draper and the merchant of decorations lived, a large crowd had gathered there and was extended densely all around, overflowing into the adjacent streets. A chain had sealed off the square and in the middle, a tree sawn through and planted in the ground supported between its branches a small platform carpeted with brocade, to which a throne had been solidly attached. Three stepladders covered with rich cloth led from the throne to the ground.

The day was superb; the sun was making all the gilt shine, and the foliage shaded the platform agreeably, which was thus brilliantly displayed to everyone, and guaranteed itself with its own gleam.

Célestine was appearing outside officially for the first time, and there, in broad daylight, in the open air, she seemed more vigorously beautiful still, filling the air with her radiance as fully as the sun above society.

The crowd contemplated her without even thinking of applauding, so absorbed were its members in admiration.

Two dignitaries each took one of the Empress' hands and guided her onto the middle stairway, while they went up either side of her. When they had climbed the few steps, Célestine installed herself on the throne and the dignitaries sat down on the top steps of their stairways.

The courtyard down below having nothing on which to sit, people ran in haste to look for stools in the neighborhood. Troops massed at the foot of the tree to defend its approaches, while others, at a distance, formed a second cordon, under Nahour's orders. The love of peoples is only employed at a distance; there is a lot of talk about it, but no one ever sees it.

180

When these dispositions were complete, Célestine asked the dignitaries sitting at her feet to summon the two merchants and their cohorts of relatives, friends and acquaintances.

As the merchants were rich, an elegant procession was seen filing past, with arrogant, self-satisfied expressions, which seemed to relish playing a role before the populace. The promise that they would be free that evening having relieved them of all worry, a succulent dinner had been ordered for them, and they had been invited to gather in the courtyard; it was a true occasion for rejoicing, this little festival, and all the more charming for being improvised.

When everyone was grouped in front of the troops at the bottom of the tree, Célestine stood up and, in an ample and sonorous voice—the kind of voice that relaxes the ear at the same time as it strikes it—said:

"Audience of affection, relaxation and joy of friendship, I have summoned you here, where your friends are, because perfume ought not to be removed from the senses that breathe it, nor tenderness from the heart in which it reposes. Isolated from your friend, you would be like a nest that is soft and decorated, but lugubriously deserted, and your friend, without you, accustomed to your tender protection, would be lacerated by the brambles of the road. Sobs break the harmonious chords, and the heart that hears them is gripped and becomes bleak, but serene tenderness expands in a suave murmur, and the agitated spirit in lulled, and then falls asleep, So, I have left the friend to amity, the nest to the bird, the melody to the dream." Célestine ceased cooing then, and suddenly added: "And I've also left behind that tearful tone, because it was beginning to irritate me.

"Relatives, friends and acquaintances, to make two crows, it requires two crows, and two crows cannot make anything except two crows. I shall not elaborate on the subtleties that might be raised on that subject, such as that a crow having neither feet nor a head might be disputed in its quality as a crow, and, in accordance with those pedal or frontal absences, Pliny, Aristotle, Jugurtha and the Monts Cévennes would not find it easy to enlighten the debate; animated with a zeal for the truth, however, I shall pass like a whirlwind over those elements of discord and say, extending over you the balm of tolerance, let us take the crows for crows and get it over with quickly."

Célestine paused momentarily, charmed by the sight of her audience, whose members, with their faces dilated by astonishment, were staring at the Empress in the same way that good children and babies stare at the amusing representations painted on the canvas of fairground acrobats.

"I deduce, then," Célestine went on, "that these two merchants, one having been able to become insolent and quarrelsome and the other a denouncer, that because the people among whom these merchants live have not destroyed these vices, it follows that the relatives, friends, acquaintances and even regular clients of these two merchants are necessarily the cause of the two merchants' crimes, as two crows are necessarily the cause of the fact that there are two crows.

"Given that, the friends, relatives, acquaintances and customers should be the only ones involved in the affair, as having made the merchants or having allowed them to be made, still in accordance with the truth that obliges the two crows to be the only ones involved in the totality of the two crows, for if the totality of the two crows isn't worth much, it's because each individual crow isn't worth much. Now, as these two merchants have only acted in accordance with the way their parents have brought them up, and the way their friends and acquaintances have guided them, and where society has allowed them to go, it follows that the two merchants are the totality of the education and direction they have received— that they are, in a word, your own totality, Messieurs et Mesdames, and that it is up to you to answer for the two merchants, just as it is up to every crow to answer for the two crows."

Having said that, the Empress sat down. Then the dignitaries descended and an officer gave the order for the camps of the two merchants to be separated. Immediately, the drapers gathered on one side and the friends of the seller of decorations on the other. Having done that, the two coteries were lined up and they were issued with solid clubs without a discern for gender.

When the process of armament was concluded, silence was commanded militarily—which is to say that a herald of arms paraded in front of the two armies, a pistol in one hand and a naked sword in the other, which caused everyone to go mute before such an amiable injunction. After that they went in quest of the judges, advocates and clerks—in sum, all those responsible for justice—and in the presence of the belligerents, the dignity of battle leaders as conferred on those robed individuals. Then an assortment of cudgels was passed round and the order was given for the battle to begin.

At that command, the apprentice combatants quivered like tender leaves in the north wind, but, unable to believe their ears, they stayed where they were, half-paralyzed, only having the strength to gaze at their clubs and the audience. In sum, only their perplexed expressions gave any sign of life, and seemed to be questioning whether the order was a joke, and wondering what they were supposed to do.

"Come on!" thundered the herald of arms, quick to become impatient. "Get on with it! Fight!"

Then a real panic gripped of the unfortunates; they looked around for a means of escape, but, with no exit being possible, they cried "Ho!" and "Ha!" and gesticulated, and became frantic, all asking questions at the same time and all wanting to make themselves heard.

"Well, you bunch of weaklings, are you going to fight?" roared the warrior.

That coarse remark restored a little courage to the panic-stricken. There was a moment of calm. "Why should we fight?" asked a fat shopkeeper.

"Why should you fight? To determine which side will be victorious!" exclaimed the herald of arms.

"Oh, if it's only for that," replied the fat merchant, "I declare in advance that I'm vanquished."

"We're vanquished! We're all vanquished!" howled both parties and the judges, in unison.

"Ha ha ha!" sniggered the man of war. "What specimens! They all eat their words, these braggarts, and cower before a flick! Go on—start hitting, and hurry up!"

"You can't make me fight against my will, damn it!" cried a junior advocate.

"Ta ta ta, Master Chatterbox—we've made many others fight against their will! If you listen to a soldier, he'll tell you that they live in barracks, that they have no hearth, that they sleep on the road, die in a ditch and have no one to defend them! Fury! That's how it is! Let's go, let's go—forward! Day of battle!" The warrior was bellowing now. "These blowhards of glory don't want to destroy for real! I'll show you what bellicose means!"

So saying, he made a sign, and the troops jabbed the points of their lances into the backs of the people who had taken root.

Like sheep prancing to avoid the dog, the two merchant cohorts stumbled precipitately and came together as they fled toward one another. Now, it happened that the men in robes, who were at the center, were very forcefully jostled, and, as they had no idea what was happening, they believed that they were being manhandled, which irritated them to the point that they began lashing out to the right and left while shouting furiously. The combatants, already exasperated, entirely lost their heads in the face of that new aggression.

There were a few who tried to explain things, but those speeches, as confused as one another, only served to augment the noise and the anger. In the blink of an eye the crowd had disarmed the judges, and, lifting them up over their heads, tried to pass them to the rear in order to receive the thrusts of the lances. As everyone in the brawl thought they were victims of personal aggression, however, they were all fighting one another and hindering the opposition. The middle was still trying to disengage, and the group oscillated like a wave that comes, goes and breaks, forms again and breaks again.

An eddy, however, launched all the gladiators toward the cordon of troops, which immediately opened up, and at the same time, the chain was released. In consequence, no longer retained by anything, the human tide fell noisily into the shop fronts facing them. There was a crash, widespread destruction, and an unparalleled mess. The fighters, overexcited by the blows and the racket, were increasingly pressed together, and lawyers and judges, men and women, wrestled one another to the ground with amazing agility.

Célestine, the court and the troops were holding their sides laughing—not to mention the crowd, whose members did not have to get any closer to be amused, and were laughing as wholeheartedly as the rest.

That hurricane of hilarity reawakened the consciousness of the warriors. They stopped, and the first to collect themselves slipped away like sylphs—but the guards having apprehended them, the others immediately got up—and as, in sum , no one had been killed or seriously wounded, the public laughed all the harder on seeing the damage that the brawl had done to the previously sumptuous appearances.

Vain but crestfallen, the discomfited held their heads high with defiant expressions, and it was in that manner that, gently directed by the lances, they advanced at a trot to the foot of the throne for a second time.

When Célestine had recovered somewhat from her fit of gaiety, she said disdainfully: "It would have been no more difficult for you to battle regularly than brawl pell-mell, and it would have been more intelligent and more profitable, for there would have been a victor, and hence an innocent party, since you must be aware that the defeated are necessarily guilty and the victors immutably innocent. In sum, I shall award the victory to whichever party has the smaller number of fallen leaders."

The guards, however, who had brought the combatants to their feet, declared that all the leaders had fallen to the ground.

"Well," said Célestine, "There will be neither victors nor vanquished, and you're all innocent and guilty, which means that, as innocents, you can go, whereas, as guilty parties, you have to stay. Furthermore, as every innocent is necessarily beyond the reach of the law, it follows that you must be guilty in order for me to judge you. Given that, here are my conclusions: Relatives, friends and acquaintances of the two merchants, you will collectively pay an indemnity to the judges, whom you have forced to go out of their way because of the incompetent way in which you have managed the individuals involved in the case." She addressed the officers: "Collect the fines—a hundred livres per head; take the jewelry of those who don't have the sum on them, and they must settle up this evening or go to the mines."

As they were dealing with prosperous people, the fines were paid immediately, and, on the orders of the sovereign, the bag containing the takings was put in the hands of the judiciary corporation. On receiving that source of delights, the sheikhs of high and low dignity were jubilant, which was touching to behold. A profound tenderness, as well as a surveillance worthy of Argus, attended every movement of the bag, committed to the safekeeping of one of them.

"Good," said Célestine, contemplating that agreeable scene. "Now, as the judges have not done any work, only being utilized by the guilty, and, in consequence, that the judges owe their titles, their positions and their emoluments to the guilty, it is only right that the judges give that indemnity to the guilty, and that they should even add to it a proportionate fee in return for services rendered—for, if the guilty were to disappear, judges would necessarily disappear, too. Thus, Messieurs of the robe, pay up and pass the treasure to the draper and the decoration merchant—who will share it, since the war didn't decide the innocence of either one."

"Blasphemy!" cried a stentorian voice. "Pay the guilty?"

"I don't know who said that," said Célestine, "but he certainly isn't perspicacity personified. Listen and learn, Man! If there were no delinquents, no government would be possible, for honest men need no army, no police, no law, no arms manufacturers, no ministers and, in sum, no government, since

186

the only purpose of government is to repress, and there is nothing to repress on the part of the honest. Now, I know that without the honest, the government, no longer having any interest to protect, would have no reason to exist, so one is obliged to recognize that, although the honest are of no value in themselves, they nevertheless have a certain utility, and that it's a sage precaution to tolerate and even to maintain them; but, on the other hand, as honest men don't produce anything without the blackguards who exploit them, it's equally just that special benefits should be accorded to knaves, detractors, denouncers and all the other species who justify protection, power and mastery—in a word, government. That's why you're going to give the purse to the two guilty parties."

Scapin[11] performing mimes never attained the heights of the judiciary physiognomies as they handed over the treasure, and were obliged in addition to bring the pennies out of their own pockets. On the other hand, no enthusiasm more profound had ever reconciled two enemies. The decoration merchant threw his arms around the draper, who was obliged to let him do it, so formidable was his grip. Seeing the purse that was presented to them, however, the terrible embracer let go and took possession of the proffered bag. "My brother," he said to the draper, "you can rely on me to divide it up; rejoice in peace while I take care of that task."

"Weigh the purse," Célestine ordered the two merchants...

"There," she said. "Very good: that's so you know the approximate value of the contents. Now, would you each please add a hundred livres to it, and bring it, thus augmented, to me. In my turn, I'll give it all to honest people, and you'll understand that nothing is more just, for, since scoundrels only live on the honest, it's in their own interest that the scoundrels should make a few small reimbursements from time to time."

---

[11] The deceitful valet who is the protagonist of Molière's *Les Fourberies de Scapin* [Scapin's Knavery] (1671).

The merchant of decorations began to tremble very visibly on hearing these words. As the officer approached in order to collect the further sum demanded, the unhappy depositary clenched his fingers around the leather and hugged the treasure fervently to his chest; but, the officer having his sword in one hand and having put the other coldly on the bag, the desolate merchant dared not hang onto it. Seeing the officer look at him imperatively and expectantly, he understood, and, head bowed, he took out his wallet and handed over the demanded sum in a melancholy fashion.

As for the draper, delighted by the discomfiture of his neighbor, he complied with the best grace in the world. Then, preceding the two merchants, the officer led them to the top of the steps leading up to the platform, deposited the purse on their behalf at the Empress' feet, and then took them down again.

"Messieurs," said the Empress, "this fortune levied on the negligence of everyone in letting vice increase will be employed by us to give a better education and endowment to abandoned children, to support old people who have no family and to aid valorous artists who are unable to support themselves. That way, all roguery will serve two ends: firstly, to justify our government, since only roguery necessitates repression; and secondly, to make that same government seem equitable and benevolent. So thank you, Messieurs."

With that, the Empress dismissed the merchants and everyone else. But there was a great tumult; as the smashed shop fronts belonged to merchants who had become involved in the affair as acquaintances, those aggrieved parties ran toward the Empress shouting: "Justice!"

"What's the matter?" demanded Célestine.

"What about the damage, Majesty? Who will pay for it?"

"The damage? Is that anything to do with us?" the Empress replied. "It's the effect of the war."

"But war isn't employed like that!" replied one of the claimants.

"And how is it employed, if you please?"

"Well, when it's a matter of major interests."

"Very good—everything is for the best in the order of things, then, for, if major interests are to be settle with the bayonet, it's perfectly reasonable for trivial ones to be disputed with the skewer, and I haven't departed from that principle, since, instead of rifles, I only gave you clubs."

"Is Your Majesty daring to joke about war?"

"Me, joke? The error is naïve. You accept that all your possessions and your government should be gambled on the heads or tails of a battle, but you find the means improper when it's a matter of a few écus? Is it, then, for a whim that one ought to be prudent, while, on the contrary, honor and liberty ought to be risked on an all-or-nothing bet?"

"It's not a matter of those considerations; the rationale of war is that one accepts it when one cannot do otherwise."

"Oh, if that's the case, you're quite right, for it must be agreed that you haven't shown any enthusiasm for combat."

"Anyway, let's leave war aside and get back to the expenses. Your majesty must know who will pay them!"

"That depends; but in order that you're content, you can each give me twenty francs."

"What!" said the shopkeepers.

"Come on, quickly—and no commentaries," Célestine ordered. Immediately, whether they liked it or not, the claimants were compelled to comply. When the Empress had received the sum, she presented each of them with a hundred sous. "Here, she said, this is to compensate you." She pocketed the rest, saying: "I'll still make a profit."

"What!" screeched the appalled merchants. "What's the meaning of this? Is this a joke? What's going on? At least give us our money back!"

"No," said Célestine. "This will teach you to reflect. You wanted me to pay you. Now, as I only possess what my people give me, it's first necessary for you to give me money in order for me to give it to you. Now, if I've kept some of it, that's a matter of retribution for my trouble, as is usual in commerce."

She added: "Look here, you're two hundred years behind the times—go and study common sense."

On these words from the Empress, the crowd was driven back with sabers and the cortege marched off to return to the palace.

When they were a short distance away, a man, emerging precipitately from a side street hurled himself impetuously in front of the royal carriage crying out with feverish overexcitement: "Justice, Majesty! Give me justice!"

"What do you want?" asked Célestine, signaling to stop the march.

"My wife is deceiving me!" the man exclaimed. "I caught her in the act. Thunder! I was about to kill her when you passed by. Decide, Sovereign, decide the fate of the vile woman!"

"Are you a good Muslim?" asked the Empress, coldly.

"A good Muslim? Undoubtedly—but why?"

"Do you believe in the mysteries?"

"Yes, Majesty, but...?"

"More than anything else?"

"Derision! It's not a matter of mysteries! What has that got to do with my household?"

"A great deal, my friend. From the moment that belief without sight is your supreme law, you're obliged to accept anything that anyone tells you; now, as your wife will surely tell you that she's innocent, believe her, even though you can't see it: it's a mystery!"

"By Allah! Does one joke about such things?"

"Truly, poor beard, you surpass in infantilism a babe in swaddling clothes! What, you believe in myths, in some god or other that you've never seen and can't explain, and you refuse to admit your wife's innocence! Understand that as soon as you have blind faith, you can't reject any absurdity, for you'd be leaving the frame of your principles if you sought to clarify anything whatsoever."

"Blasphemy! You're insulting me, when I'm the victim. What would you have done if I'd been the guilty party?"

190

"I would have sentenced you to death."

"Death for me, impunity for her! The life of a man for a woman's sin?"

"Yes. Until, in the same way as a woman, a man runs the risk of death in the suffering of giving birth, the miseries of maternity, anxiety for the present and shame forever. Yes, until man is assailed by calamities, he alone shall pay for the shared sin, from which, until now, he has only had pleasure and no preoccupation."

"Are those reasons? Can one argue in that fashion? What a scandal! But, after all, Your Majesty has just promised to cut off a man's head for a guilty woman, so that's what should be done in my case!"

"Nothing is more just. Except that, whoever demands the punishment of a fault on someone else's part must be judged at the same time as the other on the same grounds of accusation; thus, you, who are demanding a woman's head for an infraction against the laws of chastity, will have to prove your own chastity, and will submit to the same punishment if you have committed the same crime."

"Oh, I'm not worried!" cried the man, in a disdainfully boatful fashion. "I've never turned a wife's head, myself!"

"And you haven't frequented girls either?"[12]

"Eh?" said the nonplussed masculine. "Girls? What does that have to do with anyone?" His tone was mocking, with a hint of pity.

"Impudent!" thundered Célestine. "Girls concern fathers, I suppose, as wives interest husbands! You dare to put the urges of your bestial male covetousness for the female above the despair of a father before his mutilated endeavor? But if your wife deceives you, it's because she doesn't love you, so abandon her, for if you slaughter her because you can no long-

---

[12] *Filles*, here translated as "girls," also means "daughters" and, is also used euphemistically to mean "prostitutes." The triple ambiguity is exploited in the question and the judgment, and in the subsequent argument.

191

er please her, or keep her in spite of the fact that she hates you, you're not a man—a noble and sensitive being—who wants a companion of his heart, but a wild beast, who has none but bestial concerns, and obliges that flesh to remain by force or kills it. You make me ashamed on your behalf, for I'm wondering whether I'm looking at a debased carnivore with a human face, or a man degraded to the level of carnivorous appetite!" Imperiously, Célestine said: "Someone take possession of this apostle of the virginal, and let him be dispatched with his wife's seducer. Quickly—I have spoken!"

The guards had already leapt down from their horses, but the man, having seen the Empress' face, had plunged back and disappeared into his side street without it being possible to take account of where he had gone. A bitter smile creased the sovereign's lips. "Let the poor fellow go," she said. "It would be necessary either to educate him or send him to the desert."

The march continued without interruption to the palace. Célestine became morose, and the cortege of courtiers affected anxious expressions. It was time for dinner, and they were only waiting for the Empress. As soon as she appeared, Nahour, who had anticipated her arrival, came to meet her and escort her to her place of honor. Then, when Célestine was seated, he contemplated her, waiting for her to say something—but she did not say anything.

Nahour went sadly to sit down facing her. There, he interrogated that perfectly mobile physiognomy, and would have much preferred a storm to that somber taciturnity. The service of the meal continued, however, without a word being exchanged; everyone waited silently for the oracle to provide the impulsion that it was appropriate to follow.

Finally, Célestine, even more irritated by that silence, said, ironically: "Did you hear the man who accused his wife, Nahour?"

"No," said Nahour, swiftly. "I was too far away. I was told something about it, but I didn't see anything myself."

"So much the better for your dignity as a man, my dear; they are ours, as sons, fathers and husbands, but I blush for them!"

"I dare not ask you..."

"Oh, it's the old story that the human race, like a coarse and naïve lout, takes for the truth. It's the male belittling female things, and the female punished because a male has caused her to turn her head."

"I was told that the man thought he was innocent because he hadn't engendered children in other people's houses?"

"Is that your opinion, Nahour? When a man doesn't engender children in a husband's home, he does it in the home of a mother or father—it's always someone else's hearth, I think! And if the girl often destroys her child, it's because she doesn't have the refuge of the married woman; thus, the debauchery of the girl is complicated by the consequence of homicide! And don't let the man say to justify himself that he only takes lost creatures, for then, he'd be nothing but a jackal or a vulture who only feeds on cadavers!"

"But when the cadaver is made, isn't it better to make use of it than to create others?"

"Oh, let's leave it there—you horrify me! A society that requires corruption in order to live is a receptacle of gangrene. Poor insensate! A man wants virtue for his own family, but sows vice with full hands in the species, without thinking that in putrefying humanity thus he's making life such a sewer that even purity would tarnish it!

"In order for women to be noble and chaste, it's necessary for men to be noble and chaste. The delicate fern doesn't grow in the mire, nor virtue in debasement; if an exception is seen, it's pale and paltry, like everything that suffers for lack of nourishment. Man, thus far, is nothing but force, and, as long as force doesn't disappear from relationships, there'll be nothing but males and females, teeth and claws, cunning and violence—but man, that sane, just being, will only appear when woman appears, his work and his proof!

"To be just is to render justice, it's to give the creature from which one descends, and which one engenders, what one owes to one's source and to one's continuation—in a word, to oneself.

"When man achieves that, he will no longer dispute nor bargain for his bread with women; he will no longer hide his own intelligence; he will show her what she is, and by virtue of that, she will learn what he is. In the same way that man shows his force by means of the slavery of woman, he will show his intelligence by the abandonment of force.

"The wild beast proves himself by the subjugation of the female; the man will affirm himself by the liberty of his companion."

Célestine's eyes studied him. "Isn't that your opinion, Nahour?"

"Yes, Madame," replied Nahour, dolorously, and put his head in his hands.

"Come on," she went on, merrily, "when the storm has burst, the sky brightens up. Cheer up, Nahour—I want to laugh now."

"Do you know what a tiger is, Célestine?"

"I know," she said, smiling, "that you're about to let some puerility escape, and in the interest of our ears and your reputation, I advise you to stop there. If I'm a tiger, I'll reply to you that there is prey, for if there were nothing to devour, the carnivore would be obliged to forsake his blood thirst. It's necessary, dear Nahour, for you to become accustomed to common sense or dread saying anything. Anyway, you haven't understood me if you believe that I think that women ought to govern men; if that were the case, what applies to men would naturally apply to women. I laugh at masters; the masters are men, so I laugh at men; if the masters were women, I would laugh at women. I've turned the world upside down, my friend, but as it has never been upright, I've merely caused it to tilt in the opposite direction, and it still remains to be set on its feet. Instead of crushing woman, all its weight is descending upon men—but that's no better than the other, for the true law for all is to stand upright side by side."

Célestine became angry then, and shouted noisily: "I believe I said that I wanted to be cheerful, did I not? In truth, it's hardly a matter of the noble and double human creature! Whoever talks idealism to the voracious? Let's drink!" With an incredible transition, she said, in a seductive feline tone: "I've always lived among the voracious, Nahour, and if I laugh at them over dessert, I love them enough to frighten myself...

"Nahour," she went on, enveloping the man with an irresistible magnetism of movement and intonation, "if I'm the tigress, you're the tiger, and lacerations delight savage natures! You've dug your claws into me, and my ferocity finds you beautiful! The panther loves her tiger when he's strong! I love you, my tiger!"

Nahour gazed at the sorceress; he felt vanquished, at her mercy, annihilated by the whim of her caprice, and his masculine pride revolted against such servitude. A sudden rage fermented within him. He decided to sacrifice the audacious rebel to his shame and his anger, and in order to escape the power of the woman he closed his eyes and strove to stimulate himself—but memory enlaced him and enervated him; then, the man opened his eyes again, quickly, to chase away the penetrating vision, and the reality, more powerful still, gripped him with such force that all his masculine determination collapsed before the woman, as vaporous snow melts in the ardent radiation of a fire.

Slumped in her armchair, her body slackly abandoned, her eyes velveted by a vague and indefinite expression, her smile ironically bitter as well as strangely seductive, Célestine was the enchantress who terrifies, and is adored: the bizarre, indecipherable creature before whom the most battle-hardened trembles and fear, but whom he follows uniquely, because she alone moves him and vivifies him. She is the only one he wishes to vanquish, because she alone escapes him; and when his strength has run out—when, in spite of his supreme efforts, the man sees the indomitable fugitive still far away—

vanquished pride submits, weeping, hoping thus to put a stop to it.

Such was Nahour before Célestine. She was in repose there, and yet he sensed that the mind of that adored form was far away, and that nothing that surrounded her any longer counted for her. Where Célestine was, he could not go, and if he had caught her, she would doubtless have drawn further away. It seemed that she lived outside the world, and that her dream was merely an inconsequential pleasure trip. Nahour understood that he was nothing to that woman but a pastime, something tolerated, but never a goal, an aspiration; he shrank, however, and clung to her all the harder, as a victim of hallucination clings to the vision that torments him, as a condemned man clings even to the shadow of his life.

"I want stimulation," Célestine murmured, "but I no longer know how. Anyway..." She sighed, and stopped speaking.

At a sign from Nahour the tables were cleared in the blink of an eye, and the room filled up with dancers, singers and musicians.

Commencing with a prelude of graduated chords, the cadence lightly sketching delicate grace, the vibration became more animated, more gravely thoughtful, and sonorousness exploded; marrying and hybridizing the pale with the vivid, disengaging the svelte and pure colorless half-tint from the emphatic backcloth, stringing out caprice after caprice at the hazard of the bow, as a butterfly brushes the meadow at the hazard of its flight. Eventually, insensibly, an ample and rich waltz movement was detached, alternately skimming the ground and soaring until it was lost in ethereal space, sometimes rumbling like seething waves or fleeing in a long-expiring plaint.

Then, as if under the fire of inspiration, the dancers seemed to quiver, and launched into an aerial course in pursuit of the capricious winged dream. One might have thought that the bodies were molding themselves to the breath of the modulations, so much did every pose and every movement live the harmony exhaled.

Pearly voices, like sounds heard in a dream, drowned that enthusiasm with their softness, and the lulled mind thought itself in the company of visions gliding smoothly over the clouds, to the muted melancholy sounds of Aeolian harps.

Célestine was still gazing with the same smile; gradually, her eyes closed entirely and she went to sleep. Her relaxed muscles undulated like the sinuous contours of a serpent at rest. Her drowsy body communicated such an annihilation that anyone who looked at her for long felt his will escaping him like a fluid, and was numbed by attraction. Only the regular movement of breathing animated that petrifying creature imperceptibly, and the captive mind imagined that it was seeing the sculpture and the life, which only required a spark to be transformed into a human volcano. Célestine's slumber was an apotheosis.

The music, songs and dances, slowly drew away; the beings and the sounds were about to disappear, softening by degrees until they were no more than a shadow and a sigh...and finally, nothing at all.

Then, slowly, Nahour came to kneel at Célestine's feet; his head was buried in his hands and only the dull moan of a long sob troubled the silence, where everything had been agitated a little while before, where fiction and delirium had quivered...and where there was now dolor!

Chapter IX
Célestine Decrees a Ceremonial
for the Use of Physicians.
Reception of the Notables.
The Eighth Wonder of the World.

The sun dries up the dew, the wind bears away the mist; such was Nahour's experience when, having been desolate the night before, the morning found him glad.

While waiting for Célestine to get up, the large reception room filled up with courtiers who were arriving by the minute. All of them, humbly proud, hastened to go to Nahour, and then wandered around, pacing back and forth or stopping to exchange a few words, all with an indiscretion of mannerisms and an insidious insinuation, as befits such elevated regions.

Soon the Empress was announced. Nahour went to meet her and the courtiers arranged themselves in two rows.

Brilliantly accompanied, Célestine advanced, gazing frankly and coldly, and under that firm gaze the stems of the turbans inclined without resistance, as flexible poplars bend before a rapid wind.

Without addressing a word or a greeting to anyone whatsoever, the Empress came into the reception room, and all her cortege followed her. Attracted by resplendent sunlight, Célestine headed for a window that overlooked the interior gardens. Nahour immediately fell into step with her.

"It's a fine day," she said. "I'll go out."

Nahour bowed.

At that moment an officer came to present a petition to the favorite, in order that he could transmit it to the Empress.

"What is it?" said Célestine. She took the sheet of paper and read it. "Very well," she said. "Messieurs, the notables request an audience. We'll make an appointment for today. I don't like people to be late; anyone who doesn't present himself by five o'clock in the afternoon will lose his rights to our favor." Célestine added, very gracefully: "Would you like to know what I want, Nahour?"

With that, as if cheered up, she turned to the room and smiled at the audience. Instantly, every face blossomed, and the Empress seemed to spend a few seconds admiring the elevated character and instinctive nobility of the royal entourages.

What was the sovereign about to say? Which way was the wind blowing today? The courtiers waited on tenterhooks like a pack of hounds awaiting the master's order.

"I'm taking you away," said Célestine, abruptly. "There'll be an amusement at the end of the walk, the return to the palace and the reception of the notable. The day will be good, and you'll only owe part of that to me; Messieurs, the notables will gladly take responsibility for the rest. Go tell the Faculty of Medicine that it has to present itself before us immediately. I await your return."

Everyone ran out, and twenty minutes later, while the Empress was chatting to the newcomers, the courtiers reappeared in company with the physicians. The latter had a certain air of anxiety, but Célestine reassured them immediately.

"Messieurs," she said, "I have no plans against your liberty or your persons; it's simply a matter of a debate on which I want to have your opinion. This is the question: I've always heard it said that gaiety is health; do you share that opinion?"

"It is, indeed, a sign of health," replied the physicians, unanimously, "And a person who is plunged into sadness, either by virtue of obsession or by the obligation of living in a lugubrious environment, will infallibly fall ill."

"It could not have been put any better—write down what these Messieurs have said," Célestine said to the courtiers. "Now let's get to the heart of the matter. In view of the rather large number of young and vivacious lives that make the plunge from life to death on a daily basis, it's good to fill in, as much as possible, the lacunae that exist in the medical art; and, it being admitted that gaiety is health, every physician ought to occupy himself in cheering up the sick. Now, it's

199

quite evident that the current usages are the very opposite of cheerful. The physician has, by anticipation, a funereal costume, a funereal expression, and a funereal manner of speaking—let us transform that depressing condolence!

"Let the disciple of Hippocrates respire in delight henceforth, let him enter with a dance step, let him dazzle with the most radiant colors, let him speak like a candidate or a charlatan, let him gesticulate like an acrobat or an inspired person, to the point that, the invalid being convulsed with laughter or having died of fright, a conclusive result can be obtained. In that way, one would have certain effects; one would be able to follow the progress of talent, and it would be possible to study, in the physiognomy of the moribund, the monetary profit or loss of the visit.

"Furthermore, as the family has a right to surround the invalid, the family would benefit from the performance, not to mention that people could club together, and in that manner, each afflicted individual would become a subject of recreation—I dare not say desired, but gladly accepted. Prepare yourselves, Messieurs, to do your job in accordance with these orders; I shall accompany one of you to his client."

"Madame," said one of the physicians, "we would prefer death to the ridicule with which Your Majesty wants to cover us."

"I haven't made my decision on the basis of your tastes, Messieurs," Célestine said. "In any case, if you reject an efficacious remedy because it doesn't suit your vainglorious supremacy, it's because you're not physicians in order to heal, but in order to be physicians, and there is, in that case, no interest for the patients in whether you live or die. Make your choice: obedience or death?"

"Those two terms are the extremes, Majesty," insinuated one young doctor, mildly, "and wisdom is the *juste milieu*."

"And wisdom always puts things off until tomorrow," added the Empress, graciously.

"Because great actions require heroes," the diplomat continued, gallantly.

"And a dialogue requires a subject. Ours is exhausted, my dear doctor. Come now, what do you choose?"

"Madame," said the poor man, in a melancholy tone, "death is irreparable and You Majesty's decrees might change; I agree to submit to the decree." The orator turned to his colleagues and added: "And these Messieurs will likewise adhere to the reform?" That was said slowly in an interrogative manner and was approved by all the doctors.

"What are your consultations for today?" asked the sovereign.

The first case explained was a rich elderly coquette cast into despair by the abandonment of a young lover. The rage of old age and jealous spite had suffocated the lady to such an extent that she believed herself to be ill and had summoned a few young doctors to her bedside in order to give her the reward of being interesting at any price.

"There's no need to look for anything else," said Célestine. With that, she sent the Faculty away with a formal instruction to obey and, having retained four young doctors, made them put on agreeably picturesque costumes. Then, after a light snack taken standing up, she departed with the entire company for the dowager's abode.

The physicians huddled in the depths of an ample closed carriage. The excursion was very pleasant; eventually, they stopped at a house situated in an aristocratic quarter of the city.

Guards were stationed outside and Célestine, accompanied by the physicians, officers and courtiers, had herself announced to the mistress of the house. Immediately, without deliberation, the chambermaids opened the door precipitately, madly shouting: "The Empress!"

Then Célestine, advancing into the house, perceived a sumptuous room containing a bed of satin and lace, and in that bed a woman of about fifty, looking perfectly healthy and as ornamented, powdered and animated as if she were about to depart for a ball. A few ladies of aristocratic appearance were assisting the invalid.

As the sovereign penetrated into the room, the physicians, already stunned by the extravagance of their costumes and the irregularities committed, were driven forward with terrible threats. In order to blind themselves to the ridicule of their situation, the poor men sought to lose their heads completely; they made a real attempt at a fit of madness and, hugging one another tightly, they pirouetted an entrance so ludicrous that the patient, initially strangled by fear, could not help sitting up in bed, with her arms in the air, and her eyes so wide that her eyelids were frayed. Soon, having gotten her breath back, she burst forth in precipitate, uninterrupted screeches, which became shriller and shriller.

The physicians, immeasurably aggravated by that racket, were seized, in spite of their ill temper, by such an inextinguishable desire to laugh that they had to hold on to the furniture to stop themselves falling over. In the next room the court was writhing until tears flowed, and the lady's friends and maidservants alike tried so hard to muffle their giggles that they ended up guffawing louder than the rest.

Those jaws gradually recovered their ordinary concentration, however, and everyone struggled to compose a pinched and haughty physiognomy.

The invalid, still sitting up, gazed with a supreme disdain and it was evident that she was about to pour forth acidic bile, but she suddenly became anxious and briskly dove back under the bedclothes, taking care to pull them up around her neck.

This is what had happened: the lady had taken a purgative that morning; now, under the influence of such a sharp emotion, it had produced unfortunate results.

That incident avoided explanations. Having satisfied Célestine's desire, the physicians, who had a duty to fulfill, identified themselves. The Empress affirmed that their accoutrement was the result of a new ordinance, and that her presence had no other objective than to justify the conduct of the doctors. The latter then approached to take a pulse, in accordance with custom.

The invalid shook her head; the friends insisted, and the doctors, smelling certain emanations, were beginning to make singular grimaces, when the lady, in order to be rid of them, finally consented to stick out her hand. Taking and passing along that hand as briskly as if it were a game of hunt the slipper, the doctors declared that they were in accord and hastened away from the alcove. A prescription was drafted, and the society prepared to depart.

"Is she getting better?" asked the lady's friends.

"Yes, the malady has slackened its grip," replied one of the doctors, holding his nose.

"Exceedingly slackened," approved the others, with conviction. "With these words, they left the house and set off to return to the palace.

The Empress invited the physicians to supper, but they judged it prudent to decline that honor.

As the time for the audience was imminent, Célestine gave a few orders and instructed that the petitioners should be introduced when they had all gathered. A few manufacturers of apotheoses had exalted the Empress in every possible key; they represented their collections to Célestine, who threw them in the fire without even looking at them. The sovereign was informed that the individuals in question expected some recompense.

"Good, good, have them given a whipping, if a response is absolutely necessary; they're sowers of packing material, whom it's necessary to chastise rather than pay. Go tell them what I said."

In the meantime, a numerous deputation, accompanied by a crowd, arrived at the palace.

Hosts of Amazons riding back and forth controlled the recalcitrant beards with their sabers. It was remarked with astonishment that there were a few women among the deputation.

When the people had been admitted into the palace and were able to draw breath comfortably, the doors of the audience hall were opened.

Célestine, as majestic and beautiful as ever, was waiting on her throne. After the customary prostrations, a delegate advanced from the ranks and, trembling slightly, began to speak.

"Illustrious Sultana, delight of hearts, sun of the realm..."

"Pardon me," said Célestine, "but if I'm the sun, I ought to dry you up, and it's only just that I offer you refreshing dew." She ordered slaves to bring sorbets.

"We thank Your Majesty humbly," said the orator, with an ironic smile, "but we make the observation that it's not customary for an audience to be a refreshment."

"It's customary that one governs as one pleases," Célestine replied. "Otherwise, one only governs in name, and I govern in fact, Messieurs. So, it pleases me at the moment to give you the recreation of a ballet."

"Why not a feast?" mocked one joker.

"I'll take you at your word," Célestine retorted, tranquilly. "I'll order a feast; let those who are frightened go away."

The deputation thought the procedure quite ridiculous, but the lure of good food, and the attenuation they gave themselves that it might perhaps be easier to be heard at the table, must have convinced everyone, for, although they affected rather impertinent expressions, in order to appear to be merely making a condescension, they all unanimously accepted the offer, which they qualified as derisory.

Célestine looked at them shrewdly and turned toward her following, her physiognomy seeming to say: *well, what do you think?* Then, without further ado, the sovereign stood up, gave a signal, and beautiful, richly ornamented young women were introduced, who came to lean graciously on the arms of the notables and draw them along with the court to the banqueting hall. The women who had accompanied the petitioners, seeing themselves abandoned like miserable empty shells, quivered with anger and launched themselves on the heels of the guests, like Fates pursuing the living.

Petitioners and female companions having sat down side by side, the ladies were all obliged to sit down together at a corner of the table.

It was dinner time; everyone had a good appetite, the cuisine was succulent, the wines surpassed one another in exquisiteness, and the recognition of the stomach held recriminations in check. In any case, they told themselves that there would be time to do their duty over dessert, and enjoyed themselves without scruple.

The hours succeeded one another without anyone thinking about keeping track of them, except that the isolated ladies counted the minutes with bleak expressions in order to measure the duration of the insult.

By dint of eating, drinking and chatting, they had soon eaten away a considerable chunk of the evening. Then, taking advantage of a moment of respite in the general conversation, one of the sad ladies dared to say, in a tone that was half bitter and half fearful: "Messieurs or husbands, it seems to us that we're superfluous and that our presence is no longer agreeable to you."

The husbands looked at one another, a trifle nonplussed.

"So, Madame," said Célestine, "you've come to reclaim your husbands' rights over you?"

"There can't be two masters in one house," retorted the ladies, dryly, "and it's just that the man governs."

"Damn!" said Célestine, addressing the men. "Those are well-trained mechanisms. I congratulate you, Messieurs, on the confection of these automata." As the women protested furiously, the Empress added: "Messieurs, please switch your machines off; they're in good condition, but I've seen them, and that's sufficient. Mesdames, you can stand aside for those that have an interest in this. I know what you are."

"And what are they?" asked the men, insolently

"Soft dough that you've kneaded and which time has dried; I reiterate, therefore, that you should shut them up, for when they talk, it's as if you were channeling your speech though the intermediary of a mannequin, and that kind of trick is only suitable for the fairground."

"There's truth in what Her Majesty says," observed a hearty eater who had absorbed abundant victuals and liquids. "We can begin to share."

"Share what?" howled a few fat bellies.

"You make me yawn," replied the piqued *bon viveur*. "Women get hold of you and trap you for life; when they share, they make you a gift, and trust me, they have good reason to keep it."

"What, you fat mastodon, are you trying to say that my wife governs me?"

"Your wife, oh no—but your neighbor's or neighbors', oh yes—and as your wife probably governs elsewhere, that means that the conjugation of the verb is complete: I govern, you govern..." By way of conclusion, the orator drank a large draught.

His companion started laughing.

"Messieurs," said a masculine voice adopting a very lofty tone, "the honorable guest, under the influence of the sovereign's beautiful eyes, has just deserted his own side; it is appropriate to repair the damage, and if the ladies would care to hear me and these Messieurs will give me the floor, I'll try to do so."

Having spoken thus with an academic intonation and gestures, the notable bowed.

"Yes, yes," said the men, who were thinking more about their neighbor and partying than anything else.

The Empress made a sign of approval.

The personage posed his voice and his person, and with a visibly studied form, began in these terms: "Mesdames et Messieurs, in going back to the remotest testimony, by consulting the Scriptures..."

"And writing?" asked someone, bewildered.[13]

The orator stopped short and turned angrily toward the interrupter. "That observation could not be more stupid or untimely," he said, disdainfully.

"Continue all the same," said several people at the same time, with their mouths full.

"Mesdames and Messieurs," the orator explained, sarcastically, "it's not by virtue of a frivolous self-esteem that I'm offended, but if I'm interrupted so ridiculously, how can I recover my proofs?"

"Have they run away, then?" a lady asked, brazenly.

The assembly, already in a good humor, burst out laughing at that sally.

The Monsieur of the grandiose genre looked at the woman, and it was evident that he would have given her a slap if he had been able to do so. However, he said in a profoundly ironic and forced manner: "I will observe to Madame that she is almost making advances to me, in taking so much interest in me."

Basely cruel vanity appeared so nakedly in the man's tone, words and appearances, that he caused repulsion to those satisfied stomachs. A disapproving masculine murmur greeted his remark. Then, no longer knowing any bounds, the despot thumped the table and, as white as the tablecloth and gesticulating like a windmill, he grated: "Load of cretins!" and threw his napkin in the face of the Empress.

The latter, without flinching, calmly put the piece of cloth down on the table, and addressed the company with imperturbable phlegm.

"Messieurs," she said, "you will understand, given such a specimen of your sex, that we shall keep the reins, since we hold them."

---

[13] *L'Ecriture*, here translated, as intended, as "the Scriptures," would, if construed as a common noun, simply mean "writing"—hence the listener's puzzled interjection.

"Oh, Madame!" cried the men. "We disapprove of our colleague—we're not like him!"

"That's pure generosity on your part," said Célestine, "and that which is only generosity can make false promises at any moment."

"Well," said one cunning individual, "let's establish a balance. Give us something, and we'll concede on many points."

"Messieurs," Célestine replied, "I can see who I'm dealing with and I'm going to speak as is appropriate between people who can understand one another."

Having said that, the Empress looked at her audience politely, and continued: "I haven't taken power in order to destroy abuses; whoever did that would be a voluntary martyr. Now, I want to live and not to sacrifice myself; I have, therefore, simply turned society upside down, in order to give to women what men had reserved; in a word, I've inverted the roles, but have changed absolutely nothing, for that would be the work of a reformer, a friend of humanity, and I'm only my own friend. I therefore understand very well, Messieurs, that the role of women doesn't suit you, since it didn't suit women at all. But as men have never taken into consideration any protest by women, women, in their turn will take no account of what men say, for what the parrot is taught, so it repeats its lesson."

"Mesdames," said the men, ironically, "don't you want to be more than parrots? What glory it would be for you to be initiatrices of sage reforms?"

"You can't think so!" cried Célestine, with a comical expression of fright. "Women occupy themselves with politics! Aieee! What would men think?"

"Majesty, on the terrain of mockery, one can do no more than inflict wounds at every step. Wouldn't it be better to walk along the straight path and battle with reason?"

For two thousand years women have been waiting for you, my dears," said Célestine. "Let's see—what do you propose?"

"That Your Majesty recognize our legal right to be equal to our other halves."

"To be equal to one's half! That's not as easy as one might think," riposted Célestine, humorously. "Do you realize that for that, it would require each half to be intelligent enough to comprehend that a half is only a half, and as you have thus far kept the whole to yourselves, women only know one aim: to conquer that whole." The Empress maintained an affable tone. "For myself, I wish you luck, Messieurs." Then, addressing the women present at the feast, she said: "Mesdames, what is your verdict?"

The women in question were representatives of various classes of society; they had been invited in order that they could discuss and decide the questions posed by the notables.

"For myself," declaimed one of them, hotly, "before Your Majesty had put masculine government in good order, I was salaried, and to obtain any work at all from men, the men know what they demanded of me. I refused."

"Personally," said another, "in spite of the incapacity to which women were relegated, I was able to write what I thought; then, I went to request support from the apostles of humanity; except for a few extraordinary exceptions, the apostles continued their preaching, and did not budge, and we spoke in this way:

'Pardon me, Messieurs,' I said, are you not fighting for the oppressed and progress?'

"'Yes,' they replied.

"'Well, I'm one of the oppressed, and I've worked myself to destroy my shackles.'

"'So what?'

"'So, since supporting the oppressed and progress is helping everyone who is hindered and supporting all their efforts, support me.'

"'Look at this flighty thing, this pretty bluestocking,' sniggered the apostles.

"'Give up this mania for scribbling, my darling' one of them said, more gently. 'An article that we write is worth a thousand times more than your feminine whining.'

"'However, Messieurs,' I went to, clinging on even so, 'since I'm part of the suffering, I know as well as you do where the stick wounds us, and how it can be ameliorated.'

"'But my good lady, we know all that and more,' mocked the apostles. 'At this very moment, do you know what the most urgent question is? It's the perfect square.'

"'Marvelous!' I cried. 'I have a clear and precise study of the perfect square.'

"'Well, isn't that nice!' they said, looking at one another.

"'It's not a matter of the perfect square, Madame Strong-Pen' another snapped at me, going back to lining up his bread and butter, 'it's the angle of the circle that's the order of the day.' With that, a hearty burst of laughter saluted my departure."

The lady concluded, amiably: "I didn't look for the angle of the circle, but if by chance I find it, I'll accord the rights to those Messieurs."

"I can see," said Célestine, "that those apostles preach all the better because they don't practice, and it's necessary that their words take the place of virtue in the eyes of the public; that's not an accident. To you, Madame," the Empress addressed, thus giving the floor to a woman who had risen to her feet.

The latter, neat and firm, placed her right hand on the table, put her left on her hip with infinite elegance, looked at the men with aplomb and said: "I'm a courtesan, which means that masculine rights scarcely affect me, given that those lords and masters have always been obedient to the wand—except that what annoys me is that they treat us as objects of scorn. Scorn! Yes, but if our behavior with them—for we're neither debauched not enriched by women—is illicit, reprehensible and to be condemned, it's because that behavior is exactly what's required to charm men; the proof is that they seek us out and keep us rolling in money. So, Messieurs accomplices, drop the affectations! Hunt down the men—they're the ones who deprave, and thus create the depraved; let them behave with a good grace themselves, or I vote against their rights!"

Tossing her head and stamping her foot, the lady proudly scanned the horizon of turbans, and then sat down.

"We," exclaimed the mass of other women, "are artists and workers at all levels of society, but we're not schemers and we have self-respect; so, very often, we haven't eaten and we've always vegetated, because in order to produce, it's necessary not to be prudish. We therefore refuse the legality of men, who haven't even accorded us charity."

"Pooh!" said Célestine, looking at the men. "If I weren't here, I believe you'd rot on the vine waiting for reforms. Let's see, Mesdames, can't you make one concession to me, who have made so many to you?"

"Let Your Majesty acts as she wishes," the women replied, generously.

"Well," said Celestine, "let's recognize the equality that the men are demanding, but in exchange for the miseries and shame that women have gone though, the men will obey us passively until sunrise."

"Oh, Majesty!" cried the notables, in revolt.

"What!" replied the sovereign, harshly. "The yoke of a few hours in payment for centuries of obedience, and you think that's too much!"

"But what guarantee do we have that afterwards...?" hazarded the men, suspiciously.

"What guarantee?" Célestine riposted, majestically. "My word! Messieurs, a promise given is nothing to a scoundrel, but it's the supreme guarantee for honesty. I don't know what you are and I don't seek to prejudge; these are merely my conclusions—you decide. If, tomorrow, I'm brought laws that recognize the equality of men and women, by tomorrow evening I'll have quit the throne."

As she said these words, the face of the Empress was so imposing that everyone was curbed, submissive and convinced.

211

The deputation got up to discuss the matter, but a large fraction of its members had collapsed under the effect of copious libations, and it was first necessary to stimulate those nonchalant individuals.

"Come on, come on," said a few sober oldsters, shaking the arms of the sleepers. "We need to decide."

"I've decided," said one of the shaken individuals, opening one eye.

"But what have you decided?"

"It doesn't matter, I've decided," muttered the drunkard, and without wanting to hear any more, he plunged back into slumber. With a few variations, the others said much the same.

They were obliged to pass on, and make promises on their behalf.

"Now the debate is closed," said Célestine. Addressing the women, she continued: "Mesdames, thus far I have taken the initiative in everything; this time, it's you who'll throw a feast for me. It's midnight; you have six hours to astonish your sovereign."

Having said that, the Empress went to lie down on her cushions.

The men waited with their heads down for what they would be made to do, and the ladies set about deliberating in low voices.

After a rather lengthy discussion, a few ran out of the room, and those that remained continued to sup, politely inviting the men to do likewise, but the latter had absolutely no appetite—which did not prevent the ladies from enjoying themselves.

About an hour after their departure, some of the delegates came back, accompanied by slaves carrying a bundle of fancy dress costumes. Those gaudy garments of every sort were displayed in bright light and the ladies examined jackets and skirts from every angle. After much back and forth, each of them took possession of the item of her choice, and all of them came to look among the men for the subject best suited to the chosen accoutrement. At first they began measuring them at a distance, adjusting their gazes and calculating the effects, but, as such an appreciaticn was difficult, they went up to the men deliberately and began placing on the chest of each individual in turn their monkey costume, their high lama, their stevedore and their Cauchois, in order to be quite sure of the result. In a matter of seconds the same man's head was deprived of the curls of Adonis in order to be decked with the bonnet of Céladon—and the laughter of the ladies and the shrugging shoulders of the men gave the scene a certain piquancy.

One of the ladies having suggested the idea of painting the beards, the motion was welcomed enthusiastically; immediately, the men went on the defensive.

"No one has any intention of spoiling you," said a woman, coarsely. "It will wash out with a little water. It's astonishing how susceptible men are to good ideas!" she added, looking at them askance. "Anyway, if you want to play the prudes, go away; we'll keep our rights, that's all."

The men received the admonition without flinching, and the costumers set to work. Pots of paint were brought, and the question of art was recommenced. Alternately, it was decided to color one blue, and then, a minute later, it became crimson. No change of hue was ever so prompt; there was no intermediary, each shade was succeeded or moderated without any preparatory half-tint. Furthermore, no principle guided the choice; it was simply a matter of enjoying themselves. The proof is that after long debate between canary yellow and apple green, it was suddenly turquoise that supplanted them, absolutely as one sees an intruder slip between two competitors and carry off the prize without anyone knowing how.

The ladies ran around until they were sweating in order to prepare their plans, but they were careful to bedeck their accomplices thereafter, for they suspected that they would be well-advised to disguise their appearance as much as possible.

"It's necessary to draw lots in advance," said one of them, "in order that when the moment comes, everyone only looks for their own."

"That's very wisely anticipated," approved the circle, and they immediately put it into practice. Each male was labeled; anyone who took off his placard would lose his rights, the men were told; it was an obligatory decoration.

"Can you dance?" the notables were asked,

"No, Mesdames," was the unanimous response.

"Come on, you were young once," persisted one questioner.

"Leave them alone," said a shrewd individual. "When the time comes we can pinch their buttocks—there's nothing better than that; it's entirely natural and very expressive."

"Good," said the others, laughing. "We'll do that."

A full hour had passed in these preparations. A working-class woman came in. "Well?" interrogated the organizers, aloud.

"The stage is making progress," the woman replied. "The tent's almost set up. The people have gotten up; they're watching. The workers have confirmed that they can unroll canvases representing all kinds of extraordinary things. The torches are on the ends of pikes and they only have to be lit; the lighting will be superb. The musicians are tuning up and they have such beautiful costumes that I advise you to take good care with these Messieurs if you don't want them to pale by comparison with the orchestra."

"Don't worry," said the ladies.

"By the way," said one of them, "you haven't noticed any discontent among the workers and the crowd?"

"No," replied the astonished woman. "Why?"

"In fact," the lady continued, talking to herself, "man has built his own prison and his own gibbet, so it's quite natural that he should built the stage for his own exhibition."

"What did you say, Madame?" asked the woman of the people, who had not heard.

"Nothing, my lass."

"What a sight, Mesdames, what a sight!" exclaimed the questioner. "Our sovereign is difficult, but we hope that she'll be content."

Célestine did not pay any attention to what was happening in front of her; the vulgar grotesquerie had immediately bored her. Without worrying about that disdain, the women continued to talk between themselves about the savor of the fête they were about to put on.

The table, still laid, offered evidence of considerable diversion. Some of the sleepers had slipped on to the floor. Others had woken up and were seeking information about what had happened.

Shortly after three o'clock, however, the doors of the hall opened suddenly and several women came in, saying: "It's ready."

Immediately, the sovereign was asked, as she had promised, to witness the fête. Célestine got up without saying a word and, half-preceded and escorted by the ladies, was led to a carriage into which she was invited to climb. As soon as she was comfortably installed, she was covered with furs for fear that the air might be too cold at that early hour, in spite of the season. All these cares were rendered with complete silence, in order not to importune that singular character.

In the meantime, the men were placed in hermetically closed carriages; those who were drunk were deposited in baskets carried by elephants, after the fashion of donkeys. Covers were placed on the baskets and then, escorted by slaves carrying torches and supplemented by guards, the caravan emerged from the inner courtyard of the palace.

A numerous crowd was stationed at the door, and, as soon as the last rider had passed, it set off of the heels of the royal march, following precisely in its wake. Célestine, ahead of all the rest, moved with her entourage, the cavalcade unexpectedly arriving in an immense brightly-illuminated plaza.

A curious host, aggregated as thickly as grass, made a true floor of heads. A reserved passage permitted the court to advance to the center, where there was a vast square tent with a circular stage.

The four facades were ornamented with immense canvases on which were depicted a hotchpotch of all manner of fossil debris—the marvels of creation, according to the sign. Around the stage filed a cordon of astonishing productions: they were either enormous tree trunks in whose crowns human heads were growing, which moved in all directions in the midst of branches and leafy twigs launching forth in plumes; rocks ornamented with mollusks, at whose summits human faces were making a thousand impertinent grimaces at the public; or volcanoes, again with human heads, which were amusing themselves spitting, while their bristling hair released a few volleys of flame from time to time—and that collection of colorless caricatures was simply the orchestra.

When the sovereign arrived, those callosities emitted sounds from the interior of their swollen forms entirely worthy of the appropriate objects that produced them. As the crowd booed and whistled, a mariner who had voyaged in the northern seas affirmed that it was reminiscent of the bellowing of a herd of sea cows. What is certain is that it was so frightful that Célestine started to laugh.

The organizers, delighted with that success, had the Empress' carriage advance to within a few paces of one of the facades. Then, after taking the elephants and carriages containing the men and the costumes into the tent, the sleepers were left in the baskets where they lay, and while some of the women started preparing all the elements of the costumes of the notables, others, raising the curtains on the four sides simultaneously, presented themselves to put on a performance around the perimeter of the stage, in order that the spectacle would be visible from every part of the plaza.

The branched, mountainous and volcanic musicians then ceased to exhale their subsidence, and the ladies, without any superfluous ornamentation of language, tranquilly announced that they were about to display things that defied all competition.

Célestine, who was accustomed to noise, was no longer looking at the scene.

There was then a parade of stuffed dummies of all kinds and other machines of unusual nomenclature; animals, fish and plants exchanged their names without the slightest scruple; it was a true collection of family curios.

At every apparition a cavernous little rigadoon enlivened the article until its disappearance, for it is necessary to say that in order not to encumber the platform, at the same time as the marvels were passed from the tent to the actresses, the latter brandished them to the crowd, and then threw them into a hole in the basement, in order that no refuse should remain on the stage. It seemed to the spectators that some of cast-offs went past twice, but as it happened very quickly, no one dared protest.

The maneuver lasted about eight minutes, then nothing more was passed to the ladies. Showing their empty hands to the public, they adopted satisfied expressions and said: "Audience, it's finished, but don't regret it; we've reserved a choice tidbit for you, and what you're about to see is better than anything you've ever seen, or every could see!"

Hearing these words, the ladies inside had hurled themselves on the pots of paint and the costumes; then, each having taken possession of a man, they had taken hold of their labels and torn them away, during the time that the voice on the stage had continued: "One...two...are you ready?...*voilà!*"

Instantaneously, on that *voilà*, the hangings drew aside and the ladies dropped what they were holding and drew the men by the arms, leading them nobly toward the openings as the gaps appeared. The envelopes of the musicians having simultaneously collapsed, artists in formal dress surged forth, who, as prompt as thought, struck up a serious tune with orthodox instruments.

In the first seconds of the apparition, the ladies, linking arms affectionately with the men, advanced slowly with them to the front of the stage, and, the music having fallen silent, the other ladies who had presided over the performance addressed the audience, indicating the newcomers with a simple and amiable dignity.

"Humans who are looking at us, behold man and woman equal, purely by their mutual will! Have we presumed too much in announcing a unique marvel?"

Categorical approbations and vigorous bravos responded to those words. Even Célestine, astonished, shouted: "Oh, very good!"

"This time," shouted one skeptic, "it really is the world turned upside down: adversaries that forgive!"

Thus welcomed, the women let go of the men's arms and, bowing to them graciously, they retreated slowly, walking backwards to the carriages while in their midst, virtuosos sang a superb chorus well supported by the orchestra, the refrain of which—"Go, you are free, for we love you"—was taken up by the crowd as they descended from the stage. While they resumed their places in the same order in which they had come, the musicians continued to play the same tune, and only stopped playing when the last steed had disappeared.

Those inhabitants who had been up all night went to bed, and the rest amused themselves chatting.

That same day, at two o'clock, they came to present the sovereign with the declaration of the equal rights of man and woman. Célestine immediately designated representatives, men and women in equal numbers, and handed over power to them for a year, decreeing that after that interval, the representation, still in equal numbers, should be renewed by the suffrage of the nation.

Then, having had these reforms acclaimed, the Empress swore in advance her own abdication, recognizing loudly and before everyone that at midnight, the conclusion of the evening, she would reenter the ranks of simple individuals.

Scarcely had these events taken place than it was learned that a nephew of the sultan, having raised an army, had advanced as far as a mansion house not far from the gates of the city, and was camped there.

The population was momentarily downcast; one joker said that the women were pulling faces because they feared having to surrender what they had gained, while the men were scowling with regret at having paid their debt—but who takes any notice of jokers?

Chapter X
Célestine's Backcloth

Meanwhile, at seven o'clock in the evening, Célestine went back to her apartments. Nahour was waiting for her there; they had supper together.

"You've abdicated, then!" said Nahour, profoundly astonished.

"My dear Nahour," she said, laughing disdainfully, "I took power in order to find some element of diversion from the monotony of life, but I was disappointed; I counted on making humans jump, but they obeyed anyway; I've come to the end of everything, except their submission."

"You're complaining about that?"

"Like a lack of breathable air. You see, Nahour, struggle is the action of being; submission annihilates the victor and the vanquished alike."

Célestine meditated. Nahour contemplated her anxiously, but dared not question her about her plans.

"Until later," said the Empress suddenly, and then got up and drew away.

"Célestine!" shouted Nahour, carried away by his emotion. "Célestine! How the uncertainty of the future grips me! If you'd say a single word to me—just one, whatever it might be—I rather that, for if you know what was passing through my head..."

Célestine stopped and turned to Nahour, looked at him profoundly for a few seconds, and then smiled and held out her hand to him. Nahour ran to her, fell at her knees and wept over that hand.

"Oh Célestine," he said, "have pity on me!"

Célestine waited until the explosion had passed; then, gently disengaging her hand and leaning over Nahour, she took hold of his head and kissed his forehead. Then she resumed walking, placidly repeating: "Until later."

A moment later she went into her bedroom, and found Marthe there. "Have you carried out my orders?" she asked.

"Yes, Majesty; your new slaves are waiting at the little house, except for one that I had brought here."

"Good," said Célestine. "Pass me what I need in order to write, prepare our mantles and attach this purse and this bag to your waistband."

So saying, the Empress sat in front of her writing desk, which Marthe placed before her, and without deliberation she wrote:

Adieu, Nahour. If woman had not been put by man in the total impossibility of acting other than by trickery, if man had not reserved all power to himself, I would not have had to make use of you as an instrument, and you would not be in despair now, for you would never have been lured; so don't blame anyone but your own kind for what happened to you.

Tomorrow evening, at nine o'clock, I shall embark. Where I'm going, you can't know. If you want to make a tomb to my memory, have the palace where I lived demolished.

The slave who will hand you this note knows nothing; if you want to tell me something, let him go alone and immediately, for if you have him followed or delay him, it will be futile.

"Bring in the slave," Célestine commanded, folding the note. Then she put on her mantle and pulled up the capacious hood.

The slave came in.

"Today, you enter my service," said the Empress, in an imperious voice. "This is your welcoming gift"—she handed him a few gold coins—"and this is my first command: in a quarter of an hour you will hand this letter to Lord Nahour, in the palace." The sovereign added, emphatically: "I chastise as I reward."

Having said that, she went out with Marthe.

Porters, commanded by the servant, were waiting in an isolated quarter. Célestine and Marthe were transported by them to a house at the gates of the city; the two women went into it before the porters, but they went out immediately by a back door and, after a few detours, went into a rather distant building. Marthe, preceding her mistress, opened the door of a low room where half a dozen slaves were waiting. The Empress, her attitude haughty, gazed for a moment at those humbly curbed men, and then sat down, while Marthe withdrew with the slaves.

Célestine had been sitting there motionless, pensively, when Marthe returned. "Madame," she said, handing her a folded piece of paper; look at this first; then we're ready.

The Empress stood up and opened the note. It contained these words:

Célestine, you have not commanded that the palace crumble for you alone, so I shall bury myself in your tomb, and the noise of your interment will resound your departure and mine. I did not know, until today, what man was, and what woman was. Now I understand. Pardon me, Célestine, but I was quite unconscious. You are my entire being, and I don't know where you're going; to follow you, if it were possible, I would go anywhere. Au revoir, Célestine. Never adieu.

When the young woman had read the note she crumpled it with a somber expression.

"That's the way it is," she said. "One sacrifices oneself for a mirage and one blushes to live for modest and useful labor." Gravely, she continued: "Let him die; the man is already dead to the human race that has no other work than living."

The slaves were on horseback. Célestine and her servant mounted up, too. They went to the gates of the city and, the guide having spoken an imposing name, the little troop was able to go out.

After a rather long ride, they arrived at a wood surrounding the park of a mansion. When they were within sight of the residence, Célestine called a halt, dismounted, and ordered Marthe to do the same and to follow her. Then, having told the slaves to go back if they had not returned after an hour, she advanced resolutely along the broad driveway leading to the entrance.

A few paces from there a sentinel launched his challenge; Celestine replied to it, and, as the guardsmen had emerged from the post in response to the cry, the Empress, perceiving the officer, went directly to him. Turning her back on the soldiers she shifted her hood slightly and said, briefly: "Enable me to speak to the prince and your fortune is made." Removing a superb diamond from her finger, she added: "This is the password by which you will be recognized; pronounce it and know that I am your master's equal."

The lady's self-confidence imposed itself so firmly upon the officer that he made his decision immediately. He took her by the hand and led her through the interior park as far as the sentinel on the ground floor. Drawing aside slightly, he said a few words to the sentinel in a low voice; the latter gave her permission to pass, and the officer returned to his post.

Having gone through a somber antechamber, Célestine calmly lifted a curtain behind which she heard voices and bursts of laughter. Then, her arm raised and parting the heavy pleats that framed her, she remained on the threshold.

The first people who saw that tall form shrouded in the flood of brown fabric were so astonished that the others, seeing them, immediately looked in the same direction and stopped short, no less stupefied.

In response to that mute interrogation, Célestine advanced with a casual stride, and then said, in an infinitely soft voice, bending her knee: "I've come to request help from my sovereign lord."

A keen curiosity gripped the audience, but a sign was made and everyone left except for the man who had commanded. He was about thirty years old, with a handsome physiognomy, albeit a trifle grim.

Célestine extended her hands toward that individual. "Lord," she continued, "my life is in danger, so I have come to take refuge with my prince; protect me."

The young man immediately took notice of the sculptured hands of the supplicant and the richness of her bracelets. "Uncover yourself, Madame," he said. "I am the prince."

"Lord," said Célestine, in an embarrassed tone. "I was obliged to run away as I was, and my garb is not appropriate for a refugee."

"No matter," said the master, authoritatively. "Reveal yourself."

Slowly, and as if reluctantly, Célestine undid the ribbons fastening her mantle, and when the fabric slid away and revealed her in her splendid costume, she bowed her head, and two tears trickled down her cheeks.

The beauty and splendor of the woman, the time, the place and the circumstances struck the imagination of the prince so vividly that he was nailed to the spot, dazzled and fascinated. Then, recovering his senses, he came to his feet like a spring and ran to seize Célestine's hands.

"Oh, get up, Madame!" he said.

Rendered timid by the noble and dignified air of the beautiful petitioner, he sat her down and respectfully sat down a few paces away.

"Lord," the lady continued, "during the usurpation of the revolutionary they call Célestine, I suffered from jealousy. I don't know why—perhaps because of my quality as a Frenchwoman. But today, when it became known that Your Lordship was in this mansion, my doom was decided, and but for a faithful slave who warned me in time. I would have fallen prey to the vengeance of that unworthy despot."

"What is your name, Madame?" asked the prince.

"Lord," Célestine replied, with exquisite grace, "my sojourn in your company, whatever the motive might be, will always be a subject of suspicion. Permit that no one here except myself should know who I am."

"Very well—what does your name matter!" said the young man, carried away by his thoughts. "You are fascination, and will always be adored without there being any need to know more."

The supplicant straightened up, in alarm. "Lord," she said, "let me retire, or let me return to my enemy."

The master, returned to himself by these words, said to Célestine, with a certain confusion: "You can, Madame, repose without dread in this house—except that I have no woman here to serve you."

"I have my servant, Lord," Célestine said, "if You Highness would care to send for her."

The prince immediately called out, and issued a few orders. A few minutes later, Marthe was brought in, and then slaves guided the two women to the apartments of honor.

The young chief could not sleep; all night long he thought about his beautiful guest. The next day, as soon as the time came when he could present himself, he laid siege to Marthe in order to be introduced to her mistress' presence— but the servant, under the pretext of indisposition, kept the door shut all day.

The troops having raised the question of combat, the prince declared that it was not the right time, and that the matter would be put off until the following day.

At five o'clock, Célestine sent word that she was feeling better, and that in order to render her visit to His Highness, she wondered whether her presence at dinner would not be inconvenient for him.

"What time does your mistress dine?" the prince asked the servant.

"Six o'clock, Lord," Marthe replied.

"Ask her for six o'clock," said the young man, swiftly, full of joy.

A few minutes before the appointed hour, Marthe, who had gone to peep through the doors, reported to her mistress that the hall was garlanded like an arbor. Célestine smiled, and, leaning on her servant, had herself introduced to the Lord's presence.

On seeing the beautiful visitor again, the master went pale and trembled as he advanced toward her, stammering without knowing what he was saying.

"Lord," said Célestine, with a touching melancholy, "it required all the gratitude that I feel for you to persuade me to present myself before you again, for"—she pointed at her dazzling costume sadly—"these joyful garments contrast so painfully with my present situation, that I feel utterly disconcerted and fear every gaze." And the young woman turned her head with a withdrawn gesture.

"Madame," the prince replied, with no less melancholy, "Our misfortunes are parallel, let us support one another. I am Djamil, and the throne is mine by right."

"Alas, Lord," murmured the poor desolate woman.

Seeing her so sad, Djamil took her hand gently and led her to the table. Then he sat down facing her. At first he only busied himself serving her, but when Célestine had declared agreeably that it was not courteous to appear more afflicted than she was by not eating, the prince, to please her, fell upon the nourishment. As he drank large draughts in order to help the morsels down, his natural boldness gradually returned. He unleashed salvos of declarations to the beautiful lady continually, and she responded to them very cheerfully—which enchanted his adorer.

The high idea he had regarding the rank of his guest, however, prevented him from behaving too freely, so the tête-à-tête was delightful in its piquancy and originality.

They reached the dessert; night had fallen, the room was splendidly illuminated, and the flowers attached and strewn everywhere constituted a very delicate scene.

"Beautiful enchantress," said Djamil, in the expansion of his joy, "would you like to wear a crown?"

"What crown?" asked Célestine.

"Mine," said Djamil. "Tomorrow, I shall be victorious."

226

"That's not enough," said the beauty, laughing.

"Not enough!" repeated Djamil, piqued.

"No," the lady replied, coldly. "Célestine's exploits have astonished me, and not accepting to be inferior to anyone, I've sworn that I would only choose a Nahour when I was more elevated than Célestine."

"What! You're ambitious for such extravagances?"

"I don't know, Lord," said Célestine, indolently.

"Really," said Djamil, dejected, "are you telling me the truth?"

"Let's not talk about it anymore, Lord," said the young woman, in a languid and bored tone. "I see that I was wrong to tell you my secrets."

"But Célestine only reigned for six days!" insinuated the prince, after a few moments of reflection. And he looked at his companion.

The latter made no reply. Djamil continued: "Whoever reigned for twice as long would be twice as great!"

"Undoubtedly," said the lady, with an utterly impertinent indifference—and then added, in the same tone: "But I'm not content to imitate!"

"Come on!" exclaimed Djamil, abruptly. "What do you want? Tell me!"

"I'll think about it," said Célestine, calmly.

The mansion clock chimed half past eight. The beautiful lady stood up and went to a window. Djamil joined her immediately, but a very particular glance from Célestine struck such a chill into the marrow of his bones that all his temerity faded away.

"These gardens are beautiful," she said, gazing vaguely at the park.

"Would you like to take a walk there?" asked Djamil, emotionally, and, under the influence of Célestine's soft speech, he ventured to put his arm around her waist. She allowed him to do it, and they both went down the steps of the perron together, and slowly went to lose themselves in the winding paths and coverts of the park.

Meanwhile, the clock chimed the quarter-hour. The hall was deserted, the park silent. From time to time, Djamil and Célestine reappeared, and their white forms stood out against the somber background of the thickets. Soon, they traversed a lawn that brought them back to the mansion. To see them thus, advancing mutely in the pale moonlight, among the splendid gardens, one might have thought them royal shades visiting their ancient palace.

As they climbed the marble steps, pensively, a dull rumble, swelling, made them pause, but Célestine resumed her ascensional march and Djamil followed her, while the noise, which had passed in a second from loud to terrible, reached its thunderous peak. Djamil and Célestine stood still; the earth seemed to disintegrate, and then silence reposed its bleak shroud over space, and calm alone continued to reign.

"What was that?" said Djamil, when he had recovered his voice.

"It was the palace of the sultans collapsing," Célestine replied, gravely.

"The palace of the sultans!" cried Djamil, stupefied. "How do you know? And why has it collapsed?"

"Because I commanded it."

"You commanded it? You! Who are you, then?"

"Célestine, the sovereign of men, and yours, for I've vanquished you."

And quicker than thought, she shoved Djamil violently, who went down the steps backwards all the way to the bottom. The prince's hand sought the hilt of his sword, nervously; already he was bracing himself to pounce on the enemy—but, having looked at Célestine, his arms fell, his legs gradually folded, and he collapsed, inert and terrified.

Before him, at the top of the steps, Célestine upright, motionless and haughty, her head slightly tilted, looked down at him. Her moonlit face had a strangely cruel expression; it was the rictus of the panther, minus the roar; the rigidity of death sculpted her implacable physiognomy; she seemed obliged to remain there forever, petrified in her long white tunic, embroidered with silver, with sepulchral tints.

In spite of himself, Djamil was increasingly overwhelmed.

But then, like a bloody cloud gently fading to a rosy tint, Célestine's visage softened and relaxed. Djamil contemplated her anxiously; he seemed to hear his name, faintly; he started, but paused.

"Djamil," Célestine repeated, and she smiled...

Then, like lighting that passes, like the flux that reverses, Djamil leapt up, and, picking up the young woman with the fury of a hurricane, he carried her furiously into the palace illuminated by a thousand candles, and, depositing her on cushions, he devoured her with his gaze.

"Oh, I've finally found you!" he cried, and his entire being seemed to melt in that explosion.

Célestine burst into strident laughter—the kind of laughter that grates in the ear that hears it.

"Are you playing a comedy?" the lion roared.

"You know that I'm Célestine and you dare to question me?" said the superb woman, slowly raising her head and drawing out her words disdainfully.

"Célestine!" repeated Djamil. "You, Célestine!"

"Do you think that my memory would have allowed anyone to take their place there after me? Djamil, I have protected that royalty by destroying the décor that served me."

"Madame!"

"Djamil, pull yourself together. This behavior is unbecoming. You're in error, my dear; a king ought not to be preoccupied with words, whatever they are, for that would be to place himself on a level with everyone else."

In response, Djamil broke the porcelain plates, cups and lamps around him. Célestine watched him do it, smiling nonchalantly.

Silence fell.

"You're my final whim," she said. "I'm going away—would you like to accompany me?"

"You're going away!" cried the sultan, with all the violence of a master, bounding to his feet.

"Yes, I'm going away," Célestine repeated, softly, with a weary smile, and her head sank more deeply into the cushions.

The sultan was mute with anger; his blazing eyes reached a paroxysm of fury; he wanted to speak, but was foaming at the mouth.

"But remember," he finally pronounced, "remember that I'm your master. You're going away?"

"Come with me," said Célestine, still with the same smile.

"Where?" cried the sultan, drunk with rage.

"Into death," she replied, with the most perfect indifference. "I've pushed back the limits of the possible; what do you expect me to do now? Get bored? That's dying too long, and vilely. I'm leaving today, at my whim."

"But I don't want you to die! I'll prevent you from dying."

"What time is it, my dear Djamil?"

"Nine o'clock," the sultan replied, trembling.

"Well, don't waste the time ridiculously that you still have to spend with me. In an hour, I'll be dead." She held out a little bottle to him, half empty, and added, laughing: "I haven't forgotten you—look, I've kept this; it's the ticket of departure and arrival."

Then, somewhat revived by that pleasant idea, Célestine stood up and looked Djamil in the face.

"Give me something to drink," she said to him. As she held out her cup to the tremulous waves that Djamil poured for her, she murmured, disdainfully: "You look frightened. How weak men are." Then, with a charming irony, she said: "To your health, powerful lord!"

Djamil stared at her. Suddenly, with a feverish movement, he uncorked the bottle that he had kept in his hand.

"To your health!" he cried, deliriously pouring the poison into the wine—and while Célestine drank, still smiling, with his eyes fixed upon her, he swallowed it like a madman.

"Come on," said Célestine. "I'll introduce you up there, if there's society. But I deceived you when I said an hour… that was to avoid adieux… I con't like them… *au revoir*. Drink to my voyage; it will help you pass the time."

And she collapsed.

At the same time, either because the dose was stronger or because the impression aided it, Djamil fell down dead.

Conclusion

Célestine's servant returned to France. She wrote a memoir of her mistress. That consoled her a little for the loss of her idol, but she perceived that counterfeits had been made of the history; she complained about that, saying that Célestine was a true model, and that people had made her into a she-devil.

"It's to make her story useful," one cynic said to her, "for, however beautiful the things you say are, they go moldy in the light, if you don't know how to adapt them. As one knows one's saints, one honors them, mark my words..."

Marthe heard the words, but did not understand them at all. It was explained to her that virtue had no history, that only vice counted, and that if, naively, an author embarked upon an account of everyday virtues, the book would be given as a prize to schoolchildren who would already smile, in accordance with the spirit of the age, if they didn't impertinently add the familiar locution: "It's boring."

"So," her interlocutor concluded, "in order to make humans swallow the pill of education, do what the druggists do; envelop the bitterness of reason in something pleasant—and what pleases our epoch is cascades, upheavals and the risqué; otherwise, my dear, your protests will be a waste of effort, for no one will read a single word."

The poor servant tried to protest; she wrote sensible things simply, but, as no one ever read them, she was obliged to admit that what she had been told was true.

SF & FANTASY

Adolphe Alhaiza. *Cybele*

Alphonse Allais. *The Adventures of Captain Cap*

Henri Allorge. *The Great Cataclysm*

Guy d'Armen. *Doc Ardan: The City of Gold and Lepers*

G.-J. Arnaud. *The Ice Company*

Charles Asselineau. *The Double Life*

Henri Austruy. *The Eupantophone; The Olotelepan; The Petitpaon Era*

Barillet-Lagartousse. *The Final War*

Cyprien Bérard. *The Vampire Lord Ruthwen*

S. Henry Berthoud. *Martyrs of Science*

Aloysius Bertrand. *Gaspard de la Nuit*

Richard Bessière. *The Gardens of the Apocalypse; The Masters of Silence*

Albert Bleunard. *Ever Smaller*

Félix Bodin. *The Novel of the Future*

Louis Boussenard. *Monsieur Synthesis*

Alphonse Brown. *City of Glass; The Conquest of the Air*

Emile Calvet. *In a Thousand Years*

André Caroff. *The Terror of Madame Atomos; Miss Atomos; The Return of Madame Atomos; The Mistake of Madame Atomos; The Monsters of Madame Atomos; The Revenge of Madame Atomos; The Resurrection of Madame Atomos; The Mark of Madame Atomos; The Spheres of Madame Atomos; The Wrath of Madame Atomos* (w/M. & Sylvie Stéphan)

Félicien Champsaur. *The Human Arrow; Ouha, King of the Apes; Pharaoh's Wife*

Didier de Chousy. *Ignis*

Jules Clarétie. *Obsession*

Michel Corday. *The Eternal Flame*

André Couvreur. *The Necessary Evil; Caresco, Superman; The Exploits of Professor Tornada* (3 vols.)

Captain Danrit. *Undersea Odyssey*

C. I. Defontenay. *Star (Psi Cassiopeia)*

Charles Derennes. *The People of the Pole*

Georges Dodds (anthologist). *The Missing Link*

Charles Dodeman. *The Silent Bomb*

Harry Dickson. *The Heir of Dracula; Harry Dickson vs. The Spider*

Jules Dornay. *Lord Ruthven Begins*
Alfred Driou. *The Adventures of a Parisian Aeronaut*
Sâr Dubnotal *vs. Jack the Ripper*
Alexandre Dumas. *The Return of Lord Ruthven*
Renée Dunan. *Baal*
J.-C. Dunyach. *The Night Orchid; The Thieves of Silence*
Henri Duvernois. *The Man Who Found Himself*
Achille Eyraud. *Voyage to Venus*
Henri Falk. *The Age of Lead*
Paul Féval. *Anne of the Isles; Knightshade; Revenants; Vampire City;
The Vampire Countess; The Wandering Jew's Daughter*
Paul Féval, *fils. Felifax, the Tiger-Man*
Charles de Fieux. *Lamékis*
Louis Forest. *Someone is Stealing Children in Paris*
Arnould Galopin. *Doctor Omega; Doctor Omega and the
Shadowmen* (anthology)
Judith Gautier. *Isoline and the Serpent-Flower*
H. Gayar. *The Marvelous Adventures of Serge Myrandhal on Mars*
Léon Gozlan. *The Vampire of the Val-de-Grâce*
G.L. Gick. *Harry Dickson and the Werewolf of Rutherford Grange*
Edmond Haraucourt. *Illusions of Immortality*
Nathalie Henneberg. *The Green Gods*
V. Hugo, P. Foucher & P. Meurice. *The Hunchback of Notre-Dame*
Romain d'Huissier. *Hexagon: Dark Matter*
Jules Janin. *The Magnetized Corpse*
Michel Jeury. *Chronolysis*
Gustave Kahn. *The Tale of Gold and Silence*
Gérard Klein. *The Mote in Time's Eye*
Fernand Kolney. *Love in 5000 Years*
Paul Lacroix. *Danse Macabre*
Louis-Guillaume de La Follie. *The Unpretentious Philosopher*
Jean de La Hire. *Enter the Nyctalope; The Nyctalope on Mars; The
Nyctalope vs. Lucifer; The Nyctalope Steps In; Night of the
Nyctalope; Return of the Nyctalope; The Fiery Wheel*
Etienne-Léon de Lamothe-Langon. *The Virgin Vampire*
André Laurie. *Spiridon*
Gabriel de Lautrec. *The Vengeance of the Oval Portrait*
Alain le Drimeur. *The Future City*
Georges Le Faure & Henri de Graffigny. *The Extraordinary Adven-
tures of a Russian Scientist Across the Solar System* (2 vols.)

Gustave Le Rouge. *The Mysterious Doctor Cornelius* (3 vols.); *The Vampires of Mars; The Dominion of the World* (w/Gustave Guitton) (4 vols.)

Jules Lermina. *Mysteryville; Panic in Paris; To-Ho and the Gold Destroyers; The Secret of Zippeliu; The Battle of Strasbourg*

André Lichtenberger. *The Centaurs; The Children of the Crab*

Jean-Marc & Randy Lofficier. *Edgar Allan Poe on Mars; The Katrina Protocol; Pacifica; Robonocchio; Return of the Nyctalope;* (anthologists) *Tales of the Shadowmen 1-10*

Xavier Mauméjean. *The League of Heroes*

Joseph Méry. *The Tower of Destiny*

Hippolyte Mettais. *The Year 5865; Paris Before the Deluge*

Louise Michel. *The Human Microbes; The New World*

Tony Moilin. *Paris in the Year 2000*

José Moselli. *Illa's End*

John-Antoine Nau. *Enemy Force*

Marie Nizet. *Captain Vampire*

C. Nodier, A. Beraud & Toussaint-Merle. *Frankenstein*

Henri de Parville. *An Inhabitant of the Planet Mars*

Gaston de Pawlowski. *Journey to the Land of the 4th Dimension*

Georges Pellerin. *The World in 2000 Years*

Ernest Pérochon. *The Frenetic People*

Pierre Pelot. *The Child Who Walked on the Sky*

J. Polidori, C. Nodier, E. Scribe. *Lord Ruthven the Vampire*

P.-A. Ponson du Terrail. *The Vampire and the Devil's Son; The Immortal Woman*

Edgar Quinet. *Ahasuerus; The Enchanter Merlin*

Henri de Régnier. *A Surfeit of Mirrors*

Maurice Renard. *The Blue Peril; Doctor Lerne; The Doctored Man; A Man Among the Microbes; The Master of Light*

Jean Richepin. *The Wing; The Crazy Corner*

Albert Robida. *The Adventures of Saturnin Farandoul; The Clock of the Centuries; Chalet in the Sky; The Electric Life*

J.-H. Rosny Aîné. *Helgvor of the Blue River; The Givreuse Enigma; The Mysterious Force; The Navigators of Space; Vamireh; The World of the Variants; The Young Vampire*

Marcel Rouff. *Journey to the Inverted World*

Han Ryner. *The Superhumans; The Human Ant*

Pierre de Selenes: *An Unknown World*

Angelo de Sorr. *The Vampires of London*

Brian Stableford. *The New Faust at the Tragicomique;The Empire of the Necromancers (The Shadow of Frankenstein; Frankenstein and the Vampire Countess; Frankenstein in London); Sherlock Holmes & The Vampires of Eternity; The Stones of Camelot; The Wayward Muse.* (anthologist) *News from the Moon; The Germans on Venus; The Supreme Progress; The World Above the World; Nemoville; Investigations of the Future; The Conqueror of Death; The Revolt of the Machines*

Jacques Spitz. *The Eye of Purgatory*

Kurt Steiner. *Ortog*

Eugène Thébault. *Radio-Terror*

C.-F. Tiphaigne de La Roche. *Amilec*

Louis Ulbach. *Prince Bonifacio*

Théo Varlet. *The Golden Rock. The Xenobiotic Invasion; The Castaways of Eros; Timeslip Troopers* (w/André Blandin); *The Martian Epic* (w/Octave Joncquel)

Paul Vibert. *The Mysterious Fluid*

Villiers de l'Isle-Adam. *The Scaffold; The Vampire Soul*

Philippe Ward. *Artahe ; The Song of Montségur* (w/Sylvie Miller) *Manhattan Ghost* (w/Mickael Laguerre)

MYSTERIES & THRILLERS

M. Allain & P. Souvestre. *The Daughter of Fantômas*

A. Anicet-Bourgeois, Lucien Dabril. *Rocambole*

A. Bernède. *Belphegor*; *Judex* (w/Louis Feuillade); *The Return of Judex* (w/Louis Feuillade); *The Shadow of Judex*

A. Bisson & G. Livet. *Nick Carter vs. Fantômas*

V. Darlay & H. de Gorsse. *Arsène Lupin vs. Sherlock Holmes: The Stage Play*

Séamas Duffy. *Sherlock Holmes in Paris*

Paul Féval. *Gentlemen of the Night; John Devil; The Black Coats ('Salem Street; The Invisible Weapon; The Parisian Jungle; The Companions of the Treasure; Heart of Steel; The Cadet Gang; The Sword-Swallower)*

Emile Gaboriau. *Monsieur Lecoq*

Goron & Emile Gautier. *Spawn of the Penitentiary*

Rick Lai. *Shadows of the Opera: Retribution in Blood; Sisters of the Shadows: The Curse of Cagliostro*

Steve Leadley. *Sherlock Holmes: The Circle of Blood*

Maurice Leblanc. *Arsène Lupin vs. Countess Cagliostro; Arsène Lupin vs. Sherlock Holmes (The Blonde Phantom; The Hollow Needle); The Many Faces of Arsène Lupin*
Gaston Leroux. *Chéri-Bibi; The Phantom of the Opera; Rouletabille & the Mystery of the Yellow Room; Rouletabille at Krupp's*
Richard Marsh. *The Complete Advertures of Judith Lee*
William Patrick Maynard. *The Terror of Fu Manchu; The Destiny of Fu Manchu*
Frank J. Morlock. *Sherlock Holmes: The Grand Horizontals; Sherlock Holmes vs Jack the Ripper*
Jean Petithuguenin. *The Adventures of Ethel King*
Antonin Reschal. *The Adventures of Miss Boston*
P. de Wattyne & Y. Walter. *Sherlock Holmes vs. Fantômas*
David White. *Fantômas in America*
Pierre Yrondy. *The Adventures of Thérèse Arnaud*

SCREENPLAYS

Mike Baron. *The Iron Triangle*
Emma Bull & Will Shetterly. *Nightspeeder; War for the Oaks*
Gerry Conway & Roy Thomas. *Doc Dynamo*
Steve Englehart. *Majorca*
James Hudnall. *The Devastator*
Jean-Marc & Randy Lofficier. *Royal Flush*
J.-M. & R. Lofficier & Marc Agapit. *Despair*
J.-M. & R. Lofficier & Joël Houssin. *City*
Andrew Paquette. *Peripheral Vision*
Robert L. Robinson, Jr. *Judex*
R. Thomas, J. Hendler & L. Sprague de Camp. *Rivers of Time*

NON-FICTION

Stephen R. Bissette. *Blur 1-5. Green Mountain Cinema 1; Teen Angels*
Win Scott Eckert. *Crossovers* (2 vols.)
Jean-Marc & Randy Lofficier. *Shadowmen* (2 vols.)
Randy Lofficier. *Over Here*

ART BOOKS

Jean-Pierre Normand. *Science Fiction Illustrations*
Raven Okeefe. *Raven's L'il Critters; Rave's Faves*
Randy Lofficier & Raven Okeefe. *If Your Possum Go Daylight...*
Daniele Serra. *Illusions*

www.ingramcontent.com/pod-product-compliance
Lightning Source LLC
Chambersburg PA
CBHW060355030726
47497CB00003B/718